AC

A Novel

ALAN LIEBERMAN

PAGE PUBLISHING, INC.
Conneaut Lake, PA

First originally published by Page Publishing 2020

Readers, particularly those who are familiar with Atlantic City and the down beach communities, will no doubt notice that I have altered certain locations and dates. These factual discrepancies were made to meet the requirements of the story arc.

Marlborough Blenheim Hotel photo: Courtesy of the Special Collections Research Center. Temple University Libraries. Philadelphia, PA

ISBN 978-1-64462-018-2 (pbk)
ISBN 978-1-64462-019-9 (digital)

Printed in the United States of America

For the ACHS class of 1964.

"As I walk along, I wonder
awhat went wrong…"

—Charles Weedon Westover
December 30, 1934–February 8, 1990

Acknowledgments

I am deeply indebted to Dan Pope, author of *Housebreaking* and *In the Cherry Tree*. I first met Dan more than a decade ago at a writers conference at Wesleyan University. Over more than a few beers, we talked writing, agents, publishing, and our mutual love of great works of fiction. Dan read *AC*, a work-in-progress. Over the years, Dan gave freely of his time, reading each draft. His line edits and notes on structure were invaluable. His firm, gentle guidance enabled me—in spite of my occasional resistance—to realize the full potential of my vision for this paean to my hometown. So thank you, Dan, mentor, teacher, and friend.

Prologue

Summer 1979

Yellow tape stretched across the entrance to the tunnel, ruffling in the ocean breeze. A uniformed cop stood nearby.

"Who found the bodies?" Detective Sergeant Jake Harris wore a two-day growth and a sports coat to match. Seventy-two hours earlier, he'd stood at the boardwalk rail in the damp predawn chill and watched construction crews demolish the old hotel. When the rumble of dynamite charges and the squeals and creaks of collapsing steel, wood, and concrete quieted, only the minarets remained, and portions of two outer walls shrouded in a dust cloud thick with particulate. The destruction reminded him of World War II photographs of Dresden after the American B-17 Flying Fortresses and RAF Lancasters had made their runs.

"Some old rummy looking for a place to sleep. This one yours?"

"Yeah. I got the duty call," Harris replied.

"Forensic's inside. Looks like one of them archeology digs. They got construction guys putting in backup supports so they can get behind the old beams."

Harris ducked under the tape, stepped across the threshold, or what had been the threshold, and back into time. He followed the familiar footpath of tar-soaked two-by-twelve planks leading under the Marlborough Blenheim. The tunnel seemed to constrict and swallow him as he moved deeper inside. A portable generator growled like an empty belly. Thirty yards ahead, shadows cast by a strand of floodlights flickered across the mud walls.

Jake spied Jimmy Dougherty at the center of activity. Dougherty headed Atlantic City Police Department's forensic unit.

"Hey, Doc. What do you have?"

"Partial of two bodies so far. Maybe others jammed in behind the beams. This tunnel's a mausoleum."

Jake scanned the opening behind the railroad ties that had been removed from the wall then looked down at the large blue tarp carefully stretched and staked on the mud floor. A human skeleton had begun to take shape. From the layout of the bones, it looked like the right side of a body. An array of smaller bones waiting to be inserted in their proper locations lay nearby. Jake thought of the model ships and planes he and his dad built when he was a boy, how his dad taught him to lay out all the pieces in groups, put the hull or fuselage together then the smaller less obvious parts. Jake looked past the bones to the edge of the tarp, watching one of Dougherty's men set down a scrap of fabric—a T-shirt, swim trunks?—next to a single sandal, right foot, thong style.

"You hear anything new about our pensions?" Dougherty asked without looking up. "They better not mess with things. I got two more years, and I'm done. Gonna move to Florida with the wife, play golf, and fish."

Jake wondered about Jimmy's mistress. She'd miss him, or at least the monthly stipend he paid her. Jake stifled a laugh at Dougherty's concern about his pension. Jimmy had been taking cash on the side for years. Minor stuff mostly, but steady, every week. Dougherty wasn't corrupt, not really. Not like McMeekin, his captain. But the dollars did add up.

"Not to worry, Doc. The city is just opening the bidding on negotiations for the new Collective Bargaining Agreement. Just show for the taxpayers. No way City Council crosses the union. Not if they want to stay in office."

AC was a union town, even if the locals were controlled by the mob.

The bones were clean. Jake wondered whether crabs had gotten to the carcasses. He knelt beside the skull that had been placed above a clavicle.

"We're not sure if that head and body go together yet," Dougherty cautioned.

Jake took a penknife from his jacket pocket and inserted the blade in an eye socket, rotating the skull. The bones of the back of the head appeared to have been shattered. He returned the skull to its original position and continued to examine it—teeth, strands of hair.

Good, he thought, as any detective would. *Building blocks to reconstruct the crime, unlock secrets, solve the case.*

He squatted beside the tattered bits of clothing. The trunks had been white. Jake knew the style—lifeguard boxer type with a button fly. Rust from the D-ring buckle stained the waistband. He used the eraser end of a pencil to spread the T-shirt flat. It was torn along one side seam, and the neckline was ripped down the back almost to the bottom. The original color appeared to be some shade of orange, maybe tangerine. A scene of seagulls flying along the shoreline decorated the back.

"Doc, take your usual good care of these," Jake said, rising. "Tight chain of custody. I don't want some numb-nut who can't find salt in the ocean, working on this."

"By the book, Jake. I'll stay personally involved. I've already brought in an anthropologist from Rutgers to supervise the excavation and catalog the remains." Dougherty jerked his thumb toward a man with his back to them, wielding a trowel. The man stopped to shine the light from his headlamp along the wall's opening then resumed scraping packed mud from bone.

Jake walked back to the tunnel entrance. A busted electrical box trailing cut wires hung like a petrified squid from one of the beams. *Bernie's phone.* Jake had answered it just once, that long ago summer he ran with the Ducktown Boys: Vinny, Toad, and Joey. Most nights, they'd cruise Ventnor Avenue from Chelsea down to Margate in Fish Gomberg's Bonnie, windows rolled down, radio turned up, everyone but Fish a study of tough-guy cool. They'd hang out on the boardwalk, endless hours draped on the rails in their engineer boots, cigarettes dangling, and combs at the ready, watching the tourists and looking for girls. Each of them had managed to survive those bad-boy days, except Joey. Joey was the cautionary tale parents told their kids—listen, behave, work hard in school, or else you might end up like Joey Nardo. Still, Jake had never imagined Joey would come out the way he had.

From the mouth of the tunnel, Jake looked up at the hole in the sky where the Marlborough Blenheim Hotel had once stood. Destroying the hotel was like putting down a beloved dog, a loyal companion too old to enjoy life any longer. The Blenheim was a remnant of another time, another grand hotel gone to seed.

He walked toward the ocean. The sand spilled over the tops and filled his shoes. Growing up, Jake heard his parents and their friends declare with defiant pride that they were born with sand in their shoes. As far as Jake was concerned, his portion was ever present, a constant reminder of his origins. He had always hated sand in his shoes. You couldn't get the grit out of the welts. He'd take off his shoes before getting back in the squad car. Bang them against the rocker panel, turn them upside down and shake them, take off his socks, turn them inside out, flap them in the air. No matter. The sand was a permanent layer on the cruiser's floor. It stuck to your skin, got in your hair, filled your trunks, and got tracked into the house.

He could still hear his mother's voice: *Jacob, be sure to hose all the sand off before you come into my living room. And dry yourself!* It wasn't until he went away to college that he realized the problem with sand. It shifted with the wind and the tide. It wouldn't hold roots; eroding, it disappeared inch by inch.

At the water's edge, pressure pools formed in the mud around his feet and sucked at the soles of his shoes. A gull hovering over the rocks of the jetty dropped a clam with the precision of a bombardier then dove to retrieve the meat from the crushed shell. To his right, the chicken wire and plaster castles perched atop piers over the shore break were barely visible in the mist. He didn't have to see them. The Steeple Chase Pier had been a constant of his summer nights as a teen. Its giant steel wheel lit the darkness, dangling gondolas like so many charms from a bracelet, carrying lovers, and children faces pink with spun sugar.

He turned toward the boardwalk, his eyes drawn to the opening under the boards. The tunnel was indistinguishable from the shadows. Tessie's tunnel, they used to call it, seventeen summers ago.

In the hall outside Captain Eamon McMeekin's office, Jake glanced through the partially opened blinds and watched as his captain chewed out some hapless beat cop. The cop shifted and fidgeted in the chair, unable to meet his captain's glare. McMeekin had his eyes locked on the man. The captain's eyes were dead. McMeekin leaned forward in his chair and uttered a few low syllables. The cop stood, muttered, "Yes, Captain." He brushed past Jake like a man who had cheated death.

"Grab a seat, Sergeant," McMeekin said.

Jake pulled the creaky wooden roller chair to him and sat.

McMeekin knew the game and how to play it. It was common knowledge that he bagged for the top brass. McMeekin, having proved he could be trusted to manage the collection and distribution of payoffs, had been rewarded with captain's bars when his mentor retired. The joke around city hall was that McMeekin was the chief financial officer of the Unofficial Retired Captains' Benevolent Fund. He'd made captain just after Jake got his gold shield, one of the youngest cops ever to make detective. The two men had never liked each other, mainly because Jake had refused his cut of the shake off the street.

"Talk to me," said McMeekin.

"It's gonna take some time to assemble the bones, match the remnants of clothing, and get the forensics. Dougherty says maybe a week before we have the preliminary labs. Blood stains won't tell us much, but we should be able to trace the teeth."

"You talk to any reporters? I got a call from *The Press* already. Lois Lane tells me we got three bodies. How would she know the count? She says she's gonna call it the Tunnel Queen Murders."

"I haven't talked to anybody."

"Fucking Dougherty. He feeds that trim stories, hoping she'll part with a piece of ass. Anyway, we got three dead fairies."

"Maybe," Jake said.

"What maybe? No maybe about it. Location, location, location, as they say in real estate. Indiana Avenue's been the fag beach since before I been on the force. When I was on the street, I busted a lot of heads in that tunnel after dark. One sweep and I'd make my quota for the week. Jump a bunch of pansies with their pants around their ankles. Instant collars."

"You got a way with words, Cap."

McMeekin glared. "I did you a favor."

"How is that?"

McMeekin's face didn't just have pockmarks; it had bunkers and ditches that pulled and contorted with every syllable, chew, and tic. His face was always wet, slick with sweat and oil that seemed to spill into his eyes.

"I gave you three stiffs nobody gives a damn about. You can do whatever you want with 'em. Three easy stats. Take Clement."

"Clement's on medical," Jake reminded McMeekin.

"Yeah, right." McMeekin looked down at some papers in front of him. "Take Brathwaite."

McMeekin had a watch list, and Jake was at the top, a Jew with a college degree who wouldn't plant evidence or take cash. Brathwaite was right there with him ever since he'd organized the black cops, claiming discrimination in promotion and pay.

"Cap," Jake began.

"You still here?" said McMeekin without looking up.

The evidence room was deserted. An air conditioner wedged in a window dripped condensation on the concrete floor in a futile attempt to beat back the damp August heat. The small space stank of moldy cardboard. Jake fought the nausea rising in his gut and braced against the shelving's metal frame before dropping into a chair. He flipped open the preliminary forensic report Dougherty had given him that morning: three males in their twenties. John Does

1 and 2. The third had a name, identified from dental records—Jamie Wescott.

Jake pulled three boxes from the stacks, put them on a table, and removed their tops. He began picking through them, one for each body, a sealed heavy-duty plastic bag containing the remains: ulnae, radii, humeri, femurs, fibulae, tibiae, ribs still attached to sternums, three pelvises (heavier boned, thicker, and narrower than a female's), and three skulls, their occipital bones shattered. Small sealed plastic evidence bags held hair strands. Clear plastic envelopes contained tattered cloth that had clung to the bones in their crypt.

A sheet of newspaper suctioned against the narrow window high on the wall at street level and, just as suddenly, was whisked away by a gust off the beach. Sitting before the three cardboard containers, he could feel the blackness deep inside the tunnel, how it had seeped into his nostrils, his pores, lay on his hair, clung to him that long ago summer.

Part One

J ake Harris was excited like most fifteen-year-old boys at the end of the school year. Today he'd start his summer job that Rabbit had arranged for him. Norman "Rabbit" Lasky drove a cab in the summer, and he had an in with Bernie Dorfman, who ran the concessions on the beach in front of the Marlborough Blenheim.

Jake arrived early and waited on the boardwalk overlooking the beach in front of the Blenheim. It was chilly, typical for early June at the shore, and not a promising beach day. He leaned over the rail to look at the stacks of pads and chaises under heavy tarps, secured by padlocked chains strung through beams under the boardwalk.

"I'm Jake Harris," he called to the figure below busy removing the chains from the pads and chaises.

A man with a sun-weathered face and wearing a battered straw pork pie hat smiled up at him. "Come on down, kid. Give me a hand."

When Jake arrived at the stacks of pads, the man in the pork pie hat tossed him a sleeveless T-shirt decorated with a silk screen of the hotel.

"Your uniform, kid. And get a pair of life guard trunks. The ladies like them. You'll make bigger tips."

Bernie was the eldest of three Dorfman siblings. He sat at a rickety folding table and aluminum chair with a frayed web seat permanently contoured by his buttocks—his office at the mouth of the tunnel that ran perpendicular to the boardwalk deep beneath the street and under the hotel.

The Dorfmans—Bernie; his sister, Tessie; and their little brother, Sammy—all lacked high school diplomas but had successfully applied the essential principles of capitalism to the AC summer crowd: diversification of goods and services to meet the needs of their target customers, geographic consolidation, and exploitation of cheap indigenous labor.

After that first day on the job as a beach boy, Jake proudly emptied his pockets of crumpled dollar bills, quarters, and fifty-cent pieces sticky with seawater and sand on the kitchen table for his parents to see.

"You don't know where that money's been." His mother's spit hit her rag. In a continuous motion, she swept the pile of money out of the way and wiped the beach grit from the table. Sally Harris was a clean woman. And her saliva was her all-purpose cleaner.

His father just glanced at the pile of money that spilled across the table from his son's out-turned pockets. "Not bad, Jake. Looks like ten bucks at least."

Each morning, Jake set out the umbrellas, chairs, and lounges. Weeklies had their favorite spots, and Jake quickly memorized them all. Jake was what the locals referred to as a beach rat. He wore the uniform: white lifeguard trunks and a tank top with the image of the Marlborough Blenheim's twin minarets across the back. Beach rats took pride in their tans; the darker the better. Back then, nobody worried about skin cancer or how they'd look at fifty. You started the summer with a second-degree burn that blistered and peeled. Hurt like hell when you showered. But it was the foundation, the necessary first stage to the ebony tone that marked you as a native. It was an honest tan, acquired while hustling the hot sand, not lying on a towel like meat on a broiler.

Jake soon had one of the best. He oiled up with Bain de Soleil and smoothed the residue on his hair for highlights. He had the kind of skin that took the sun. The Italian kids he knew from high school called him the Sicilian. He never wore the tank top when the sun was shining. He tied it around his head like a desert headdress. He wore his trunks low on his hips, just tight enough to show the lines that mattered. At fifteen, he was sinewy, but you could see the beginning of the man in his shoulders and chest.

On rainy days, the beach rats lounged under the boards on stacks of pads piled a dozen high, cracking on each other, listening to the gulls and the boom of thunderheads. One morning that first summer, Jake was watching storm clouds move across the sky. The dark clouds discouraged beach traffic. The other boys had disappeared, probably to meet girlfriends at their summer jobs, serving burgers, hot dogs, pork roll, and greasy French fries to tourists strolling the boards.

Bernie had gone up to the street to settle the weekend action, leaving his brother, Sammy, to mind the phone. Sammy had a weak bladder. Jake watched Sammy walk further inside the tunnel to piss in a milk bottle behind a stack of wooden chaises. Sammy needed to pee every thirty minutes, or so it seemed. Before Sammy finished, Bernie's phone rang, and Jake thought it would be a good idea to answer it.

"Who's this?"

"Jake."

"Where's Bernie?"

"Not here."

"Sammy around?"

"Taking a piss."

"Okay, kid. Tell Bernie to put one large on My Gal Sal in the sixth for the Geator. Got that, kid?"

"Yes, sir."

"Repeat it back to me."

Jake did.

"Good kid."

This was where Bernie Dorfman's real money came from: making book. The phone hanging on the beam just inside the entrance to the tunnel was his only overhead. Life was a cash business for Bernie, and the government got only enough to keep the IRS from getting curious.

Jake ran up to the street to find Bernie standing at the base of the ramp. When Jake relayed the Geator's message, Bernie looked at Jake like he was seeing him for the first time, a half smile on his face. Bernie never said much, just cocked his head at a slight cant and, with the barest of grins, conveyed he had cut through the bull by whoever was tossing it.

Bernie would then say something the listener didn't expect or understand: *Keep your mouth shut and make like you got all the answers and nobody will know you don't. Keep 'em guessing, kid.* That was Bernie's imparted wisdom. Years later, Jake decided that was the reason Bernie had always seemed so wise—he didn't say enough to sound dumb.

"From now on, kid, leave the phone to me or Sammy. You stick to the pretty ladies in the cabanas."

"Yes, sir."

As soon as he could slip away, Jake ran the few blocks to the Arkansas Avenue beach—Chicken Bone to the locals. He figured he might catch Rabbit in time to drive to the track for the sixth race and still get back in time to break down the setups. During the day, Rabbit shuttled carloads of Negroes from the bus terminal at the north end of Arkansas Avenue. He would jam eight in his cab—six in the back and two more in the front. Shoveling coal, Rabbit called it.

Rabbit, a rising freshman at Franklin and Marshall College, had first noticed Jake in the high school cafeteria, backing down a bully who was baiting a frightened kid. Jake cowed the bully by offering to stand in for his victim. Rabbit liked what he saw and decided Jake was worthy of his friendship and guidance.

Jake spied Rabbit parked in his usual spot at the ramp, dropping off fares. "Yo, Rabbit!"

Jake had learned not to stare at Rabbit's two front teeth.

"You got time to make a run to the track?"

"Maybe."

"I answered Bernie's phone."

"Shoulda said so in the first place. Let's go."

At the track, Jake camped by the hundred-dollar window two minutes before post and watched a string of ten-percenters play My Gal Sal to win. Rabbit stood ready at the ten-dollar window and, on signal from Jake, bought six win tickets. The ten-percenters had driven down the odds, but My Gal Sal still went off at thirty to one. My Gal Sal broke first and never lost the lead. She won by two and a half, going away.

"Good job, Jake," Rabbit said. "Beats shoveling coal."

Young Jake was a hustler in a city of hustlers, humping lunches and snacks, cigarettes, and cold drinks for the hotel guests who lolled in the cabanas, scoring a half buck, maybe a dollar each run. Jake watched people, not fully conscious of what he was doing, but learning. He knew how to get the good tips, but there was no guile in him, no premeditation; it was all instinct.

Usually, the wives became his advocate. "Oh, honey, give him more. Such a handsome boy."

Jake put his best effort into the cabana guests. These were the regulars, usually monthlies, though a few rented for the season. The day-trippers—shoobies, they were called by the locals because of the cardboard shoeboxes stuffed with food they lugged to the beach, along with the kids and the lawn furniture—rarely spent a dime. Shoobie men wore white guinea tees tucked into bermuda shorts hiked high on their waists. Gartered black silk socks rising from mesh-toed dress shoes were stretched to transparency, exposing bony knees and an inch or two of thigh, white as powder.

Jake followed the same routine each morning. He swept the cabanas—three-sided black-and-white-striped canvas tents, a privacy flap over the entrance, with a peaked roof and wooden plank floor—and wiped down the surfaces of the tables and chairs. He put out fresh towels and pads for the chairs and lounges.

One morning, he became conscious of her watching him as he set up chairs and umbrellas. He walked toward her cabana, thinking she wanted him to run an errand. But she didn't call him over until her third day.

She looked directly in his eyes. "A tonic with lime, no ice; garden salad, Italian dressing on the side; and a pack of Marlboros." She spoke in a low, husky tone. Her words conveyed an intimacy that made him blush.

He was back quickly. She did not speak. She motioned him into the tent. He put her drink and salad on the table. She scanned the shore break before lowering the flap of the beach tent. Her body movements pulled him in their wake, invisible but real. He could feel her from three feet away. He wasn't frightened, exactly. He was aware only of his heart thumping. He had never before been conscious of his heart.

She sat on the edge of the chaise. "Come closer, honey."

She undid the D-ring buckle of his trunks and the buttons of his fly. Her hands were deft and efficient, her touch impossibly light. She wore no makeup. She smelled fresh, as if she had just stepped from the bath. She tilted her head, and her hair fell to one side, a sheet of silk she gathered to the back of her neck, Philadelphia's answer to Lauren Bacall. She took him in her mouth, her tongue a butterfly, her fingers velvet. He shivered with the force of a thousand wet dreams.

I'm sorry, he thought.

Her smile was gentle and assuring. She buckled his trunks, stood, and kissed his forehead.

"You'd better go. He just went for a dip." She brightened. "Here," she said, reaching in her purse to produce a five.

He did not extend his hand. He'd never gotten that much before, and it didn't seem right to take it. She took his wrist and pressed the bill into his palm. He didn't know how to express his feelings, tell her he didn't want her money.

Outside the cabana, he spied a man emerging from the shore break and walking toward the cabana Jake had just exited. The man's scalp glistened through strands of hair plastered to his head. His middle was soft, his arms shapeless.

* * *

The Atlantic City boardwalk—a sixty-foot wide, four-mile long promenade—rested on trestle-like supports ten feet above the powdery white beach sand farthest from the ocean's reach. The Marlborough Blenheim loomed hard against the avenue edge of the wooden strand, the doyenne of the beach front hotels, oblivious to the adit-like opening under the boards centered beneath her lobby.

The tunnel, perpendicular to the boardwalk, extended from Bernie's office at the beach to its terminus deep under the Blenheim: Tessie's, the luncheonette operated by Bernie's sister. Here, Tessie Dorfman reigned over a subterranean world. Everything about Tessie was big: conical breasts, her face pan-caked and rouged, topped by a teased meringue beehive giving her the appearance of an aging drag queen.

The tunnel entrance leading to the luncheonette was a kaleidoscope of pinwheels and stars where sunlight met shadows. The walls were packed with railroad ties to hold back the mud. The tunnel ran fifty yards beneath the street with about six feet of headroom at the beach end before widening into the luncheonette, the ceiling higher so that the tallest patrons were able to stand upright.

The luncheonette had an aluminum-edged linoleum counter about fifteen feet long, with red vinyl-topped stools that swiveled 360 degrees. Behind the counter were soda spouts and stainless steel containers filled with lettuce, tomato, onions, peppers, cheese, and lunchmeats. A metal hood vacuumed the smoke and pungent aroma from a grill segmented by food group—hotdogs, hamburgers, bacon, onions, and peppers—lining the back wall.

Jake would pick his way through the crowd to place an order for a cabana family. Oiled bodies were tightly bunched at the counter. They were known as Tessie's Boys, and that was how Tessie thought of them. She was the

Queen Mother. In her place under the boardwalk, her boys were royalty; they belonged. She was their confessor, the one they turned to when there was no one else. She listened to their stories of love and heartbreak and brutality, comforting them the best she could.

The denizens of the luncheonette seemed to speak with their eyes, offering promises to be kept or broken, tentative pleas, and preemptive apologies. Jake was aware of their glances and sensed a vague power over them.

One afternoon, he was surprised to see a familiar face among the oiled bodies: his Uncle Sandy. Sandy Gordon was his father's uncle, but Jake had always called him uncle. He was a small trim man, his bronzed face open and readable.

From his expression, Sandy seemed not to have noticed his nephew. Jake's first thought was to turn away to avoid being spotted. Neither of them should be in Tessie's, for different reasons. But Jake didn't want to hide from his uncle.

Sandy looked startled as their eyes met, but then he half sighed and smiled. Jake hugged his uncle, just as he did at the family's annual High Holiday gatherings.

"Where have you been hiding this one, Sandy?" one of the men said.

"He's my nephew," Sandy said. "And he's off limits."

Sandy pulled Jake by the elbow. "Jake, I'd like to introduce you to my friend Jamie Wescott. Jamie, my nephew."

"Well, hello, young man."

Wescott was years younger than Sandy. Thick curls streaked blonde with peroxide fell over the tops of his ears and the back of his neck. His arms and shoulders were muscled.

"Pleased to meet you, Mr. Wescott," Jake said, extending his hand.

"Jake," said Sandy, "do me a favor and don't mention—"

"I know, Uncle Sandy."

"Thanks, Jacob."

"It doesn't bother me. I mean, it doesn't change a thing—"

Sandy patted him on the back. "You're one of the good ones, Jake."

At night, Jake sold newspapers on the boardwalk for Bernie's brother, Sammy. He operated from a stand on the boards at Kentucky Avenue—not a stand really, just a couple of stacks of papers topped with a brick to keep the wind from blowing them away. KY was the center of the action on the boards after dark. With three shows a night at the Warner Theater and the mobs of tourists at the Steeple Chase Pier, he had plenty of customers.

One night, papers were selling as fast as he could pull them from the stack. His right hand, black with newsprint, ached from nonstop transactions. In a seamless motion, he would grab a paper and, with a flick of his index finger, fold it in half over his thumb while extending it with his palm upturned to catch the coins dropped by the customer. The grimy carpenter's apron tied around his waist sagged with quarters, dimes, and nickels. He had sold out twice, and it was barely nine o'clock.

He glanced at the headline in large bold type across the top of page one: "Marilyn Monroe Dead, Found in the Nude." She was a big star, but he hadn't been allowed to go to any of her movies. He first saw her in the pages of one of his father's magazines, which Jake discovered in its secret place in the utility room behind the heater, under his father's toolbox. Her platinum hair flowed in waves to her shoulders. Her head was tilted slightly back and to the side. She was kneeling, thighs tight together. Her back was arched, and she supported herself on one arm. Her free hand cupped the back of her head, pushing her breasts up and forward. Her skin was flawless, the color of cream, her nipples erect.

His parents must have discovered what he was doing because the magazine disappeared from its secret place. That didn't stop him. He conjured her image at night, and in some ways, that was better than the photograph. He could be alone with her in the dark, in his own bed. At about this time, his parents left a book in his room—*Puberty and Adolescence*—their response, he realized much later, to the stains on his sheets and underwear.

Now she was dead.

Sammy Dorfman waddled penguin-like toward his newsboy, lugging two bundles of late editions. A potbelly the size of a beach ball hung over the waistband of his bermuda shorts. The bottoms reached nearly to his ankles, covering the eczema scales on his shins. Scraps of rice paper filled both pockets. Sammy ran a small-time policy game, and he used rice paper to record the code names and numbers of his players because it dissolved easily in water and could be flushed or even ingested, if necessary, in a vice raid. Numbers and newspapers were the Dorfman family enterprises conducted above sea level.

Sammy talked around the stub of a soggy, unlit cigar wedged in a corner of his mouth. He wore sunglasses even at night—blocky black plastic Roy Orbison frames—and a newsboy's cap too big for his bald head.

"Papers here! Get your papers!" Jake was shouting his usual hawk when he spied Sammy.

"Hey, kid. Whatta the seagulls say?" Sammy's spittle sprayed the boy's hand as Jake extended the money pouch. "Schmuck! Schmuck!" said Sammy, mimicking a gull's squawk, answering his own question, as he always did. "I wanna hear: 'Marilyn Monroe Dead, Found in the Nude!' Got that, kid?"

"Okay, Sammy."

"Well, let's hear it, kid."

"Marilyn Monroe Dead, Found in the Nude," Jake repeated in a monotone.

"Louder, kid." Sammy dropped the bundles at Jake's feet, produced a pair of rusty wire cutters, and snipped the straps. "Schmuck, kid," he muttered under his breath. To Sammy, anybody with a heart, a conscience, and who wasn't putting it over on the other guy, was a schmuck.

Jake wouldn't use the words Sammy wanted. He wouldn't say anything. He'd stand there and hand papers out and collect the quarters, dimes, and nickels because that was his job. But he wouldn't betray her. He watched Sammy waddle out of earshot down the ramp to the street and went back to his regular hawk.

"Papers! Get your papers here! Papers here!"

He'd sold out the late edition, and Sammy had made his last pickup of cash. The crowds of tourists had dwindled. The rasp and clang of metal security gates being lowered in front of the souvenir shops and clip joints along the boards signaled the close of another day in AC's nickel-and-dime economy.

Jake rolled the grimy carpenter's pouch into a tight cylinder and tied it off with the apron strings. A breeze off the ocean had driven away the humid August heat, and he decided to walk home along the boards. Hi Hat Joe's at Chelsea Avenue and the boards would still be open, and a crowd of mostly Jewish teens from Philly would be congregated out front.

As he approached Texas Avenue, he could see the small gathering along the rails on the beach side of the boardwalk. Every kid in the high school knew Joey Nardo and his corner boys, Vinny Nicastro and Toad Carbone. They'd stand out there most of the night, leaning against the rails, hands in their pockets when they weren't slicking back their pompadours.

Jake watched as the three boys suddenly straightened from their tough-guy slouch. He followed their line of sight and looked down the ramp leading from the street to see a figure approaching: Michelle Nardo, Joey's sister. Jake recognized her from school; there was no mistaking her. Jake moved to the rail on the street side of the boardwalk to watch her.

Vinny and Toad inched away from Joey as if to get out of the line of fire. Michelle said something to her brother. Then she abruptly pivoted from her audience and headed toward the ramp to the street. She would have to notice him, Jake realized; she was coming straight at him. He looked down at the soiled pouch he carried and his newsprint-stained hands.

Michelle Nardo. He'd seen her for the first time sitting in the front row of the auditorium balcony in study hall. He hadn't the nerve to approach her, the prettiest girl in school by far. He'd studied her profile, the drape of black hair that fell in a soft curl just below her chin, and that had been enough to fall in love. He had never seen any girl as beautiful. And from that moment, he knew he would do anything for her. It did not matter to him that she was *his* sister.

Now, she stepped in front of him. "You're Jake Harris."

"Yeah." He looked up, swallowed, shifted his feet, and looked back down at the boards.

"You watch me in study hall," she said, a statement of fact, not an accusation.

"I'm sorry," he said, still looking down at the tops of his sneakers.

"Don't be sorry. I kind of like it. It's cute."

He blushed and slowly raised his head. Her eyes were one shade lighter than the black of her hair. He had never looked—really looked—in a girl's eyes until then. He understood at that moment why. It took courage.

She smiled. "Try talking to me instead of just staring all the time."

It took all he had to put aside his insecurity and ask her out. On their first date, they went uptown to the Warner Theatre on the boardwalk to see *Breakfast at Tiffany's*. By the time Audrey Hepburn had cried in George Peppard's arms, Michelle had snuggled against him, her arm laced with his. He was conscious of the gentle pressure of her breast against him, of her warmth. It was imperative that he remain perfectly still, neither breathe nor move a muscle, for fear of disturbing the feel of her against him.

The boardwalk was empty when the movie let out. They stopped at the rail and looked out over the Atlantic. He liked the beach late at night, the quiet of it. The breeze off the ocean had cleared out the greenheads and cleansed the air of the wet heat of the day. The surf had calmed and held the lights of Steeple Chase Pier on the water's surface. The movie's theme played in his head. *Moon River, wider than a mile, I'm crossing you in style someday…*

He knew he had to see her again, no matter the consequences.

* * *

Jake lived with his mom, dad, and younger brother, Ben, in lower Chelsea, the best of Atlantic City's neighborhoods, if "best" was measured by middle-class small-business owners and single homes with intact families.

The Harris house on Aberdeen Place was landlocked. Sally Harris had insisted on the location because she was convinced living any nearer the water would result in her children's death by drowning. Buddy Harris went along even though he could have afforded a small bungalow on the bay and knew water property would prove more valuable. The narrow alley next to Jake's house, like all the others separating the houses in the neighborhood, had an outdoor shower, where mothers washed the beach sand from their children.

Michelle lived uptown in the Italian section. Little Italy, they called it—Ducktown to its denizens. Ducktown spanned Texas Avenue to Mississippi Avenue, from Arctic Avenue to the boards. St. Michael's RC Church, the heart of Ducktown, dominated Mississippi Avenue between Atlantic and Arctic. Every kid in the neighborhood had been baptized and made first communion at St. Mike's. They attended the parish school as their parents had, at least those who had not been banished to public school for disciplinary problems.

Confessing the sins of adolescence was a regular practice. "Forgive me, Faddah, for I have sinned." Dante Hall—Danny Hall to the locals—doubled as St. Mike's gym and bingo parlor. Saturday night, the hall filled with teenaged boys combing pomade through DA haircuts and eyeing parallel lines of teenaged girls in teased-up beehives, shimmying under the stern watch of Mother Superior and her minions.

Ducktown was a different world to Jake, edgy and risky to outsiders. It might as well have been a foreign country. His family only ventured in for an authentic meal at a respectable *trattoria*, or his father would pick up an order of White House subs, their Sunday night staple. But the conventional wisdom of his parents' circle was that its pool halls, bars, and side streets were inhabited by toughs, juvenile delinquents, and dead-enders and were to be avoided.

But after that first date with Michelle, feeling her against him, none of that mattered to Jake.

Jake had to get permission to date Michelle. And since her parents were gone—gone forever—Jake had to talk to her older brother.

"Yeah, sure," Joey Nardo said in his deep voice, not even hesitating. "You can take her out, Beach Boy." He paused, and Jake's heart raced as Joey's hand landed on his shoulder. "On one condition."

"What's that?"

"That you ride with me and my crew so I can get to know you a little better."

Jake knew their reputation, the toughest of the tough. But he would have agreed to almost anything to see Michelle.

"Deal," he said.

They cruised in a shiny black-and-chrome 389 V8 Bonneville Coupe, the disembodied voice of the Geator with the Heater, the Big Boss with the Hot Sauce, turned up high on the radio, spinning the latest teeny-bopper hits, serenading pedestrians through rolled-down windows. "Sherr-ee won't you come out tonight with your red dress on." The Bonnie's five occupants moved their heads in time to the music. Vinny "Two-Tone" Nicastro rode shotgun and sang lead. Franco "Toad" Carbone, wedged between Vinny and the driver, provided backup vocals. Joey Nardo sat in his usual spot in the back seat on the passenger side, silent and motionless. Joey at eighteen was the oldest, unless you counted the driver, "Fish" Gomberg, who had Joey by six months. But nobody counted Fish. Fish was just the driver, not a Ducktowner, not even an Italian. Jake sat in the back with Joey, thinking about Michelle, hoping the ride would end without trouble.

"Yo, Fish. Stop singing so loud, will ya?"

"Lay off him, Toad," Vinny ordered.

"Christ, Vinny, he ruins the fucking song."

"Too bad, douchebag, it's his car."

Artie "Fish" Gomberg was from Downbeach, a rich boy by Ducktown standards. Downbeach was Ozzie and Harriet Land. As Atlantic City began to change in the 1950s, the whites that were able to afford it pushed south into Ventnor, Margate, and Longport, communities of single-family homes with manicured lawns, neighborhood schools, churches, and libraries—buffered from the undesirable elements of the big city to the north by the unwritten, inviolable whites-only code of the Downbeach Board of Realtors.

Fish didn't say much. But he became agitated when it came to protecting his car, which was anytime one of the others lit up. Fish and Jake didn't smoke, but Joey, Vinny, and Toad did. It was part of "the look": packs of Marlboros rolled up in the sleeves of their T-shirts, Zippos at the ready, cigarettes dangling from their lips. "Don't get any ashes on the upholstery! It's real leather. Blow the smoke out the window, will ya? The smoke makes the car stink." Fish whined more than he talked, but when it came to protecting his car, he didn't care how he sounded. His Bonnie was the most important thing in the world to him.

Toad liked to let the ash burn, holding his cigarette at an angle, delaying gravity as long as possible—just to prolong Fish's anxiety. Fish would shoot pleading looks, his bulging eyes darting from Toad to the ever-lengthening ash. This went on until Vinny intervened. They were just having fun with Fish. Toad didn't really want to mess up Fish's car. Fish was an honorary Ducktowner, a sort of mascot—and besides, none of them had a car. They needed Fish for his wheels.

Vinny Two-Tone was the smoothest-talking, the coolest of the crew. Vinny bought the beer (quart bottles of Schlitz, which they passed around) with a phony age card he'd gotten from one of the wiseguys at Victory Billiards. Vinny had the stones to pull it off. They would hit a different liquor store each Saturday night outside of Ducktown—where every liquor store clerk knew them— and Vinny would work his magic. In a pinch, when the card didn't work, they'd find a rummy to buy the beer for them.

Joey Nardo always rode in the back seat like he was being chauffeured. He could keep an eye on his companions that way. He lived at the corner of Arctic and Texas, in a walk-up, with his sister and their alcoholic aunt. Their parents were gone; no one knew where, but no one was brave enough to ask Joey about the subject. Joey carried a Louisville Slugger fashioned of white ash, its handle black with pine tar Joey had rubbed on for a better grip—his prized possession. Joey had the bat with him whenever the Ducktown boys cruised the streets. He kept it at his feet, tucked under the front seat. Jake had never seen Joey hit anyone with it or, for that matter, even threaten anyone. But he always had it with him. All the guys had a nickname except Joey. Joey was just Joey. Some called him Crazy Joey, but never to his face, because he *was* crazy.

That first night Jake rode with them, the Ducktown boys called out to pretty girls, hurled insults at guys whose faces they didn't like, but that was it. No trouble. Joey let

Jake out at ten after busting on him for being a momma's boy.

"See you tomorrow, Beach Boy."

Some nights, they'd stop for a homemade dinner at Toad's house, the best Italian food Jake ever tasted. Toad Carbone lived with his mother and Nonno, his grandfather. The first time Jake met Nonno, the old man squinted at him, picked up a knife, and cut a chunk of Parmesan from the wheel in the center of the kitchen table.

"*Morta Cristo*," the old man said, motioning in the direction of Jake with the wedge of cheese impaled on the knife point.

"He likes you, Beach Boy," Toad whispered.

"How can you tell?"

"He gave you a nickname. That's an honor."

"*Morta Cristo?*"

"Yeah."

"What's it mean?"

"Christ Killer."

"What time you come home, Franco?" Nonno never referred to his grandson as Toad.

"It's *titsoon t'tell*, Nonno."

Toad croaked his laugh. He cracked himself up every time. *Titsoon t'tell. Titsoon* was Italian for "charcoal," dago street talk for Negroes, which to Jake didn't sound as bad as the other names the Ducktown boys used. Ducktown punks policed their turf on the boards between Mississippi and Texas. When a colored passed by, Jake would hold his breath, hoping they'd forgo their slurs. But they never tired of the same dumb-ass routine, and standing there with them Jake felt ashamed of his silence. Jake's best friend, Alfie Braithwaite, was Negro, and Jake cringed to think how Alfie would feel if he saw him with the Ducktowners. "Yo, Toad. Whattayiz wanta do tonight?" Joey would ask whenever a Negro strolled by. That was the cue. "I dunno. Titsoon t'tell." You'd think they were watching Martin and Lewis at The Five, the way the corner-boys roared.

"Stay outta the dark neighborhoods, Franco," Nonno Carbone called after them.

At midnight, a land breeze picked up, making for a sticky summer night. The boys had tired of cruising the streets.

"I need a cheesesteak," Vinny said.

The White House Sub Shop was located on the corner of Mississippi and Arctic. The White House made the full array of submarine sandwiches, the best on the island, but the cheesesteak was its specialty: fresh-baked Formica's rolls, guts out, virgin olive oil, premium steak, melted provolone—none of that Philly yellow cheese whiz crap—*cheesesteaks to the stars*. Jake's mother always said it was the water that made Atlantic City Italian bread the best in the world. *White House* was to *cheesesteak* what *Kleenex* was to *tissue*.

"I gotta get home. Nonno's been on my ass." Toad never crossed his grandfather.

"What about you?" Vinny asked Joey.

"Fish and I got some business," said Joey.

"C'mon, Jake," Vinny said. "It's just you and me tonight."

Inside the White House, three men in stained white bib aprons—cheesesteak impresarios—stood equally spaced over a six-foot grill. Each wielded a large rectangular spatula corralling peppers and onions into geometric piles and flipping thin slices of prime sandwich steak in various stages of readiness. The men turned from their work only as long as it took to snatch a slip of green grease-stained paper from a wire running along the edge of the business side of the counter. There was nothing careless or random about them; their movements were methodical and continuous. They didn't converse or joke among themselves. They responded to the sights, smells, and sizzle arrayed before them, focused on the work of preparing the White House cheesesteak sub, the best in the world. No three-star Michelin chef brought greater pride to his creation.

"What're you havin', hon?" Marie said, poised at the cash register with her pencil and pad of green slips.

"Steak, double cheese, works."

"Whole or half?"

"Whole."

"How about you, hon?"

"Whole cheesesteak, no onions." Jake was ready. You didn't keep Marie waiting.

"In or out?"

"In," Vinny responded.

She tore their order slip off the pad, clipped it to the wire with other orders waiting for execution, punched one of the flashing buttons on the black telephone on the counter beside the register, and spoke into the receiver wedged in the crook of her neck. "You want onions…hot peppers? Fifteen min." She scribbled on her pad, tore off the sheet, reached back without a glance to place it on the wire, and punched another flashing button.

The boys walked down the narrow aisle between the counter and booths. They took two freshly vacated stools. Jake tried not to stare at the men in the closest booth. He scanned the wall above, every inch of it covered in photos personally inscribed by the biggest names in sports, politics, and entertainment. The sentiment, variously formulated, was the same. "To Angelo and the White House crew. Thanks for the greatest subs in the world!"

As he studied the Brown Bomber's photo, Jake glanced at the men seated below and then quickly away.

It *was* them.

Skinny D'Amato was holding court. On the table was a tray piled with cheesesteaks and a variety of other subs layered with Genoese salami, capocollo, prosciutto, provolone, lettuce, tomato, onions, and hot peppers all seasoned with oregano stuffed in fresh-baked rolls, guts out, drenched in olive oil. In a lot of ways, Skinny D'Amato was Atlantic City. He was the legendary owner of The Five Hundred Club, the crown jewel of AC's nightclubs. All the biggest acts and headliners played The Five, of late more out of loyalty to Skinny than the payday. Skinny had supported them before they made it to the top, and they never forgot him, especially now that his town and club were on the decline.

"Hey, kid." The speaker was a thin man sitting in the middle of the semicircular booth surrounded by his companions.

Jake could only stare, place an index finger on his chest, and mouth, "Me?"

"Yeah, you."

He knew the house rule about not bothering the famous, and the White House fed them all—Joey Giardello and Rocky Marciano, Chuck Bednarik and Richie Ashburn, Abbott and Costello, the crooners and comics who played the Five and the Pier, and the stars of Philly's professional sports teams.

Jake looked toward the counterman for approval.

"Angelo, it's okay," said the skinny man who had called him over.

Jake stared into pure azure eyes set in an olive face, an amalgam of sharp angles topped with a Bryl-creamed pompadour that dropped a curl over one brow.

"Kid, you know who this is?" he asked, motioning to his right. The deep timber of his voice was surprising for such a thin man.

Jake recognized the second occupant of the table from the Dinah Shore and Ed Sullivan shows, regular television fare in the Harris home. "Yes, sir. That's Mr. Dean Martin."

"That's right, kid. Good. Now as exceptional as he might be, I do everything better than my *Paisan*—and I mean everything. I outsing him, outdrink him, and outfuck him. We got a bet on you, kid. I say you're Calabrese. Dino here says you're kosher. Which is it, kid?"

Jake stared at the eyes. For a reason he could not explain, he did not want to disappoint their owner.

"Well, don't keep us waiting, kid. You a wop or a Jew?"

He hesitated. "Jewish, sir."

"I coulda told you that." The nasally voice came from a horsey, boyish face topped with a crew cut seated between Dino and Blue Eyes. He looked ten years younger than the others. Jake recognized him as the funny half of Martin and Lewis.

"Kid, you cost me a C-note." Blue Eyes smiled. "Here, get yourself and your guinea pal a couple of cheesesteaks on me." He took Jake's hand and pressed a crisp twenty-dollar bill into the palm.

* * *

He met Michelle on the sidewalk in front of her apartment. She took his hand, smiled, and sensing his jitters, assured him they would have a wonderful time. They walked hand in hand to St. Mike's. As they neared their destination, the Virgin beckoned with outstretched arms. He'd seen Vinny and Toad make the sign of the cross whenever they passed before the statue of Mary in a small grotto beside the church. Joey never did. Joey just hunched his shoulders and never looked at the stone figure. Just before entering Dante Hall, Michelle let her hand fall from his.

He had never been inside Dante Hall before. The hardwood floor glistened. The sweet-and-sour aroma of hormone-fueled perspiration overlain by *Lestoil* permeated the air. When Michelle asked him to the St. Mike's dance, he did not think about Dante Hall; he only thought about holding Michelle when a slow dance played.

At the far end of the hall, behind a backboard and next to a score clock enmeshed in protective wire hung the body of Christ nailed to the cross. Even from the entrance to the hall, a basketball court away, Jake could make out the crown of thorns and droplets of blood spotting the figure's forehead.

"Let's stroll!" came the voice over the loudspeaker. Two parallel lines—one female, one male—hurriedly formed. "Ladies and gentlemen, the Diamonds!" "Come, let's stroll, stroll across the floor…" Michelle grabbed Jake's hand and pulled him toward the dancers. AC High held dances in the gym over the lunch periods but Jake never danced. He had, however, watched enough line dances to fake it. Michelle squeezed in line on the girl's side, and Jake did the same on the boy's trying his best to line up directly across from her. The lines moved in perfect sync, the dancers shuffling two steps right, two left, left foot back cross, right foot back cross, lazy hand claps on alternate steps. At the head of each line, two dancers came together and strolled down the lane, followed by another and another, each couple taking their places at the end of their respective lines, keeping perfect time with the music. The more accomplished did fancy pivots and spins as they moved down the lane. Jake was relieved to see that he had counted correctly. Michelle and he would arrive at the top of their lines together.

"Let's slow it down," the deejay crooned over the last bars of "The Stroll." The Platters. "They asked me how I knew my true love was true…" Jake held Michelle as close as her billowy skirt would allow, his arms around her waist, hers draped loosely on his shoulders. Their cheeks touched. Neither saw her approach. Ruler in hand, Sister Don Bosco firmly tapped Jake on his shoulder with her weapon of choice. She placed the ruler between them in the proximity of their waists to guide them apart. The mother superior of the Daughters of Mary in full habit, headdress, wimple, wooden crucifix and beads gave Jake a stern look before turning toward the next couple in violation of Mother's decency code. Jake felt as if all eyes were on him, which of course they were not. "I'm sorry, Michelle," he whispered. She responded by pulling him close once the nun was a safe distance. "Mother's been upset lately," Michelle began. "One of her novitiates refused her vows and ran off with a young priest." Jake did not pursue the subject, instead snuggling closer to Michelle.

When the Platters faded into the *Mashed Potato*, Michelle led Jake from the dance floor. "Let's get some punch," she said. As they neared the table holding the punchbowl, Jake saw Vinny and Toad slouched against the wall. Theresa Salducci was draped around Vinny. She wore a tight-fitting skirt, pink cashmere sweater complete with a carefully placed virgin pin and pumps. Toad was wearing a similarly attired Maria Del Bene.

"Yo, Jake." Vinny motioned him over. The three girls exchanged somewhat cool greetings as Vinny grabbed Jake in a playful bear hug. "Looks like Mother caught you having too gooda time," Toad said.

"Hello, Franco," Michelle said, more a rebuke than a greeting. She turned to Vinny and offered an equally chilly greeting. In unison, the two boys mumbled respectfully "Hey, Michelle."

Theresa and Maria had reputations. Jake heard one of them whisper to the other something about Michelle "acting better than everyone with no parents and a crazy brother." But Michelle never turned around and gave no indication that she'd heard anything. It was clear Michelle didn't care one bit what Theresa Salducci or Maria Del Bene thought of her.

Vinny shed Theresa and motioned Jake to follow him out of earshot of the girls. Toad did likewise and huddled with Jake and Vinny.

"What are you doing after the dance?"

"I don't know. Probably hang out with Michelle."

"How about meeting up with us. Joey and Fish are picking us up after the dance."

"What about Theresa and Maria?"

Vinny smirked and winked at Toad. "That business was taken care of before the dance."

"Geez, I don't know. Michelle will be pissed."

"Yeah, well, sometimes you gotta choose. Do whatever it is you two do. We can meet up after outside the White House. What do you think, Toad? Can Jake handle Miss Nardo? Take my advice, kid. You make the rules. It's easier that way."

Jake returned to Michelle, who was standing in awkward silence a few feet removed from Theresa and Maria. "What was so important I couldn't hear?"

"Nothing. Vinny wanted to know what I was doing later."

"Later when? Tomorrow? Tonight? You're with me. Don't think you're going to ditch me for Vinny to do whatever it is those guys do."

"He said Toad and he are meeting your brother and Fish. Wanted me to hang with them."

Michelle rolled her eyes. "Jake, you know how much I worry about Joey when he's with Fish—which is all the time. I can't do anything about that. But you're smarter than that. They're only going to cause you trouble."

"C'mon, Michelle. They're harmless. We'll probably end up at the White House for cheesesteaks."

She sighed. Tommy Edwards's "All in the Game" came over the sound system. She took his hand and led him to the dance floor. Ignoring Sister Don Bosco's earlier warning, she pressed close against him and placed her hand gently on the nape of his neck. "I just worry, Jake," she whispered. "I don't want anything bad to happen."

"Nothing bad is gonna happen, baby. I promise."

* * *

Pageant Week. The gang had front-row seats for the Parade of States thanks to Jake's dad who had reserved one of the rolling chairs lining the parade route along the boardwalk. The chairs were rented at a premium during pageant week, but Buddy Harris had an in with the guy who owned them, a Polish Jew named Max.

Max had survived the camps; a *sonderkommando*, a Jew who ran the showers and the ovens for the *SS*. Jake's mother had never liked Max. He was crude, she said, and reflected badly on the *rest of us*. The first time Jake saw Max with his father, they were in the boiler room of one of Max's buildings in the Inlet. Jake had stared at the blue-black numbers, fuzzy with time, on Max's forearm. Jake's mother told him that Max and his wife, Faiga, swallowed gold filings and diamonds buffered in bread, shit them out (his mother didn't use the word *shit*), cleaned them off, and swallowed them again, and that was how they were able to survive: bribing guards, ushering their fellow Jews to the showers, and burning their corpses. By the time Auschwitz-Birkenau was liberated, they had swallowed and shit enough gold and diamonds to start over in America.

But Buddy Harris admired Max. He told his son Max was a "survivor."

Jake loved the old-style rolling chairs. They were as AC as Mr. Peanut, the pageant, and the diving horse. When he was much younger, as a special treat his Poppa Joe would take him for short rides in the wicker chairs along the boards in front of the Steel Pier. Vaguely Victorian, the original rolling chairs—some with canopies, some open-topped— were a boardwalk fixture. Mostly, Negroes pushed them up and down the boards, carrying tourists, woolen throws across their laps to protect against the night chill off the ocean.

Max decided motorized chairs would be an improvement. His bankers questioned his judgment and wondered whether visitors would ride the motorized version. The bankers said the tourists would prefer the European charm of the wicker push chairs. Max responded to the bankers that he'd lived in Europe and there was nothing charming about it. Max prevailed. He knew how to make money, and his bankers underwrote his project. Max's chairs smelled faintly of battery acid. He called his business the Blue Chair Company, and Buddy Harris worked for Max during the summers to keep the Blue Chairs rolling.

The Miss America Pageant was held the week after Labor Day. It marked the end of the season, the perennial finale. The seasonal tourists were gone, back to Philly and their work-a-day lives. The local kids were back in school, which started the first weekday after Labor Day. The pageant had begun in 1921 as a gimmick to squeeze one more week of tourist revenue out of the summer. Now millions across the nation were glued to their TV sets to learn who would be this year's *Ideal.*

The swimsuit competition defined the pageant. All the rest—the talent portion (tap dancers, baton twirlers, and singers from church choirs) and the questions to the five finalists—was included to keep the pageant from being dismissed as a skin show. "What would you do to make the world a better place?" Bert Parks would ask every year. "I would encourage everyone to attend the church of their choice," Miss Stars & Bars would answer. At least half of them responded with some variation on the church-faith theme. One thing was certain: none had to suppress the impulse to respond, "Fucked if I know. We're all doomed."

Oddly, or so it seemed to Jake, each of the contestants had the same shaped buttocks. The height and width of each bottom varied with the overall size of its owner, but the contour of each was eerily similar: an upside-down heart. The top two-thirds of the misses' butts were flattened from just below the waist. The bottom third bulged and spread slightly to meet the crease at the top of the thighs. The cheeks did not protrude; the assembly of young buttocks seemed deliberately designed to discourage male viewers from commenting how they'd like to *do it to them doggie style.* Bosoms were controlled as well. Protruding nipples encased in rigid, pointy cups offered just a glimpse of cleavage.

The winner would have fair skin, long legs, and the facial features of a porcelain doll. Everyone knew that, expected it, and demanded it. That paradigm had been broken only once, in 1945, when a dark-haired, olive-skinned Jewish girl from New York got to walk down the runway as the new Miss America. *That* showed the Nazis. Since then, only Barbie Dolls from the Deep South or Midwest had won. That's what America wanted, and that's what the pageant officials made sure to deliver. They were pushing a product, no different from the carneys selling blenders and phony antiques to Mr. and Mrs. Whitebread in town for a week of wholesome family togetherness at the seashore. It was all a harmless hustle: the Boardwalk, Miss America, corndogs, skeeball, auction joint "estate" sales, miracle blenders, and Mr. Peanut.

The Parade of States, the highlight of the first night of the pageant, was a slow moving procession of white Oldsmobile convertibles—the official Miss America cars that would be sold after the pageant as mementos to wealthy locals—interspersed with high school marching bands from around the country. Each convertible carried a "Miss" who, from her perch on the folded-down top, waved to the onlookers with a perfect, unchanging smile. It was the first opportunity for pageant-watchers to pick their favorites and predict the winner.

The pageant had talent winners, Miss Congeniality (the kiss of death), swimsuit winners, and evening gown competition.

"Yo, Toad, watch where you're putting your fat ass."

"Fuck you, Vinny." Toad squeezed in between Vinny Two-Tone and Joey Nardo on the padded bench seat, made to fit three adults. Jake shifted over to the edge.

Vinny stood and reached his arms toward one of the misses as her convertible passed close by the front of the boys' position. "Here she is…" he sang giving his best rendition of Bert Parks "…our ideal."

Toad yanked Vinny back into his seat.

"Yo, Toad. Look at those tits." Vinny cupped his hands around his mouth. "Yo," was all he shouted. The girl turned toward the boys, waving.

"She smiled at me. You see that?"

"You're nuts," Toad said. "She'd smile at Fish if he was here."

Fish wasn't there since he was managing Sammy Dorfman's enterprises: running numbers, stocking newspapers, and hooking up call girls with pageant week conventioneers. (Sammy expanded his business interests to include girls during pageant week.)

"I'll bet you I can score with her."

"Right. Tonight in your bed at home. Only it'll be your right hand." Toad made the universal jerk-off sign.

"Five bucks says I get at least a hand job."

"You're on. But you gotta have proof."

"What proof, Toad? What am I gonna do? Let you watch?"

"Take a Polaroid. You know, like with Theresa Salducci."

Jake thought if anybody could pull off a hand job from Miss Stars & Bars, it was Vinny.

"I'll see you losers tonight outside Victory. You'll get your proof. Just have your five bucks, Toad."

It was nearly 2:00 a.m. when Vinny finally showed at Victory Billiards. Toad, Joey, Jake, and Fish were leaning against the Bonnie.

"Get your fin out, Toad."

"Bullshit," said Toad.

Vinny smiled. "She's staying at the Chalfonte. Frankie No-Neck is workin' the lobby. He lends me his uniform jacket. I get a tray, two glasses, two Cokes, and a bucket of ice, and I go up and knock. The chaperone opens the door. Miss Stars and Bars is standing right behind her. I look at her. She looks at me. I give her the Vinny wink. She tells the chaperone she ordered the Cokes, which is a lie, of course. I leave and wait down the hall. It could go either way, but I'm betting I'm in."

"Just get to the good part, Vinny." Toad grabbed his crotch and thrust his hips forward.

"I wait until the chaperone comes out of the room, on her way to the elevator. I head back to the room, and the door is cracked open. "Here she is…." Vinny did his Bert Parks again. "Two minutes, she tells me. She says she sent the chaperone downstairs to get her a personal hygiene item. She says I have to come in two minutes like I'm some soft-boiled egg. And don't get any on her or the furniture, she tells me."

"Two minutes—that's a long time for you, Vinny."

"I says, it ain't my style to come that fast. But I'll try. I want to show her my towel trick. She asked me what it was, and I told her. She said, 'Next time, sweetie.' She called me *sweetie*."

The Ducktown girls loved Vinny's towel trick. A quantity of small towels was needed and a source of water to soak them. Vinny would get hard, and one by one he would drape wet towels on his unit. His personal best: fifteen hand towels.

"So she sez, 'Y'all have a wonderful pecker. So big—and what an interesting color.' Then she jacked me off. I musta shot ten feet. That's the truth. Five bucks, Toad." Vinny held out his hand, palm up, and jabbed it with his index finger.

"That story don't mean diddly without proof."

Vinny reached under his T-shirt and produced from the waistband of his jeans the signature white sash with red lettering each contestant wore. Written on it in a feminine hand were the words "To Vinny, with love."

"Fucking A," said Toad, reaching for his wallet.

* * *

School started the day after Labor Day. It had been a week since the new *Ideal* had been crowned, but it still felt like summer. The seasonal renters had gone back to Philadelphia, to pick up with their lives where they had left them the previous Memorial Day. The hardcore still hit the beaches—the marathon tanners and Tessie's boys. Tessie kept her luncheonette open weekends after pageant week

until the High Holidays. She closed for the season sometimes in late September, sometimes in October, depending
on where *Yom Kippur* fell in the Jewish lunar calendar.

A cool September night, Jake headed down Texas
Avenue on his way to see Michelle. Fish's Bonnie pulled up
to the curb. Seeing the black and chrome vehicle made Jake
feel like he'd been caught cutting class.

"Get in, Beach Boy," Joey Nardo said, leaning across
the backseat. He opened the door.

"I dunno," Jake said. "I got a date with Michelle."

"Get in the fuckin' car. You wanna play kissy-face with
my sister tonight, Beach Boy, you got a date with us first."

"Yo, Joey. Get off the kid's ass. He's in love."

Vinny was the only one who could get away talking to
Joey that way. Nobody, even Joey, seemed able to get angry
at Vinny. He had an impish charm that worked on the corner boys as well as the girls.

Jake didn't want to get in, but he also didn't want to
land on Joey's bad side. He climbed in the back, his toe
accidentally nudging the barrel of Joey's Louisville Slugger
protruding from under the seat. Toad extended the brown
bag containing the half-empty quart bottle of Schlitz.

"No thanks."

"Aww, Beach Boy don't want beer breath when he
kisses his girlfriend," Toad said.

Fish drove down Ventnor Avenue all the way to
Margate, windows down, so everybody would see him
with his boys. The Margate Jews hung out Saturday nights
at Kramer's Delicatessen at the corner of Ventnor and
Lancaster, just at the top of the Parkway where the avenue

widened into median strips of manicured landscaping and alabaster fountains bordered by manorial homes.

The Margate kids looked down on the Ducktowners, but they were afraid of them, too. And there was Artie Gomberg in his black and chrome Bonnie with the Ducktowner feared above all others—Joey Nardo. Fish could feel the awe, no longer his invisible self.

Fish stopped at the light on the corner of Lancaster and Ventnor. Toad and Vinny Two-Tone jumped out of the Bonnie and sprinted to Kramer's front window. The booths against the window were filled with Fish's Margate classmates eating corned beef specials, French fries, and drinking cherry cokes. Toad and Two-Tone dropped their pants. Toad pulled his underwear down—Vinny wasn't wearing any—and pressed their butts flush up against the window. Toad called it pressed ham.

Vinny turned and hung his unit in the window. That was what he called his dick: the unit. The tip was almost snow white, the shaft was tan, like Vinny had taken it sun-bathing and carefully lathered the head with protective cream. Vinny Two-Tone was proud of his unit, and the girls adored it.

They hopped back in the car, and Fish peeled out, Vinny and Toad laughing about the looks on the Margate kids' faces. Uptown, Fish turned his Bonnie onto KY, the stretch of Kentucky Avenue between Atlantic and Arctic. The Club Harlem, the Negro answer to The Five, was located mid-block and gave KY its hustle and jive. Fish slowed the Bonnie alongside several couples outside the club. Jake knew what was coming next. He shot a glance at Joey, who had pulled the Louisville Slugger from under the seat and was breathing heavy with anticipation. Jake slid down and turned away from the window, hoping Joey wouldn't notice.

Toad leaned across Vinny and stuck his head out the window. "Yo, jungle bunnies."

"Hey," Vinny snapped, wiping his cheek. "You got spit on me."

"Yo, sorry, Vinny."

Jake stole a glance out the window and there was Alfie Brathwaite. "Why you gotta do that?"

"Do what, Beach Boy?"

"Call people names out the window. They're not hurtin' us."

"You wanta run with the moolies?"

"Yo, Joey. He can't help it. He's a Jew. Ain't that right, Jake?"

"Shut up, Toad."

Toad croaked his laugh and gave Jake a swat on the back of the head. Everything was cool with Toad.

Fish made a sound somewhere between a laugh and a moan. Maybe it was just his adenoids, Jake thought. Whatever caused it, the sound was creepy.

Jake was the only one who seemed to be aware of Fish's presence. The others acted like he wasn't there, unless they were directing him to drive to a particular place—or until he opened his mouth, usually to protest a perceived injustice.

Fish was soft, short, and round, his chin embedded in layers of jowls. His eyes were puffy, like he'd gotten woken up too early, bulging beneath hooded lids, wide-set, nearer his temples than the bridge of his nose. He didn't breathe air so much as ingest it slowly using thick Darwinian lips to scoop oxygen from the atmosphere. The lower protruded, closing over the upper with each breath. Adenoids made him sound like he was whining and caused him to breathe laboriously through his mouth. He was an easy target for his classmates.

When Nonno first saw Artie Gomberg, he told the boys gathered in the Carbone kitchen about a huge fish, some of the specie grew to six hundred pounds—a bottom dweller and very clever. He caught one in Florida on a fishing trip. It had thick lips, bulging eyes and moved very slowly. The captain of Nonno's charter boat called it a jewfish, which Nonno Carbone thought fitting, after seeing Artie Gomberg. So Nonno Carbone honored Artie with a nickname: *Jewfish*. Fish for short.

Although Fish was nearly three years older, Jake had caught glimpses of Fish's struggles growing up. Fish had no success with girls, though he wanted them like every other boy after his first wet dream. He had bigger breasts than most of the girls in his class at school. He was lousy at sports. Team captains would rather go short-handed than choose Fish. When he turned seventeen, he got his license, and his father bought him the Bonneville. It was a cool car, but it did nothing to improve Artie's social standing. No girl would ride with him.

Fish must have known that the car was the only reason the Ducktown boys allowed him to be part of their gang. But Fish would have been just another rich, Downbeach

Jew, even with his 389 V8 Bonneville Coupe, if Vinny Two-Tone hadn't adopted him. Fish was Vinny's Jew.

Vinny noticed Fish one summer night on the boards running one errand or another for Sammy. A few nights later, some young Ducktown punks began razing Fish pretty hard. Even then, Vinny was a planner. His parents told him that Jews were smart at business, and Vinny figured Fish was a smart Jew driving a car like that. Vinny had his eye on the future, and it wasn't going to be hanging on the rails or running errands for the wiseguys at Victory Billiards. Vinny would need people like Fish. So Vinny Two-Tone looked out for Fish and kept the corner boys from riding him too hard. That was how Fish Gomberg, a Jew from Margate, became the wheels for the Ducktown boys.

The Negroes outside the Club Harlem did not respond to the taunts. Jake was grateful for that. Had they said anything, the confrontation might have escalated with Joey jumping out of the car, Louisville Slugger in hand.

"Indiana?" Fish wanted to know.

Indiana Avenue had a string of leather bars from Pacific to the beach.

"Sure," Joey answered.

Jake had had enough. "Fish, lemme out here."

"Turnin' pussy on us, Jake?" Toad chided.

"Fish, swing by Victory, then take the kid to see his girlfriend." Vinny again the voice of reason.

Fish said nothing, gulped some air, and hung a U-ee down Atlantic to Mississippi Avenue.

The street had offered little trouble that night, and Jake breathed easier. That was how Jake always felt, getting out of the Bonnie at the end of the night, lucky to avoid disaster. But that was the price he had to pay for peace with Joey, and Michelle was worth it.

Fish pulled to a stop at the curb in front of Victory Billiards. Vinny and Toad exited to hang with the wiseguys. Jake managed to climb past Joey to follow Toad out of the Bonnie. Shouts of "Pussy!" trailed the Bonnie as it squealed away from the curb, laying rubber up Mississippi toward Pacific.

Jake ran the six blocks to the corner of Arctic and Texas and took the stairs two at a time to the second floor landing.

She was waiting there, leaning against the jamb in jeans and a boy's white T-shirt.

"You're sweating."

He wiped his forehead. "I ran from Victory."

"You've been with Joey?"

"Yeah."

"Anything bad happen?"

"Not tonight."

"Where is he?"

"Tooled off in Fish's Bonnie."

"Fish scares me."

"Fish?" He laughed. Jake wondered how soft, short, fat Fish could scare anyone.

"He's creepy. I wish my brother would stay away from him."

"He couldn't hurt anybody if he tried. He's got adenoids."

"All the same, I worry about him. She reached out her hand, grabbed his arm, and pulled him inside."

"Where's your Aunt Theresa?"

"Mario was here, asking for money. They got into it then made up over a bottle of gin. He left after she passed out."

They went into Michelle's room. Her Philco was permanently tuned to *WMID AM 1340 on your radio dial.* A song ended, and the DJ came on with a dedication:

"This is the Geator with the Heater, the Boss with the Hot Sauce, for all you young lovers. Let's slow it down for some Saturday night cheek to cheek. This one from the great Tommy Edwards goes out for the beautiful Michelle in Ducktown from her guy, my main man, Jake."

Michelle smiled, draped her arms around his shoulders, and the two shuffled slowly to the song over the radio.

"Many a tear has to fall, but it's all in the game…"

An hour passed before they stirred from their embrace on her bed. Jake kicked his legs over the side of the bed and stood, stretching. The thought of his mother's anger at his being out so late animated him further.

"Jake?" Her voice husky with sleep sounded sultry.

"Michelle, I have to get home. My mom's gonna kill me."

"I need you to find Joey for me. He didn't come in last night and I'm worried."

"Why is this night any different?"

"I just have a bad feeling, that's all. Please, for me?"

He was already in deep trouble with his mother and additional delay getting home wouldn't really matter.

"Okay, baby. I'll find him." He bent over and kissed her forehead.

"Thank you." Her eyes closed and a contented smile appeared on her lips.

Outside Jake raised his jacket collar against the damp chill of the night air. There was no sign of Joey or the others at the White House. He turned up Mississippi Avenue. The Bonnie was not at the curb in front of Victory. He walked to Pacific Avenue. It was deserted, a black corridor lined with worn-out motels, pawnshops, and the occasional all-night burger joint. Synchronized traffic lights stretched to the Inlet blinked yellow. The Jitneys had stopped running for the night, so he walked to the boards.

He headed uptown a few blocks, stopped across from the Marlborough Blenheim, and stood at the rail facing the ocean. The mist felt good on his skin. Leaning out over the rail, he could make out the black hulks of tarp-shrouded wooden chaises, lounge pads, and beach umbrellas.

As he pushed away from the rail, he heard a faint mewling cry, maybe a cat. He went down the steps to the beach to investigate and peered into the mouth of the tunnel. A prickly-cold wind howled down the gullet, stinging his face with debris. The smell of the sea was heavier in the narrow, confined space. The darkness was flawless. He knew that Bernie's phone was attached to the beam at the entrance, two feet from where he stood, yet he was unable to see even its outline.

He extended his arms reaching for a stack of pads; he knew there would be two other stacks to guide him deeper inside as his eyes adjusted. He hoped Sammy hadn't left a full piss bottle in the narrow aisle. He heard the cry again, fainter, a guttural moan. His vision still had not adjusted.

Halfway to Tessie's gate, a gust off the ocean whistled through the blackness. He wanted to turn and run, but he didn't, afraid to expose his back to whatever was down the tunnel.

Grunts and thuds echoed. He inched forward, his hands probing the blackness. His foot caught the edge of a plank, and the other one stubbed against the make-shift walkway, causing him to almost fall. Someone yelled. Panicked voices penetrated the darkness. He froze momentarily then turned and ran.

When he had the night sky over him, he pivoted at the sound of labored breathing closing behind him. Jake took the steps two at a time and raced across the boardwalk to the ramp leading down to the street. He glanced over his shoulder in time to glimpse a shirtless figure emerge from the tunnel in a half run, half stagger across the sand. At the base of the ramp, polished chrome reflected the hazy yellow streetlight, piercing the darkness.

* * *

1964

As a hunter might say, the city was in the dying quivers. The Democrats were in town to nominate Lyndon Johnson. Bobby Kennedy, gaunt and haggard, spoke to the convention in his brother's memory. Members of the official Mississippi delegation dropped water balloons from hotel balconies on the heads of Negroes. "Hey, pennyhead!" they yelled to get them to look up. When the Mississippi Freedom delegates were seated, the water balloon delegates walked out. Pearl Mesta, the Hostess with the Mostest, threw lavish parties for the powerful in her rented mansion on Atlantic Avenue.

The Knife & Fork—a Tudor landmark located across from the high school where Pacific and Atlantic Avenues came together—was doing well. It was operated by the same family that had opened it fifty years earlier. Lew Tendler's Steakhouse and Dock's Oyster House further uptown on Atlantic Avenue were hanging on. Teplitzky's had a monopoly on the kosher-only crowd. Ducktown offered family owned trattorias specializing in homemade southern Italian cooking and the White House Sub Shop drew the famous and powerful along with the locals.

Mainly though, Atlantic Avenue was a wall of plywood, irregular seams, and crudely cut padlocked openings, headstones marking the empty shops behind them. The families that owned the stores had given up on the city. Some simply closed their doors one night and never opened again. Many moved their businesses offshore to "villages" of boutiques where families could window-shop, strolling from store to store along manicured tree-lined paths, undisturbed by addicts, the homeless, or other undesirables.

The way the city fathers sold the Democrats on the grand beachfront hotels, the cavernous convention hall—home of the Miss America Pageant—and the city's world famous "wooden way" as the place to hold their national convention would have done a boardwalk auctioneer proud.

The cops rousted the leather bars, shut down the bathhouses, arrested street addicts and pushers, and ran the hookers and pimps across the bay to West Atlantic City. The hotel lobbies were freshened with plaster and paint to hide years of neglect, but their guts—corroded pipes and overloaded electrical systems—were beyond saving.

All summer, Jake and his friend Alfie Brathwaite hustled the beach. Chicken Bone was one huge picnic, or so it seemed, and Alfie was raking in the tips. Jake was having a big summer too. The delegates had plenty of cash to spread around, and the cabanas in front of the Blenheim were booked solid even though Bernie Dorfman had tripled the rent.

Jake worked the hotel suites hooking up the big spenders with everything from White House cheesesteaks to passes to The Five. Bernie Dorfman was the connection to Skinny D', who always had a couple of tables for his bookie.

That summer, Jake didn't spend much time riding with the Ducktown boys. He'd run into Toad and Vinny on Texas Avenue waiting for Joey outside his apartment. Fish had traded in his Bonnie. Their new ride was a two-door muscle car with a 389 cubic inch V-8 under its shiny black hood, scoops and aftermarket pipes to give it some street growl. When Fish saw the ads for the Pontiac Grand Tempest GTO he had to have it, and his was one of the first off the line. He used some of his dad's life insurance money to make up the difference left after the trade.

Joey had given up ragging Jake about not running with them. The two would nod as they passed on the stairs to the Texas Avenue walk-up, Joey to the GTO, and Jake to see Michelle. All that summer, Jake spent evenings with Michelle alone in her room. Aunt Theresa was usually passed out, but she wouldn't have minded. She liked Jake in her way. They listened to music and talked about the life they'd have after high school. They both swore they'd get out of AC. Neither was sure how or where, but they would. The only thing they knew for certain was that AC was a dead end. When they were sure the gin had taken well hold of Aunt Theresa, they would strip to their underwear and climb under the sheets. They would push against each other, their legs entwined, he pressed against her belly and she against his thigh.

Sometimes she would read to him, usually Edith Wharton. She read without inflection in a soft, natural voice. *The Age of Innocence* was her favorite. What must it be like to love someone more than life and not have that person completely? Her eyes filled with tears when she read the last page.

"Why didn't Archer go up to Olenska's apartment?"

"I think because he was frightened. He'd lived each day yearning for someone he couldn't love. Sad, huh?"

"Jeez, Michelle. How do you come up with that stuff?"

He ached for her as only an adolescent could for a first love; it was real, and it was exquisite. He did not tell her when he bought a copy for himself. At night, when he was not with her, he would read passages, hearing her voice until sleep came.

Labor Day was two weeks away, and Jake would be leaving for freshman orientation at F & M the next week.

* * *

Rabbit had been the one to guide Jake to Franklin and Marshall, a small men's college in Lancaster, Pennsylvania. Jake had never heard of it until Rabbit selected it for himself. Rabbit had gone to Franklin and Marshall on a full scholarship, majoring in poli-sci. Rabbit had his eye on law school: Norman Lasky, Esquire. This all seemed like a good idea to Jake. He already knew an upperclassman. So it was settled. He accepted early admission without visiting or applying to any other school.

Norman "Rabbit" Lasky, born and raised in the Inlet section of Atlantic City, had never gotten out. The Inlet was "changing," a euphemism the locals employed to describe the influx of Puerto Ricans and Negroes. The Inlet back in the day had been a thriving, lower middle class community of mostly Jews and Irish until the 1950s, when families with ambition and the means left for bigger and newer homes in lower Chelsea, Ventnor, and Margate. Parents went deep into debt for homes Downbeach to give their kids opportunities they never had.

Rabbit's family never had the money to make the move. Being raised in the Inlet had its benefits though. It taught Rabbit how to get the edge on other people, in a fight, in a deal, driving a cab. He had attitude and instincts. Mostly, he was able to spot bullshit and weakness in others. Rabbit had a gap between his two front teeth, precisely one sixteenth of an inch. The Puerto Rican girls loved him. Word spread, and Rabbit was besieged. "Please, Rabbit. Do that thing to me that you do with your teeth."

Rabbit pulled his cab to the curb, reached across, and opened the passenger door. "You look lost, man. Get in."

"Hey, Rabbit," Jake responded as he slid into the front passenger seat.

"You ready for F & M?" Rabbit asked.

"Guess so."

"How about showing a little more enthusiasm. Who knows? You might get lucky with some cute Amish farmer's daughter. Where you headed? Don't tell me. Let me guess. Texas and Arctic."

Jake nodded.

"I'll give you a lift. Speaking of girls, what's the plan with you and Michelle?"

"We're gonna see each other on breaks."

"Maybe. But there's lots of girls waiting for you in Lancaster, you know."

"You sound like my mother. She's always nagging me. Tells me I'm too good for Michelle. She's hoping when I go away, that'll end it. Wants me to meet girls from *good families*."

Rabbit laughed. "Let me tell you something about girls from good families. They're spoiled cunts who think their shit doesn't stink. You remember I was seeing Gail the summer before I went away to school?"

Gail was Gail Liebgott of *the Margate Liebgotts*. Her father was prominent in Jewish charities, a past president of *Avoda* and *B'nai Brith,* and had been chairman of the Golf Committee at Linwood Country Club before becoming its president. He was a Penn graduate, and Gail's brother was a freshman at Penn. They called him a legacy. Mr. Liebgott sold cars—a lot of cars. His dealerships supplied the official convertibles for the Pageant.

"Gail's old man hadn't counted on me dating his little girl. To him, I was a coal-shoveling, meter-juicing, whore-running cab driver from the Inlet, not good enough for his princess. But I had the bastard's number from the start, with his Ivy League education. He is a fucking car salesman."

"What's his problem? You're Jewish."

"Not the right kind."

"There're different kinds?"

"Wise up, Jake. To the goys we're all the same. But to the Jews you got your *Litvaks*—that's the Laskeys—and the high Germans. They would be the Liebgotts. The German Jews got here first, unless you count the *Sephardim.* Those were the Jews who left Spain during the Inquisition. Some of them were here during the Revolutionary War. The Liebgotts and their kind came to America in the nineteenth century. They brought their art and German culture. The Eastern European Jews just wanted to get away from the Tsar and his pogroms. They came with the clothes on their backs. But they were tough. That was a benefit of taking regular ass-kickings by the Cossacks. To the German Jews, the Litvacks were coarse, an embarrassment, the kikes that gave Jews a bad name."

"My mother used to say that about Max, the guy my dad does work for. Owns Blue Coal and the rolling chairs."

"I know Max. He's the lowest on the ladder, a Holocaust refugee. Anyway, her old man sees me at the country club with his daughter. Next thing I know, Gail says I can't pick her up at her house anymore. 'Daddy' says she can't see me. She'd thank him someday, he told her. But she won't listen to him. So I pick her up outside Kramer's, and she jumps in the cab, crying, 'What are we going to do, Norman?' I know what I'm going to do. I think to myself, I'm going to get a blow job."

Rabbit's face broke into a grin.

"So she goes down on me. When she finishes, I zip up and drive back to her house, not saying a word. We get to her house and she says, 'Norman, tell me you love me.' I don't look at her. I reach across her, open the door, and tell her to get out. Those were the last words I said to her."

"That's cold, Rabbit," said Jake. How could Rabbit treat someone so cruelly? Gail was a nice girl. He didn't understand then that what Rabbit did had nothing to do with Gail. It was all about Rabbit and Mr. Liebgott.

"No loss. Plenty of girls with fancy pedigrees looking for something different to bring back home to Darien to shock the folks. You'll see. Your first mixer at Bryn Mawr, and you won't remember Michelle's name. No offense. She's a beautiful girl, but still."

Jake knew there was no point in debating Rabbit when he was on a roll. "Where's Darien?"

"Connecticut. Half of F & M's preppies come from Greenwich or Darien or New Canaan. A bunch of Harvard rejects with Roman numerals after their names."

"What are they like?"

"I just told you. Members of the *Lucky Sperm Club*, living off family money. The way I see it, Jake, a preppy WASP is no different than an Inlet spic with a tattoo of Jesus on the cross between his shoulder blades."

Jake figured that vision allowed Rabbit to be Rabbit. Different tribe is all.

"Corner's fine."

Rabbit pulled his cab to the curb at Texas and Atlantic.

"Thanks for the ride. But you're way off about Michelle. I'm not giving her up."

"Maybe not."

From the corner of Texas and Atlantic where Rabbit had left him, Jake spotted Michelle waiting for him on the sidewalk. He broke into a trot and soon could hear the angry voices coming from the open window above the street. The whole neighborhood could. Mario and Theresa were into it again, fighting over money, like they always did.

"Jake, thank God you're here. I couldn't stand being in the apartment one more minute," she said taking his arm. "Let's get out of here."

They walked to the boards and down to the beach. A gentle breeze came off the ocean. The night sky was cloudless and the stars were visible over the water beyond the amusement piers. The Perseid meteor showers were peaking and an occasional arcing tail of light streaked across the sky out to sea. They turned right and headed toward Margate.

"When are you leaving?" Her tone was flat.

"Orientation starts next Monday. My folks are driving me to Lancaster on Sunday. When does Trenton State start?"

"Day after Labor Day. I've got my bus ticket. Jake, this is hard for me to talk about. You've never taken me to meet your parents. Sometimes I think you're ashamed of me."

"I love you, Michelle. I want to be with you for the rest of my life. Tomorrow night you and I are going to have dinner at my house. My dad will love you the moment he meets you. It might take my mom a bit more time, but once she gets to know you, she won't be able to help herself—especially once she sees her first beautiful grandchild."

She laughed. "Slow down, Jake! I just want to meet your parents."

"I'm just saying I know you'll be a hit."

The boardwalk ended where Margate began. They walked to the water's edge, easier going than the soft, dry powder out of the ocean's reach. Michelle huddled against him. He put her under one arm, and she reached across his chest and snuggled closer.

"Jake, do you think you'll ever be happy?"

"I'm happy right now."

"Sometimes when we're in my room, you're off somewhere. I can feel it. You pull me tighter like you're holding on, but you're not there. It's a feeling I get sometimes."

"I used to get sad for no reason when I was a kid. I never could figure out why. My mom would get mad at me for it. Like I could control it. But I don't feel that way anymore."

"Do I make you happy?"

"Yeah, Michelle. You're all that does."

"Maybe that's what I mean, Jake. There has to be more."

"Why?"

"Because there has to be. People change. They die. They go away. My mom and dad went away. So there has to be something that makes you glad to be alive, something only you control."

"Don't you wonder about them?"

"No. Maybe sometimes I wish they hadn't left Joey and me. But they did."

"Would you change that if you could?"

"I don't know."

"Would you change anything?"

"You make me feel good about myself, Jake. I know it sounds corny. But you make me feel safe. Before I even knew you existed, I'd wish for you. What about you?"

"I liked to know more about my grandfather."

"Your Poppa Joe?"

"No. My dad's father, Isaac. I've never even seen a picture of him. My mom says he was a good man. He got sick when my dad was just a kid and couldn't leave the bed they set up for him in the living room. He couldn't climb stairs. Something with his heart. Anyway, he died when my dad was still in high school. He was a carpenter. My dad never talks about him. It's like he never existed."

"Why don't you ask?"

"My dad and I don't really talk about that kind of stuff."

"But that's what you should talk about with him, Jake. If my mom and dad were around, I'd want to know everything about them."

At the bulkhead separating the beach from the street Lucy the Elephant, a sixty-five foot colossus of wood and metal stood sentinel at Margate's southern boundary. Woodrow Wilson in his pre-presidential lawyer days paid the dime admission to tour the interior and climb the spiral staircase to the canopied howdah astride Lucy's back. Eight decades of sea air had eaten through the tin to expose the structure's wooden ribs. Tear-like streaks of rust tracked down Lucy's cheeks from each massive eye. Long neglected, abandoned as a hotel, she had been condemned as unsafe even for tours.

Michelle turned from him and took a few steps toward Lucy. Her hair glistened like black silk. Even in the darkness her eyes drew him. She made a small gesture with her hand to follow.

At the base of the old structure, he took off his windbreaker and spread it on the sand. The warmth of their bodies warded off the night chill. Michelle fixed him with her eyes then slowly reached under her skirt and slipped off her panties. As she did, his heart began to race. He had never had intercourse with anyone. He and Michelle had kept their underwear on when they held each other in her bed. They had pushed against each other, and he had climaxed, the first time entirely unintended. This was different. Michelle was in control, and he gave himself over to her.

She took his hand as she knelt on the windbreaker. He lowered himself over her body, positioned between her legs, his arms extended, supporting his weight inches from her. He was certain she could hear his racing heart. He remembered the first time he saw her, in study hall. He had watched her then, undetected, or so he had thought.

She slipped his trousers and shorts down and guided him inside of her. She moved beneath him. He was conscious of her breathing and his own. She pulled his face gently to hers, touched her lips to his cheek, and folded into his arms.

It was 3:00 a.m. when they returned to her building. The apartment was dark and quiet. Through the half-open door, he could see her aunt passed out on the couch. Mario was nowhere to be seen.

"We'll see each other on Thanksgiving," he promised.

The words hung between them. As soon as they were out of his mouth, he wanted them back. Despite his intention, they sounded hollow.

She kissed him and went up the steps.

He walked along Ventnor Avenue, slowly as if his pace would ease the abruptness of his goodbye. At his front door, he turned and headed back to Texas Avenue. He wanted to tell Michelle that he loved her, that they'd be together always, no matter what.

From the corner of Texas and Atlantic, he saw white and red flashes against the walk-ups lining the street. Black and Whites, roof lights flashing, formed barricades at both ends of the block. Cruiser radios and handhelds crackled with the clipped jargon of cops. The disembodied voices were flat, no urgency in them. On the street, cops leaned on open doors of squad cars nosed into the curb outside the apartment building. They were shooting the breeze about the Phillies' late summer swoon, families, what they would do with their lives when they retired.

An ambulance was parked perpendicular to the curb, its rear hatch open to the sidewalk. The crew leaned against it, smoking, their demeanor devoid of any expectancy that they would be in a life-saving race to the ER.

Jake sprinted the last half block, ignoring the shouts of the cops at the corner. He pushed past neighbors gawking on the sidewalk dressed in whatever they had been wearing to bed. They whispered behind cupped hands as if someone might overhear, their eyes riveted on the scene, not wanting to miss the excitement, enjoying their role as spectators.

The sidewalk directly outside her building was cordoned with wooden sawhorses painted white with "ACPD" in blue lettering.

"Where do you think you're going?" the officer asked.

"Upstairs." Jake looked past the cop, up the second-floor landing. He could see yellow tape stretched across the door of Michelle's apartment.

"You live here?"

Jake's silence gave the cop his answer.

"Afraid not, kid."

The smell of grease and week-old garbage hung in the stairwell. He heard Michelle's voice:

"Please don't hurt him!"

Three figures appeared on the landing. Two cops had Joey by the crook of his elbows, hands cuffed behind him. From that angle and distance, it looked as if he were wearing a red T-shirt. His hands and arms were covered in blood as well, his face splattered with it. Joey offered no resistance, his face expressionless, his eyes empty. The trio pushed past the cop, guarding the entry. Only Jake stood between Joey and the squad car waiting to take him away. Their eyes locked.

"Take care of my sister, Beach Boy."

The cops stuffed Joey into the rear seat of a squad car.

Pulsing lights, statical voices, the stench of grease and blood filled the steamy August night. At the top of the stairs, Michelle struggled vainly to free herself from the embrace of two cops and join her brother. Jake bent over the gutter, stomach rising. He felt the hot liquid move up from his belly until the bile heaved from his gut.

The killing of Mario Cippolone made the front page of *The Press*, a two-column below-the-fold account headlined: TROUBLED TEEN BEATS UNCLE TO DEATH. HACKS OFF HANDS was the subhead. The account did not scrimp on the details at the crime scene. The linoleum floor in the living room was "sticky and thick with blood." The victim's face had been pummeled into a "grotesque mask." The reporter's description of Mario Cippolone's face called to Jake's mind Carmen Basilio's following his championship bout against Sugar Ray Robinson. Jake had watched that fight on TV with his dad. Basilio's nose, lips, and cheeks, broken and split and engorged with blood, formed a Cubist portrait. His left eye was swollen shut and had the appearance of an overripe Jersey beefsteak split open from rot. Crusted rivulets of blood ran from his nostrils and ears. But

Joey had outdone Sugar Ray; he'd knocked his uncle's right eye from its socket. Joey had beaten Mario unconscious with his bare fists, the article said, then hacked off both his hands at the wrists with a butcher knife.

Vinny told Jake what he knew. Joey had come home right after Jake dropped off Michelle. Turns out Mario had been in the apartment all along, passed out on the floor. Joey and Mario had argued. Vinny wasn't sure what set it off.

His mother's reaction was predictable. "Jacob, this does not happen in nice families. Whatever it is you think you have with this girl, she is not for you. She is beneath you. You will not see her again as long as you are under my roof. Do you understand me?"

His mother divided the world between Jews and those who didn't like Jews (everyone else). There were genteel, polite anti-Semites, like the Kennedys, discreet *lace-curtain Irish*, and then there were *shanty Irish*—beer swilling, wife beating, vulgar. But lace curtain or shanty, they were all anti-Semitic. So were the Slovaks, as she called them. "Butchers," she said. In Sally Harris's world, Italians were the most mysterious of gentiles, Catholics who truly believed in the body and the blood, the incarnation, and the resurrection. Although she had never met Michelle, Sally Harris was certain she knew her kind.

Jake had never seen his mother as forceful and resolved. She came at issues from the side, attributing her feelings or wishes to an anonymous entity, her personal doppelgänger. But this thing with this Italian Catholic girl with the hoodlum brother and no real parents, this girl who lived in a third-floor walk-up demanded her full attention. She had saved up whatever influence she would have over her older son for something of great importance. And this, in her mind, was it.

She had expectations for him. His father did too. College, graduate school, a profession. "You'll be my lawyer. You'll marry a nice Jewish girl. You'll give me grandchildren so I can brag on the beach to the ladies."

No one had expectations for Michelle.

On the ride to F & M, Jake stared out the backseat window of his parent's sedan, watching the Lancaster countryside roll by. The last words he had said to Michelle played over in his mind.

"We'll see each other Thanksgiving."

But already, Ducktown seemed a lifetime away.

Part Two

October 1979

The guy working the grill at the White Tower was new, part of the vanguard of latter-day Okies looking for a piece of AC in the new era of casino gambling. They were strangers, without sand in their shoes.

"Y'iz want onions?"

Sixteen silver-dollar sized White Tower burgers sizzled in day-old grease, the aroma irresistible.

"Yeah," Jake answered.

"Me, too," Alfie added.

"Whataya want to drink?"

"Coffee, black—if it's been in the pot less than two days."

"You're a funny man."

"Just water for me. I don't know how you drink that sludge, Jake."

"Alfie, you remember that guy I told you about? Buddy of mine from school that went with the Bureau? Bill Perry."

"Yeah."

"He's in the Philly field office. He's working both sides of the river on the joint task force with the Jersey crime commission. We've been feeding each other since I got my shield. He called. The New York and Philly families are jockeying for control of gaming and the unions in our little town by the sea. The feds flipped an insider and wired him. Perry wants me to keep him posted on our little dig."

"Since when do we answer to the bureau? Besides, what do three vics that have been dead for seventeen years have to do with the feds?"

"We don't answer to them, Alfie. We'll work with them. Perry's interested in the location, not the bodies. The Blenheim is prime casino real estate."

"McMeekin will have our asses if he finds out."

"He's not going to find out. Bill Perry knows the importance of going dark, if only to protect his own investigation. I trust him."

"I don't know, Jake. Sounds like no good can come of working with the feds. But okay—for now. But you had better not leave me out of the loop. It's my shield too if McMeekin finds out."

"You sure you want in on this? Plausible deniability can be a wonderful thing."

"Now that you mention it…"

Jake felt like a high school freshman again, trying to find his courage to call the prettiest girl in school. All his shame and guilt came rushing back. She told him she had a faculty meeting after the school day but agreed to meet him at her home when that was over. Until now, he had protected his memories of her, a precious possession to be managed with care, kept inside. The ache of first love had become all the more exquisite with time. He realized his remembrances could be entirely his own, not shared by Michelle. Now, he risked losing her again.

She lived in a small bungalow on Sovereign Avenue that backed up on the bay. Her features had shed the soft roundness of a teenager, but her eyes hadn't changed.

"Hello, Jake." No pretense, no agenda, no reproach. Same Michelle. "Want a cup?"

"Black, no sugar."

"I know. I remember."

She returned with two cups of coffee and handed him one.

She looked at the cup cradled in her hands, uncertain where to begin or whether even to try. Jake could practically read her mind. *You ran away when I needed you, Jake. You never once tried to see me. And now you suddenly reappear, a cop with a notepad.*

"I'm not good at this, Jake. What do you want from me?"

What he wanted was to be a kid again, standing at dawn in black and white, at the boardwalk rail with Michelle pressed close against him, "Moon River" playing in the background.

"I'm here about Joey."

"Of course."

Joey was the only reason anyone ever came. Truant officers, social workers, cops, probation officers, sickos—they'd all come for Joey.

"Do you still have any of his things?"

"Let me guess. You think he killed those men they found under the Blenheim?"

"It doesn't matter what I think."

"It does to me."

"Michelle, the lab puts the deaths all around the same time—'63, maybe '62. Joey was still on the streets then."

"I'm sorry, Jake. I know you're just doing your job. You know what the shrinks at Farview told me? They tested him, some kind of genetic screen. They claim he's got an extra Y chromosome." She paused and seemed to be trying to digest the implication for her family tree. "They say that makes him a *supermale*, prone to violence and sick behavior."

She'd been palming a cigarette, like a teenager hiding it from a parent. She lit it in that semiconscious way that serves to occupy pauses in conservations. She took a deep drag, turned her head away, and exhaled toward the ceiling.

"I know you hate these things. It's on my list to quit. There's a chest of Joey's things in the hall storage closet. Take whatever you want."

He didn't get up. That would make it look like he didn't care, that he had gotten what he'd come for.

She saw his hesitance. "Go ahead, Jake. It's okay. Really. And thanks."

"For what?"

"Coming alone."

He lifted the lid of the chest. The bat was on top, placed cross corner to fit, a first-class relic of summer nights, stained with resin and sweat. He used a handkerchief to grasp the handle and lifted the bat from the trunk. He held it to the light and rotated the barrel.

She barely glanced at the bat when he returned. He leaned the Louisville Slugger against the table and sat down.

"How have you been?" Even before the awkward words were out he braced for her put-down. In that instant, he reconciled to a reply that ranged from sarcasm to disdain.

"Got my degree at Trenton State—delayed a year— and a job at the high school, teaching freshman English. Married Jimmy Walcott. You remember Jimmy. Fancied himself a poet. I thought I could create life as I pictured it should be. You know—bungalow, picket fence, dog, two kids."

Of course, he knew—about Walcott and her teaching at the high school and where she lived, though he never had the courage to call her, even after he moved out of his marriage. He'd imagined their meeting, planned it. There were a dozen ways to make it happen, casually with no apparent risk. But he had done nothing. He forced something between a grimace and a smile.

"What?" she reacted to his expression.

"My brother calls that the 'Ozzie and Harriet' fantasy."

"Your brother's right. I love my little bungalow on the bay. Even has a picket fence out back. Still working on the dog and kids part. Anyway, I enjoy teaching, and I've got tenure. Pays the bills."

He looked at the nub of the bat handle then down at his hands placed awkwardly on the table. It was too late to withdraw to the safety of small talk.

"Michelle, I'm sorry—"

She reached for the cigarette in the ashtray before pulling her hand back. "Jake, I don't want to go there. It's over—long ago." She sighed, one that conveyed she opted to get it all out. "You hurt me. I didn't understand how you could walk away so easily. I waited for the phone to ring, to hear your voice. It's silly, I know. We were just kids. But the sound of your voice made everything all right. All the ugliness with Mario and Joey, Theresa's binges—your voice made it all disappear. I needed to hear your voice, Jake. You could have told me anything. It wouldn't have mattered. But you never called."

"What Joey did to Mario scared me. I let myself believe what my mother was telling me. That was the easy way out for me. I was afraid, and I needed an excuse. I've never stopped being ashamed of it." He looked down. "I've thought of you every day."

"Really, Jake." It wasn't a question. It carried a cut-the-shit edge. "Life has a way of distorting memories—good and bad."

She paused. It was apparent to him their walk down memory lane was over. "Listen to me, Jake. These murders. I know my brother. Joey didn't do this."

He nodded, unable to meet her gaze. "I'll do my best, Michelle."

"You do that, Detective."

She got up from the table and a carried the empty cups to the sink.

Alfie straightened from his slouch against the cruiser parked around the corner and out of view of Michelle's bungalow. Jake wrapped the bat in clear plastic secured with yellow tape, the word *evidence* and the date printed at intervals along its length, and tossed it into the trunk of the cruiser.

"How'd it go?"

"She says her brother didn't do it."

"What do you believe?"

He shrugged.

"Come on, Jake. Be serious. You're not sixteen anymore, trying to get into her panties—" Alfie frowned. "Sorry. But McMeekin's been all over me about wrapping this up. Wants to know who we've interviewed, see the forensics when they come back—shit he never cares about. Something or someone has crawled up his ass on this one."

"Maybe we'll get some usable prints off the bat, with all that pine tar on the handle."

Alfie slid behind the wheel of the cruiser and turned to Jake in the passenger seat. "To hell with McMeekin. I don't care what he wants. We'll get it, Jake."

"Get what?"

"The truth."

The truth, Jake thought. *Just how much of the truth could he survive?*

The building was a derelict, boarded over, condemned. He wasn't really sure why he needed to see it again. He had no cop reason. The hinges of the street level entrance had been ripped from the jamb. The door looked like the entry to a cartoon-haunted house: wedged askew in the opening and held in place by a couple of warped two-by-six boards. The vestibule smelled like a toilet. He stepped through syringes, burned spoons, and empty bottles of Ripple littering the floor.

Upstairs, the door to the apartment was open. It was empty of furniture and had the look of having been hastily and carelessly vacated by its occupants. An irregular near-black stain vaguely shaped like one of the lakes near Ginny's family cottage in Bar Harbor, complete with the outline of an ovoid islet at its center, covered a large section of the linoleum floor in what had been the living room.

Ahead of him was the door to her room—the room that had been their sanctuary. It was open a crack, but from where he stood, he was unable to see inside. He stood where he was and remembered. Then, without entering, he turned and left the apartment.

At the third-floor landing, he paused. The dark walls were coated with decades of cooking grease, grunge, and odors that had seeped under the doors from tiny kitchens. Names of couples, punks, and street gang logos were carved in the wood and spray-painted on the cracked and pock-marked plaster. He stared down at the particulate-laden ray of light filtering through the door on the street below and began his descent.

* * *

The Barrens sprawled across seven counties, home to the Pineys and the mythical Jersey Devil. Brackish tea-colored waters of the Mullica wound through a million acres of white cedar, giant oak, and pine forests to the salt marshes separating the mainland from the coast.

The two-lane hardpan that led from the Black Horse Pike cut a narrow corridor that bulged every ten miles or so to accommodate a general store and a gas station. Streaks of sunlight sliced through the dense forest canopy dappling the road. Thirty miles in, the hardpan teed into an unmarked, black-topped state road.

Jake turned left in the direction indicated on the small green sign with white lettering: *Farview State Correctional Facility and Psychiatric Hospital.* He drove another half mile and coasted to a stop outside the first of three chain-link fences topped with coils of razor wire. He flashed his credentials and the guard activated the first gate. At the second gate, the guard waited for the first gate to close, glanced at Jake's identification, and opened the second gate. The same procedure was followed at the final checkpoint.

Farview was a campus of five flat-roofed orange brick structures. He parked at building 1, which housed administration, to pick up his escort. The deputy superintendent—a taciturn, humorless man—led him outside, down a concrete path lined with tufts of crabgrass.

"Haven't seen you up here in a while, Detective."

"I got promoted to homicide. Most of my perps are sane."

They passed building 2, the hospital and infirmary—a charitable description given the level and type of care provided. Buildings 3, 4, and 5 housed the inmates: serial killers and sexual predators, men who tortured and mutilated without passion or remorse, without purpose other than self-gratification. Like any population, Farview's inmates had specialties. Their victims defined them: young girls, young boys, gays, women. Women were divided into victim subcategories based on age, race, profession (nuns and school teachers were favorites), hair color, eye color, type of clothing (particularly shoes). Buildings 3 and 4 housed serial rapists and pedophiles, the latter despised by their fellow inmates and were themselves at risk of dying at the hands of others.

As a newly minted detective, Jake had sent one of his early collars to Farview. Sonny Days had been the superintendent of an apartment building on South Carolina Avenue between Arctic and Baltic. The owner fired him when female tenants complained that Sonny made them uncomfortable with his sexual innuendoes. Sonny believed he was descended from African princes. He also believed that his mission was to perform cunnilingus on the women who lived in his building. He used his duplicate set of keys to let himself into their apartments. At his competency hearing, he had described himself as the *Prince of Cunnilingus*. He was certain that once he had performed his art the women would not only be forgiving, they would be grateful. They weren't. Sonny confessed at the time of his arrest. His principal concern as he told Jake was the ingratitude of the women. The former building super expressed genuine puzzlement at their lack of appreciation for the pleasure he bestowed on them.

Building 5 was reserved for inmates considered dangerous to themselves, other inmates, and staff. It was not the violence of Joey's murder of his uncle alone that earned him a cell in building 5. Joey's entire history had been meticulously detailed in school and juvenile hall files and the record rooms of three police departments, in addition to Atlantic City's. The discovery of Joey's extra Y chromosome confirmed the state criminologist's assessment and the decision to place him in building 5.

Entering building 5, Jake wondered what he could possibly hope to learn from Joey that he didn't already know. What would he ask him? How would Joey answer?

Hey, Joey.

Yo.

Seen any of the guys?

Vinny came up once when I first got here.

How they treating you?

Great. Just great. Most of the time I sit on the floor of my cell. Naked. That way when I shit myself it's easier to clean up. Turn on the fire hose and wash it all down the drain in the middle of the floor. Did I tell you my room has a floor drain?

Sounds nice, Joey.

The electric shock is kinda neat, too. They put this leather strap around your head and a hard rubber wedge in your mouth. That way you don't swallow your tongue or bite it off when they hammer your brain with the juice.

Interesting.

Haldol makes everything nice.

Joey, did you beat three queers to death with your Louisville Slugger and bury them behind the railroad ties in Tessie's tunnel?

At St. Mike's, the nuns had described Joey Nardo as "unruly," "sullen," and "in need of constant discipline."

His behavior could have been predicted by Joey's fifth birthday, had he been taken to a child development specialist. He did not begin to talk, at least to others, until he was five. He pointed and grunted. His parents were gone by then, and he lived with his aunt and two-year-old sister. He spoke words only that he deemed necessary to achieve a specific need. *Hungry, milk, more, no, yes, potty, go bed.*

His baby teeth rotted in his mouth before they could fall out, the result of his aunt filling his sippy cup with Hawaiian Punch. He would suck on the sippy cup, drawing the pink liquid sugar across his teeth while endlessly watching cartoons on the TV.

His one toy was a fire engine, which his aunt bought him secondhand at a St. Mike's rummage sale. For weeks after she gave it to him, he pushed it around the linoleum floor in ever-tightening circles screeching and whirring to provide what he imagined to be the authentic sounds of the truck racing through the streets. That stopped when his Uncle Mario smashed it against the wall. But the truck must have made an impression because when the nuns asked him what he wanted to be, he responded, "Fire truck." "No, Joey. You mean *fireman*." "No, Sister. Fire truck."

Joey careened between agitation and withdrawal. His aunt turned to Jesus. She took Joey to mass every Sunday, convinced that the priests would help her control him. By his seventh birthday, Joey had made his first communion and was eligible for altar boy, but his conduct with the sisters in class eliminated him from the list. Altar boy was an honor reserved for the well behaved.

But the priests were willing to do what they could for Joey, and for that, his aunt Theresa was grateful. Each day after school, Joey went to the rectory for instruction and discipline by the parish priests. On Sundays after mass, Joey assisted the priests with their weekend chores.

His time with the priests seemed to help. His episodes of wild agitation, which had always frightened Theresa, became less frequent. Theresa was so relieved by this that she did not allow herself to become concerned when Joey stopped talking with anyone except his little sister. He fended for himself for his basic needs, rarely asking his aunt for anything. He lived on soda and Devil Dogs. He put himself to bed after first making sure that his sister had eaten, brushed her teeth, and was tucked snugly under her covers.

In school, he sat quietly and stared at his desktop. The sisters stopped calling on him because he had conditioned them to expect nothing. Soon after his twelfth birthday, everything changed. The report from St. Michael's and the juvenile authorities said he "went berserk," attacking a priest with his fists, hurling lamps, ashtrays, bottles. He turned on the gas of the rectory's kitchen stove. Only the arrival of the police prevented his burning the rectory to the ground.

The story seeped out in fragments, whispered among neighbors and parishioners. According to the priests, Joey's Sunday chores included collecting the soiled linens and clothing from the priests' bedrooms and taking them to the laundry room. Each Sunday one of the priests was assigned to escort Joey from bedroom to bedroom. Joey would enter each room to collect the sheets and towels while his escort waited outside. That Sunday, Father Frank was the boy's escort, instructing Joey in his catechism while Joey helped with the laundry. The priest's face required twenty stitches to close the gashes in his cheeks, above his right eye and over his lip.

Aunt Theresa begged the priest not to press charges. He agreed. He had done everything in his power to help the troubled boy. But Joey was expelled from St. Mike's Parochial.

At Chelsea Junior High School, Joey got into fights nearly every day, in the gym, in the cafeteria, in the schoolyard, on the way to school, on the way home from school. He repeated the seventh grade, which did nothing but prolong the inevitable. Joey moved on to Atlantic City High School, even though he lacked the reading and math skills of a sixth grader. He left school for good on his sixteenth birthday, beginning his career as a full-time street punk.

Joey lived without a safety net, without any notion except to do the opposite of anything and everything others—normal people—expected. According to the judge who sentenced him, Joey was *depraved. But what of Michelle?* Jake wondered. Had her gentle nature diluted the purity of her brother's evil?

Jake waited in the interview room, a cinderblock bunker with a sheet of shatterproof one-way glass. A metal table sat between two metal chairs, one of which was bolted to the floor. Jake eyed the cameras set in each corner of the ceiling.

The shackled figure shuffled into the room between two guards. The leg and wrist irons connected to heavy gauge chain that served as a hobble and a lead extending from his waist. He wore a pair of flip-flops, loose-fitting khaki pants, and a white T-shirt. Most of his hair was gone; his face slack, his mouth expressionless, and he was a hundred pounds heavier than the nineteen-year-old Jake had known. But Jake knew immediately that it was Joey. His eyes had not changed. He was still in there; Jake could feel his presence, his intelligence—even if his keepers didn't.

The guard guided Joey to the unoccupied chair, squeezed him under the edge of the table, forced him down, and locked the chain connecting his ankle shackles to an iron ring set in the floor.

"You want me to stay with you?"

Jake shook his head.

"I'll be just outside the door, Detective. It'll be locked from the outside."

He pointed to a toggle switch by the steel-reinforced door. "Flip that when you're done."

Joey rested his hands on the table. He appeared serene. Haldol had done what all the others—the nuns and the priests, Uncle Mario and Aunt Theresa, the juvenile authorities and the cops—could not.

"Joey." Jake spoke the name softly, more than a simple greeting. Joey remained silent, his eyes, fixed beyond his visitor, registering nothing. Jake nudged the press clipping across the table. "McMeekin is pushing hard to hang this on you." Jake paused, searching Joey's face for any understanding of what he had said. Nothing. "Your bat is at the lab for analysis. If forensics can tie it to the victims, case closed. Crazy Joey Nardo did the crime." The reaction Jake had hoped would be triggered by using the label Joey hated never came.

"Joey, I remember one of those nights back when we started to run together. We were cruising like we always did. Toad and Vinny pulled their usual act at Kramer's window, raised some hell outside the Club Harlem. It was still early. Michelle was expecting to see me. Vinny told Fish to drive Toad and him to Victory, then drop me off at your place to see Michelle. I jumped out at Victory and walked to Texas Avenue. I gotta be honest. I was thinking Fish and you might decide to drag me along if I stayed in the car. You want to know why I remember that night, Joey? When I was leaving your place, Michelle asked me to look for you. She was worried about you. She wanted you home. I walked by the White House and Victory. I didn't see the Bonnie. I walked home on the boards. I stopped at the rail in front of the Blenheim, and I heard a noise that sounded like it came from the tunnel. I had promised your sister, and I needed to find you. I had to find out if you were in the tunnel. I got partway in and tripped on the planking. I heard shouts. When I was back on the boards, I saw a figure run from the tunnel. He was shirtless. As he half ran, half stumbled down the beach he shot glances over his shoulder in the direction of the tunnel entrance.

"Was that you in the tunnel, Joey? After Fish dropped Toad, Vinny, and me in front of Victory, where did you go? I'm asking, Joey, 'cause I think I saw the Bonnie parked at the ramp that night. When I got to the top of the stairs, I saw a glint of chrome reflected under the streetlight. I didn't think about it at the time. I just wanted to get out of there as fast as I could. Inside the tunnel, when the bodies were being dug out from behind the beams, what I saw that night when I went looking for you came back to me. It was a long time ago. But as I stood by, watching the bones being arranged on a tarp, my recollection of that night became vivid. Am I right, Joey? Did I see Fish's Bonnie? Were you guys in the tunnel that night?"

Joey did not speak a word or look at the man across the table. He gave no sign of hearing the words spoken to him. Jake got up from the table. Before flipping the toggle switch to summon the guard, Jake stopped and turned to face the slouching figure seated in chains.

"I saw your sister. I told her I would help you. What should I tell her, Joey?"

No answer. Jake went to the door and hit the switch. As the door opened, he heard two words: "Beach Boy."

Joey's eyes were narrowed, focused, cognitive. Then, just as suddenly, they faded back to their Haldol stare.

Alfie was waiting in their usual booth at the White Tower.

"How's Joey?"

"Living large. State feeds him, clothes him, hoses him off once a day, and keeps him high on Haldol."

"Tell you anything?"

"Not a single word."

Jake wondered about Joey's demons. They had to be real, powerful, and terrible to have made Joey who he was.

Then he wondered about his own.

"Jake, you got to stop this Lone Ranger routine. I'm your partner. This isn't *your* case. Leave whatever it is that's eating at you out of this. Cut me out again, and there won't be a next time."

Jake didn't like his partner's tone, but he choked back a *fuck you.* "Understood."

His efforts to fall asleep were futile, more and more typical of his nights since Ginny and he split up. He threw on the clothes he had tossed three hours earlier on the chair by his bed and headed down a deserted Pacific Avenue to the White Tower.

"Jake, you're a handsome man, but you make it hard to see," she said, taking the crumpled bills from the counter. "Your hair sticks up where it shouldn't, and a shave now and then wouldn't hurt."

Personal grooming pointers from a woman in a hairnet who served coffee on the graveyard shift.

"Thanks, Mary. Keep the change."

"And take an iron to your pants," she called after him.

Outside, he raised the collar of his sport jacket, pulled the lapels across his neck, and hunched against the wind blowing off the ocean. The warm daytime breezes of Indian summer yielded to the bone cold of the early morning. The heavy air clammed up his skin. He inhaled the aroma of dead clams and horseshoe crabs simmered in seaweed.

Home.

He headed to the boardwalk. He stopped at the bottom of the ramp and sipped from the paper cup, wincing when the hot liquid hit his tongue. He tossed the cup into the wire trash basket chained to the "No Parking" sign.

He trudged up the ramp. At the rail, he stared at the hole in the sand where the Blenheim had once stood. The cool film forming on his skin refreshed him.

He looked down at his feet: scuffed shoes, knots marking the breaks in the laces. The elbows of his sport coat were threadbare without the Mr. Chips patches; the collar of his shirt was frayed and separating. Sackcloth and ashes.

He felt lousy, probably the result of his diet: a rotation of pizza, White House cheesesteaks, and White Tower grease burgers. He never cooked. Families cooked. And he was unable to sleep. He missed the normalcy of his wife and son.

The Venice Apartment Building on Atlantic Avenue where he moved after his divorce was in the Chelsea section across the street from the Dairy Queen and a block from the high school. He had lived there nearly a year now but moving boxes remained stacked along one wall largely unpacked. He had opened those only of necessity to retrieve flatware, plates, dishes, a favorite sweatshirt he was certain he had packed, a wool watch cap when the windchill drove temperatures into negative territory. Pant legs and shirt sleeves draped over the sides appeared to belong to flat-limbed zombies attempting to escape their corrugated crypts. He had not noticed the movement of the clutter on his apartment floor, but it seemed to have extended toward the center of the room, a necrotic creep.

Ginny had insisted he take the couch when he moved out.

The couch. *Their* couch. Pocked with dark-rimmed holes from dropped joints. Spotted with their lovemaking, "Gallo red," Danny's infant spit-up. It was pushed against the living room wall, an all-purpose artifact from a previous life. Why had he agreed to take it, to comfort, taunt, or exorcise? Maybe it was just that he needed a place to sit and didn't have the energy to replace it.

He thought of the first night they had made love on it in their own apartment. They were unmarried, in open defiance of both sets of parents. A lamp in a far corner of the room had cast enough light so they could see each other's bodies. He was seated on the couch, and she stood before him. Slowly, she removed her sweater and jeans. She reached down and undid his buckle and knelt to remove his pants and boxers. "I want to watch you get hard," she had purred as she straightened to undo her bra and let it slip from her breasts.

Her breasts were firm and round, as perfect as breasts could be. Their areolae and nipples reminded him of those he had seen as a boy in his father's magazines. She watched his penis fill with blood then rise toward her. "That's what I want," she murmured, staring, as if his erection were a separate being from its owner. She placed a finger in each side of the waistband of her panties. Moving her gaze from his now fully erect member to his eyes, she slid her panties to the floor and kicked them to the side. She stood there, allowing him to look at her naked body, enjoying the involuntary twitches of his erection the sight of her caused.

She moved closer, placing her legs on either side of his. The slit between them glistened through a flawless vee of fine auburn hair. He could feel the heat radiating from her. She took his hand and placed it between her thighs, moaning softly when he slid his finger inside. They made love three times, and both were certain their son was conceived that night.

Exhaustion was a prerequisite for sleep. To shorten his nights, he never had dinner before 8:00 p.m. It hadn't occurred to him that eating so late might contribute to his malaise. His energy level was zero. He watched old movies until his eyes closed. When they popped open at three in the morning from a mental jolt out of nowhere, he knew sleep would not return.

The bed, a foldout, was missing a box spring and sagged in the middle. The sheets and bedcover—unchanged for a month—were braided together by restless sleep on those occasional nights he'd made it into the bedroom.

He figured he deserved all this.

The walls of his apartment were empty but for grimy outlines of the previous tenant's framed photographs. He imagined the lives of the people in the missing pictures. Maybe they were of a young family, and the apartment was a temporary way station on the road to buying a home. *No,* he thought. This place was the last resort; it could not be otherwise. At night when sleep would not come, he became one with the lonely souls that preceded him.

One framed photo sat on his dresser. He remembered the day he'd snapped it. The three of them were in Bar Harbor, Maine, where Ginny's family summered. Danny was three.

It would have been easier if he and Ginny hated each other. But no, they'd parted as friends.

One day Ginny announced it was time for them to separate. Ginny could be decisive like that. She could reach back beyond him, to generations of her people, to that place where giant hardwoods stood for millennia against the strongest gales. She knew her past, knew that she was part of a continuum, knew the good and the bad that happened to people in every life would be smoothed by time.

He had only the present.

Ginny had attended Bryn Mawr College on Philadelphia's Main Line. They met for the first time when Jake drove down from Lancaster with a carload of his F & M classmates for a mixer. She didn't need makeup. Her face was somewhere between pretty and handsome. Good bone structure, people always said. Virginia Hale Fitzgerald was lace-curtain Irish, as different from him as she was from Michelle.

She was tall, nearly five-nine, and fair-skinned with fine reddish-blond hair. Her eyes were blue-white. She had an innate confidence borne of the knowledge she needed only to build on the life she had been given, wrapped in a genuine grace that put others at ease.

He decided to be himself around her instead of putting on a preppy act, like his New Canaan classmates. He was a rough-edged kid from AC, and if she rejected him for that reason, it wouldn't sting as much. Better to be the street kid than be caught trying to hide it. She'd attended Miss Porter's School. Her father was an investment banker; her mother was Mistress of the Hunt and chairwoman of the Horticultural Society (Ginny left out her membership in the DAR). They wintered at their place in Aiken, South Carolina. After she told him her family history, he offered his congratulations on her membership in the LSC. On cue, she asked what that meant, and she cracked a you-got-me smile when he told her the Lucky Sperm Club. He silently thanked Rabbit for that one.

She came back with her best Katherine Hepburn imitation—a Bryn Mawr alum. Ginny did a good one, exaggerating the lock-jawed, upper-class manner. He reciprocated with stories of the beach, Ducktown (he didn't mention Joey), and his rendition of Sammy Dorfman waddling like a penguin, chopping on his stub of a cigar imploring him to *get the money.* She laughed at his recollections of the Miss America Pageant (he did not recount Vinny's towel trick or his encounter with Miss Stars & Bars), the boardwalk auctions, the carneys, all of it.

That first night, they talked into the early morning. Jake called her the next day and made a date for the weekend. He drove down in a borrowed car and took the Local to Philadelphia. They strolled along South Street between Front and Sixth, observing the street life and browsing the offbeat shops that offered everything from kitschy porn and sex toys to theatrical costumes, tattoos, used books, secondhand clothes, and everything else that could not be found in Saks or Lord & Taylor. They skipped the artsy movie at the TLA, ate burgers and fries, and hopped the last Local back to Bryn Mawr.

A few days later, a piece of torn notebook paper tacked to his dorm room door contained a scrawled message with her name and number. He returned her call immediately. She was going home the next weekend and wondered whether he would like to come along.

Her hometown, tucked in the farthest corner of northern New Jersey, was a village of manorial homes surrounded by manicured grounds, mature hardwoods, and circular drives. Trees and shrubbery cushioned schools and commercial buildings. Neat little shops surrounded the village green.

The Fitzgeralds lived in a Georgian mansion; a tree-lined tipple stone drive wound fifty yards from the front gate to the house. They owned a horse farm in Aiken, South Carolina, some twenty miles from Augusta National, where they wintered beginning after the first of each year, and attended the Masters before returning north.

Everyone smiled—her father, mother, three brothers, even Grandma Hale. They smiled for two days. These weren't wiseguy fuck-you smiles. But neither were they warm, the kind intended to welcome and put at ease; stiff, well-mannered smiles, all appearance and nothing more.

Questions meant to determine his suitability were casually layered with polite conversation: "Where did your parents attend college? Where is your family from originally (*no one is from Atlantic City. How in God's name did your family get there?*)? Jake—is that short for John?

Oh, for Jacob. How nice. *Harris—is that anglicized from Hershkowitz?* What sports do you enjoy? *Sailing, golf, skeet or trap, tennis, squash? No? Baseball, wrestling, basketball! But what will you do for recreation after you graduate?* They asked questions that weren't asked of the boys Ginny typically brought home. But he was a stray, a mongrel. Perhaps by the end of the visit, Ginny would realize how unsuitable this boy was.

Saturday evening was the family dinner, the intended highlight of his visit. It featured a *fuck-you* entrée (baked ham) proceeded by a *fuck-you* grace. They joined hands around the table, as Mr. Fitzgerald recited, *Thank you Lord for these Thy gifts we are about to receive, in Jesus name, amen. (And fuck you, Jacob Hershkowitz.)*

But Jake got the best of them.

Ginny's acceptance to Penn med kept her close to AC. She had a killer schedule, but Jake traveled to see her on weekends whenever possible, even if only to sit in her apartment and rub her shoulders as she studied. They married during her third year at Penn. Her classroom work had ended, and she was beginning the mandatory rotations of the third and fourth years. He was a third-year cop on the ACPD. They lived in a walk-up in Chelsea, and Ginny commuted to her rotations at hospitals, clinics, and office practices.

Ginny found a rabbi in north Jersey, took instruction capped off by a full immersion *mikva*, complete with clipped finger and toenails and a symbolic trimming of her hair. She emerged a Jew, or *Jewess* as Grandmother Hale commented. Jake had not asked her to convert, but his mother fell in love with Ginny for it. Sally Harris had her Jewish doctor after all.

The Fitzgerald-Hale clan placed an announcement in the Sunday *New York Times*:

> *Virginia Harris (née Fitzgerald) of Sparta, New Jersey, Aiken, South Carolina, and Bar Harbor, Maine, and Jacob Harris were wed at Beth Judah Synagogue in Fair Lawn. Rabbi Seymour Aronson performed the ceremony. The bride attended Miss Porter's School and is a graduate of Bryn Mawr College. She attends the medical school of the University of Pennsylvania. The bride's father is a senior managing director of J. P. Morgan and a member of the board of trustees of Princeton University. The bride's mother is Mistress of the Hounds of the Bergen Hunt and chairwoman of the Preservation Society. She is a member of the board of trustees of the Horticultural Society and a past president of the New Jersey chapter of the Daughters of the American Revolution.*
>
> *The groom graduated from Franklin and Marshall College.*
>
> *The couple resides in Atlantic City.*

"You became a cop to spite your mother, Jake," Ginny had told him. "Now you bring home a Catholic wife. Only an Irish mother could love that combination."

At the birth of their son, he had supported Ginny's head as she curled her body to push. He could find nothing beautiful about a bloody, purple-veined skull nickeling from the birth canal. He felt guilty about that. The act of birth had a familiar violence to it. Maybe he had been working the streets too long. He couldn't bring himself to stand between her legs with a camera. He had seen enough of those home videos, capturing every splash of blood and gush of fluid.

He inched to her side, careful to keep his eyes on her face. He would be the best coach AC Medical Center's obstetrical unit had ever seen—from the neck up. He leaned in close to her and locked her eyes with his.

"Breathe, baby, breathe."

Ginny sucked and puffed, belched and farted. She grunted and blew drenched strings of hair from her mouth, snot and sweat flying. Cottony gobs of saliva mixed with mucous and perspiration sprayed his face. He had witnessed it all: her wild groans, her anger, her strength, the taste of her, the smell of sex coating her skin.

"Fuck you, you bastard! Breathe your fucking self!"

Honest words. A slap. A wail. Life.

God, he wished he had it all on tape.

* * *

"How's she doing today, Mrs. McKenna?"

The chief administrator, surrounded by walls of manila folders, sat behind the reception counter of the Alzheimer's unit.

"She's had three ice cream cups and a Hershey bar. She's been entertaining us with recitations of her lyrics. She's wandering into other rooms, though. We have to keep an eye on her." Mrs. McKenna smiled. "She's still after the men, I'm afraid."

Jake laughed.

"She's been asking for her *Jacob.* Wants her smoke."

"Has my brother been in lately?"

"No. But Linda visited last week."

He took the pack of Winstons and matches from Mrs. McKenna. His mother's room was at the end of a hall hung with crayon drawings by the artists in residence. The one with his mother's name on it hung by her door. He passed the old men and women, walkers and chairs with stainless tubing holding them in, moaning syllables to no one he could see. The dayroom was a gallery of open mouths that didn't move, sunken cheeks, and frozen eyes, tentpole bones angling translucent skin.

At one time, Jake's mom could carry a tune and play the piano well enough to be featured on the local radio kiddie talent show. In her black-and-white serrated-edged Kodaks, he saw the sixteen-year-old yearbook editor smiling out at him, the proud naval aviator's war bride, and the Little Theatre lead at center stage. Jake could almost picture her as she had once been in her youth, before he came along.

When Jake was a child, his mother always had two books in her bedroom: one open, her eyes on its pages, the other on the night table beside her, at the ready. They had been important books too; he knew that even then. Gradually, unnoticed, the hardcover books and *New York Times* yielded to puzzle books. Now there was only a ten-by-twelve room with an unwatched television screen suspended from a metal bracket in the corner.

"Hi, Mom."

He looked around the room. A life squeezed and jammed in a ten-by-ten space. The bridge table from the den crowded the dresser from the master bedroom; the Queen Anne chair from the living room was wedged between the dresser and the Danish modern leather recliner that had come from the sitting room. Framed family pictures that once had room to tell a story in his boyhood home, now edged one against another, a line of dominoes, all but the first mostly hidden. How had his brother and he decided what to take, what to leave behind? He couldn't remember.

"Which one are you?"

"You tell me, Mom."

His tone was gentle, his "challenge" intended to have her exercise her mind in the hope that one spark of memory might ignite another.

"Ben."

"Close. Try again."

"Jacob."

At least she remembered both of her sons, even if she didn't know which was which. That was a good day for her.

Jake had her driver's license pulled after she sideswiped two of the neighbors' parked cars. He and his brother hired a driver and a live-in when the police found her wandering Atlantic Avenue in her nightgown. They tried to keep her out of a nursing home. But she got too difficult to handle, and the decision was made; the brothers went through the house, deciding what to keep, what to sell, who would get what, what should go to the home with her.

"Jacob, I don't want to go to the home."

"I know, Mom. We're just looking into some options."

They told her it would make her life easier, and she would have a garden and be able to see friends and make new ones, that if she didn't like it, she could come back home. The lies children told their parents on their way to *the home* were not all that different from the lies the SS had told the Jews on the way to the showers, Jake thought.

They lied so they could do what they had to do.

"Where is the pretty lady?"

"Ginny, Mom. We're divorced, Mom. Remember?"

"Such a pretty lady."

The set piece, she would recite what she could each day. He heard no regret in her voice when she dropped a line, no more than a lost second of daylight with the passing of the summer solstice.

"Yes, Mom. She's a very pretty lady. I got lucky."

"Where is that nice man?"

Buddy, his father, her husband.

"Pop died."

He wasn't being cruel. These were his lines.

"I got the pick of the litter." She pointed at the framed poster across from her bed. "Is that him?"

"No, Mom. That's Frank Sinatra."

"I got a real catch." She paused. "What was his name? That nice man?"

Her own mother had been just fifty-two when she had started asking that same question.

Since junior high school, for a lifetime, he was her only love.

"Buddy, Mom. His name was Buddy."

"Ben will be my doctor. He's good at math. What's that lady's name?"

"Linda, Mom. Ben's wife." He had become adept at understanding her unconnected references.

"Jacob, you'll be my lawyer. I'll have a doctor and a lawyer."

He knew an apology to her would be meaningless, yet he wanted to make one. It would be more a confession. He had blamed her for driving him away from Michelle. The brief time he remained at home before leaving for college he had been sullen. He was unsure how much of that had been due to what had happened that last summer with Michelle. And he had been generally unhappy ever since. He acted in self-destructive ways because he believed that would hurt her. He turned down Harvard Law to become a cop; he married a *shiksa*. That would show her! Show her what, exactly? Everything seemed so petty now sitting here by her bed.

Her eyes went to his hands and the pack of Winstons.

"You didn't forget. You're a good boy." She threw her legs over the side of the bed. "Come. Help your mother."

They went for their walk, he holding her arm. Outside, she took one last drag and dropped the butt on the sidewalk.

He had done his duty.

"It smells in there. I don't like the way it smells."

When Buddy was alive, she had written lyrics. Jake and his brother referred to them as her "Ode to Buddy." A friend put them to music. She had a demo made and dreamed of Edie Gorme´ singing her song. She began and ended each of his visits, reciting her lyrics, her eyes welling at her favorite passages. Each visit she had fewer words. Then one day the gnarled balls of protein hardening her brain took even those words from her, along with her books and the *New York Times* puzzle.

"When can I go home? I don't like it here."

"Soon, Mom. Promise."

She wouldn't remember his lie. She might not even remember to ask again when she could go home.

Alfie pulled the cruiser to the curb in front of Formica's Bakery. Victory Billiards in faded gold lettering bubbled across the top panel of the windowless door directly across Mississippi Avenue.

"Ready to shake the tree?" Jake asked.

Alfie nodded. "Your show, partner."

The permanent odor of stubbed-out cigarettes floating in stale beer wafted down a narrow stairway lit by a single bulb. The second-floor landing led to a foyer configured to block direct access to the main parlor. A single drop lamp hung over each of the eight tables lit the green felt surfaces. Shadows and smoke obscured the perimeter lined with cue racks and wiseguys. They had always been there; had never left. Through the haze he recognized Meatball, Bushman and Socks—neighborhood guys who'd graduated from Dante Hall CYO basketball to running the hotel workers' local. Uniforms, supplies, bartenders, waitresses, chambermaids, bellmen, laundry services—it all went through Victory Billiard's backroom.

"Pootaan! Yiz made me scratch. I tole yiz. No talkin' when I'm over the table."

"Yo, Ant. *Manja* this," Cheeks said, grabbing his crotch.

"Y'know, Cheeks, yiz got a real mouth on yiz."

"Heeey. Look who's here. Howya been, Jakey?"

"Been okay, Cheeks. You?"

Cheeks Spagnola was an old corner boy, a punk who'd spent his summer nights hanging on the rails at Texas and the boards. Now he banged heads for the union. He racked his cue, picked up a shot glass, and approached the two detectives.

"Yeah. Yeah. I'm good. Whattaya need?" Cheeks said, all the while looking at Brathwaite. That's the way wiseguys did it. Cheeks could say "Fuck you!" with his eyes, and he was saying it now to Brathwaite.

"How about an anisette, Jake? We can send out for a bottle of Ripple for your friend," Cheeks said, flashing a big grin at Alfie. Alfie smiled back with one of his own.

"Maybe next time," said Jake.

"Sure. *Cent'anni!*" Cheeks drained the shot of syrupy, clear liquid and spit three espresso beans back into the bottom of the glass.

"Toad here?"

"In the back."

"I need a couple of minutes."

"Wait here."

Jake could have muscled in with his badge, but he knew better. Everything was about protocol, respect. Cheeks opened the door to the backroom and disappeared inside. When the door reopened a few moments later, it was Toad who motioned Jake to enter. Alfie found an empty chair, sat down, and rocked it back on two legs in a half lean against the wall.

In the backroom, Nonno Carbone, sporting a two-day growth of white chin stubble, unchanged by time, sat peeling an orange at a table with four other men. A plate of prosciutto, block of Parmesan, and slices of melon was in front of each along with water glasses filled with homemade jug wine. Broken loaves of Formica's fresh-baked bread lay on the table by dishes of olive oil and roasted peppers. At a smaller table against the wall in shadows, Nicky Zitto sipped a sambuca-laced espresso.

Jake looked past Toad at the mob boss. Little Nicky was five-six if you counted his pompadour and Cuban heels. He was all slick and shine, manicured nails, clear polish, star sapphire pinky ring, shooting two-inch cuffs out of a sharkskin jacket. These days, Nicky was making his move. The Tri-State Organized Crime Task Force had Nicky on the second line of the org chart, a capo in the Gambino family. The casinos raised the stakes for everybody. Now, there were nothing but square-block craters along the boardwalk, but soon steel and glass money factories would rise. It was time for bold action. Nicky Zitto stopped killing for others and started killing for himself—or rather his nephew, Crazy Walter, killed for him. Nicky was a vengeance killer, motivated by some perceived slight or disrespect. Walter Lucci did the business killing, not that Crazy Walter discriminated between killing for business and killing for pleasure.

"Heeey. Howya doon, Jake? Nonno, you remember Jake. Used to bring him around when we was kids."

The old man smiled, just like that first time in the Carbone kitchen. He eyed Jake, spit pips into his loosely formed fist, and deposited them in the orange peel on the table in front of him.

"*Morta Cristo*," he said.

"He still likes you, Jake. C'mon. We'll sit over there."

Toad pointed to a table in the corner opposite Nicky Zitto. He took Jake by the elbow and led him across the room.

"Boom-Boom," Toad called to a dull-looking young man in a white apron, "bring us a coupla black sambucas and espresso."

Jake knew there was no point in declining. The two men sat at the table, swapping "Yo, remember that time" talk until Boom-Boom placed the coffees and liqueurs in front of them.

"Okay, Jake. What's so important you gotta come in here like Dick Tracy?" Toad's expression remained unchanged, like he was reminiscing about mooning Kramer's.

"The bodies under the Blenheim."

"Yeah. I read about that. You working that case?"

"It's looking bad for Joey Nardo. He's got the rap sheet for it and probably the murder weapon—the Louisville Slugger he used to carry around with him in Fish's car, you remember it. We're waiting on forensics to come back."

"Yeah. Too bad for Joey. Is that what you came here to tell me?

"There were three victims. That's a lot of killing for one man to accomplish."

"A baseball bat can do a lot of damage real fast."

"Sure. Take out one, but you'd think the other two guys fighting for their lives would be able to overpower the guy swinging the bat."

"Sounds to me like you're reaching for something that ain't there. What are you after here, Jake?"

Jake sat back in the chair, poured some sambuca into the espresso, and took a sip.

"How's Fish? Talk to him lately?"

"What are you, *stoonodz?* You're talking about a man who's been honored by the pope, the State of Israel, and the governor of New Jersey. He builds hospital wings and gives to the Little Sisters of the Poor."

"He and Joey always seemed to have something going on, just the two of them."

Toad's cheek twitched. "That was a long time ago. Arthur Gomberg's an important man. He's got a lot of friends."

"Friends in this room, Toad?"

Toad smiled, the tic suddenly calm. He took Jake by the forearm with one hand and by the shoulder with the other. Toad leaned in close, so close Jake felt light-headed from the odorous blend of garlic and Aqua Velva radiating from Toad's pomaded head.

"You make me look bad comin' in here like a cop. You need somethin', Jake, you got it. But you come alone. You come in here with a moolie cop we don't know, everybody gets nervous, especially Nicky. That's not good."

Toad hadn't stopped grinning and squeezing Jake's shoulder and forearm the whole time he was talking, just like they were reliving old times.

"Be smart, Jake. Leave the rocks where they are. Don't go digging."

Toad walked Jake to the door. Outside, Brathwaite waited until they were back in the cruiser before saying anything.

"So what'd you get?"

"Judging from the Irish jig his face was doing, he's nervous about something."

"What's he got to worry about?"

"Not sure yet. I'm guessing McMeekin will be hearing from Nicky. Maybe Carbone's worried for Gomberg, maybe for himself. Let's go give his *goombah* a visit. I have a feeling that will stir the pot some more."

From Victory the two detectives headed uptown to a third-floor office suite at Ohio and Atlantic.

Vinny Two-Tone. Vincent Nicastro. Mr. Nicastro. The street charm had been buffed and polished, leaving a satiny glow. He had traded walrus-tusk collars for Brooks Brothers spreads. Vinny from Ducktown had gone corporate, and he wore the uniform: navy-blue chalk-stripe

Hart Schaffner & Marx, custom, monogrammed French cuff dress shirt, red silk pocket square, Italian silk tie, and English hand-sewn black wingtips polished to a high shine.

"Mr. Nicastro will see you now," the pretty young receptionist said.

No more *Yo, Vinny.*

It was *Mr. Nicastro.*

Vincent Nicastro was the deal maker, the *Facilitator,* in the new game of Casino Monopoly. He wasn't the man with money. He was the man who connected city hall to the Casino Control Commission to Trenton to the backroom at Victory Billiards. That made Vincent Nicastro important. Arthur "Fish" Gomberg paid Vincent to make those connections.

"Jake, it's good to see you. Please sit. And your partner, Detective…"

"Brathwaite."

"Brathwaite. Something to drink, gentlemen?"

Mr. Nicastro was refined and soft-spoken, the attitude under wraps. Jake wondered whether the pretty receptionist knew her employer's street name and its origin.

"I'm good, Vincent." Jake thought *Vincent* was a good middle ground between Two-Tone and Mr. Nicastro. Jake pushed the temporary restraining order halting construction on the Blenheim site across the desk. "This gives us another two weeks to work the site."

Vincent smiled. "You didn't need this, Jake." Vinny Two-Tone was getting restless, dying to come out. "You know Mr. Gomberg is only too happy to cooperate with city hall, always."

"I know that. Just a formality. Captain McMeekin insisted," Jake lied. He pictured Vinny jumping out of Fish's car to moon Kramer's Deli.

Vinny looked at Brathwaite then back at Jake. He didn't need words. His expression said it all.

Why're you doing this, Jake?

On the street outside Nicastro's office building, Jake smiled at his partner. "I'm guessing our little visits to Victory and Nicastro will rattle a few cages. Let's see who takes the weight."

"Let's just hope it's not us, Jake."

* * *

Eamon McMeekin flashed his signature grin, one that told the recipients that they were about to pay for a serious transgression. Jake and Alfie sat before him like schoolboys. It was the day after showing the colors at Victory and their meeting with Vincent Nicastro.

"How long you guys planning to milk this case before I get something on my desk to send the county prosecutor?"

McMeekin knew something about opportunity. It was common knowledge around city hall that McMeekin bagged for his superiors and protected the local mob. No one had the stomach to go after him. Taking on McMeekin meant taking on Nicky Zitto. That was a fight you'd better be sure you could win before starting it—assuming you lived long enough to see a courtroom.

Jake had most of the facts from Bill Perry, his FBI friend. Perry was assigned to the Tri-State Organized Crime

Task Force, a consortium of federal and state law enforcement from New York, New Jersey, and Pennsylvania. And what Jake didn't get from Perry was filled in by scuttlebutt around the stationhouse. McMeekin was keeping Nicky one step ahead of the task force, and for that, Nicky made regular contributions to McMeekin's personal retirement fund.

The New York mob was making its move on AC. The unions whose rank and file serviced the hotels were big business and would be bigger still once the casinos were operating. The local mob had a long and successful history of controlling the unions under the Philadelphia *cosa nostra*.

Nicky was restless. He knew he had to stay on the sidelines until the Gambino and Bruno families sorted things out. Then he'd make his move. Angelo Bruno—the Gentle Don—head of the Philadelphia family, had lost his taste for killing. That made him weak even as Zitto was gaining strength. The New York family reached around Bruno to form an alliance with Little Nicky and his nephew Crazy Walter—proven killers and ambitious. Zitto had grown tired of Bruno's restraints, and an alliance with New York had been the quickest way for Nicky to get out from under the Philadelphia mob boss's control.

Philly wiseguys started turning up dead—one, sometimes two a week. The three Philly papers ran stories every week with body counts. The *Daily News* included fresh-kill photos of mob hits, marking Nicky's rise from local punk to regional power. Angelo Bruno was shot in the head sitting in his car outside his favorite restaurant in South

Philadelphia. He'd eaten there six nights a week for twenty-five years. According to Bill Perry, Phil "Chickenman" Testa, one of Bruno's top lieutenants, ordered the hit because he had tired of the Don's reluctance to murder. Testa, who was as ugly as he was mean, was killed by a nail bomb exploded on his front porch. Nicky was earning his place at the table, and Crazy Walter was having fun.

But the money to be made shaking down the casinos with threats of strikes and violence was small-time in comparison to having control of a casino. That made Arthur Gomberg a valuable asset, one that needed to be protected.

McMeekin pointed his index finger at Jake.

"That was quite a stunt you two pulled at Victory, Harris. And what's that bullshit you gave Nicastro about my approving the extension of the restraining order on the Blenheim site?"

"We need more time," Jake said. "We assumed you'd be on board with that, Cap."

"Stop assuming. We ain't extending the restraining order. You're not gonna embarrass important people because you got a wild hair across your ass. Gomberg's lawyers are callin' in chits."

"Fuck Gomberg," Jake said.

Alfie shifted in his chair.

McMeekin smiled. "That's what I like about you, Harris. You got balls where your brains should be."

"Give us one more week."

"No way. Midnight tomorrow. This ain't that difficult, boys. Get your asses out of the sandbox. Work Nardo. Now get the fuck outta my sight. Both of you."

* * *

The cruiser's radio squawked over the churn of the ignition. Alfie tapped the dash panel switches activating the flashers and cut a screaming right angle across Atlantic Avenue south onto Indiana. At the boardwalk, the two detectives hunched against the stiff breeze coming off the ocean, humped up the ramp, and stared down at the hole that had been the Blenheim.

The wind-whipped yellow tape at the entrance to the tunnel had blown free at one end. The cop leaning against a piling straightened when he spotted the two detectives on the steps leading to the beach.

"Anybody inside?"

"Dougherty and two of his techs," the cop responded, nodding a greeting at Brathwaite.

The day was chilly and overcast, the tunnel cold and dark, even with a portion of the ceiling gone. Dougherty and the two techs were deep inside, beyond where the luncheonette had been and twenty yards further in than the spot where the last remains had been found. Floodlights plugged into a portable generator illuminated the wall of mud and rotted railroad ties where the two men were working. Four-by-six boards angled against the ties for support.

A decent replica of Michelangelo's God-hand reached from the muck between two of the rotted ties. The forearm was rotated underside up, the wrist bent slightly, the hand half closed, index finger extended. Purple and yellow bruises streaked up and down the arm from blood pools at the elbow joint. A deep slice creased the palm from pinky to thumb pad.

Dougherty nodded at the two new arrivals and turned back to the young techs who were probing the mud wall with trowels.

"We're honored by the presence of AC's finest duo," Dougherty announced with faux fanfare. "Gentlemen, the dapper one is Detective Brathwaite. The refugee from a rummage sale is Detective Harris."

The two techs nodded and turned back toward the limb protruding from the mud.

Dougherty turned to the two detectives. "Any bets on an ID?"

"Yeah," said Jake, eyeing the familiar star sapphire ring on the pinky finger of the corpse's hand. He had seen that ring many times in court.

"That shit bag has made his last ruling."

They had found Eddie Blatstein, Judge, New Jersey Superior Court.

Eddie Blatstein had started out as Little Nicky's pit bull trial lawyer. He graduated from the mob to become Arthur Gomberg's "fixer." When Eddie had all the money he thought he needed, he did what a lot of well-connected lawyers did: he had Gomberg buy him a judgeship. And that suited Gomberg. He liked the idea of reaching into his pocket and making some scumbag a judge. Gomberg had plunked down an envelope containing $25,000 cash on the desk of the party's patronage boss and Eddie the mob lawyer became His Honor, the judge.

The techs had cleared mud from around the head. Bone protruded through the scalp, and Judge Eddie's eyes bulged from their sockets. "From the looks of it," Alfie said after a closer inspection of the corpse, "somebody must have been seriously pissed off at one of his rulings."

"I have a short list of who could've ordered the hit: Nicky Zitto."

"And?" Alfie asked.

"And no one."

"Pretty sloppy job. I would expect more professional workmanship from Crazy Walter, two .38s behind the ear, and a trip to the Meadowlands. The judge didn't buy it here. No sign of a struggle."

"Alfie, you think Arthur Gomberg was on notice his boy had to go?"

"I'm guessing not. If you're right that Zitto had this done, I'm pretty sure he wouldn't look for Gomberg's permission. Of course, the New York family is not gonna be happy with the publicity. They've got the tri-state task force up their ass already."

"Wonder if Nicky had the good sense to clear this with New York, Alfie."

"Nah," they answered in unison.

"What are you two doing here?"

Jake and Alfie turned their attention from the dead judge to face Eamon McMeekin, who had moments ago arrived on the scene. "Hey, Cap," Alfie began, "came over the radio, and we figured since the vic was in our hole, we'd handle it."

"You figured wrong. I'm putting McTierny on this. Now go do your job and nail Joey Nardo."

"McTierny," Jake spat the name once he and Alfie were back in the cruiser. Dennis McTierny was a detective lieutenant and ranked both of them. He was also McMeekin's protégé. "You curious why our captain shows up at a fresh crime scene and assigns his butt boy to the case?"

"Jake, slow down. The vic is a sitting judge. McMeekin may just be showing the colors for the press."

"Not the response I was looking for, partner. I'm going to give Bill Perry a call."

"Don't get stupid, Jake. Best to leave this one alone. Blatstein has nothing to do with our tunnel case."

"Maybe. Can't hurt to buy Perry a cup of coffee. You in?"

The White Horse Diner, a classic all-night hash-and-eggs joint that looked like it belonged on the set of *Happy Days*, was situated on the Jersey side of the Delaware River, ten miles from the Ben Franklin Bridge. Bill Perry, flipping absentmindedly through the cards of a table top jukebox in a corner booth, had a clear view of the entrance. He made eye contact with Jake Harris as soon as he crossed the threshold.

"Hi, Bill. Thanks for meeting on short notice."

"Happy to accommodate, Starsky. Where's Hutch?"

"We thought it'd be better for him to sit this one out. Two of us meeting with you would look like official business. This way, we're just a couple of sorry-ass loners with nothing better to do."

Perry grunted something approaching a laugh. "I'll give you this much, Jake. You are looking a lot like a lost soul these days."

"I earned it. Divorced, living in a third floor walk-up on Atlantic Avenue, and my mother thinks she was married to Frank Sinatra. So, you going to tell me why Eddie Blatstein showed up dead in my crime scene?"

"I expected your call. Here's the executive summary. We served Eddie with an invite to appear before the special grand jury. We put the word out on the street about Blatstein's grand jury appearance, thinking Eddie would come to us for protection once Nicky found out we wanted his testimony. According to our CI, two wannabes did the hit. They were sitting on a stoop in Bayonne, drinking beer and listening to Vic Damone when Nicky called with their big chance. Two weeks ago, a Trooper cruising the Garden State spotted the trunk of a car poking up through the reeds on the bank of the Mullica near Tuckahoe. Vehicle had been reported stolen a week earlier. Blatstein's fingerprints were all over the interior. Looked like a kid went crazy with red finger paint.

"Messy hit," Perry continued. "Eddie kicked the windshield out, *Godfather* style. The dash was splattered with bits of Eddie's skull and brain. Looks like the lads from Bayonne got spooked and dumped the body in your pit so they wouldn't have to risk driving the body ninety miles north on the Jersey Turnpike."

"What did you have on Eddie?"

"He had a side business taking a cut from a ring smuggling untaxed cigarettes up from North Carolina. AC's finest had a piece along with Eddie. Your boys would bust a load now and then for appearance's sake when Eddie was the duty judge. Eddie set OR bail, and the crackers went back to their swamp. ATF had a guy inside. We paid Eddie a visit and read him the menu. We told him we'd arrange for a very public appearance at the federal courthouse, followed by an all-day session in front of the grand jury. We explained how it didn't matter whether he actually testified. Nicky would think he did. It doesn't take all day to plead the fifth. So Eddie cut a deal."

"Guess he's not going to get the benefit of the bargain," Jake cracked.

"He wore a wire for six months. Zitto was getting suspicious. Eddie was not winning any Oscars, and his nerves were shot. We shut him down and started the process to put him under. Too bad for Eddie—and us—the paperwork to get him into the witness protection program got bogged down in Washington. Fucking suits in the Justice Department can't get out of their own way. So we stashed him in a motel on the boulevard in West Atlantic City. You know, rent by the hour, bring your own sheets and towels. Eddie hated it. He crawled through the bathroom window to find some trim. The Bayonne lads must've been sitting on the place."

"Tapes worth anything?" Jake asked.

"There's enough on them to take down Zitto, his nephew, and the business agents of three hotel unions. But we were counting on Blatstein in court. Without him to authenticate the tapes, they could be suppressed. But even if we can convince a judge they're admissible, we need a live witness to talk the jury through them, set the scene, put the conversations in context. You know the drill."

"Yeah. Where do you go from here?"

"The wiseguys will hang tough, but Eddie walked a wire in on a state senator and a Casino Control Commissioner.

We'll let them listen to themselves arranging to take money from the mob. See if we can't persuade them to come over to the white hats."

"Hell of a choice," Jake said. "Cooperate and risk permanent residence in the Meadowlands or refuse to cave and hope no one else does."

"Yeah," Bill Perry agreed. "A jail sentence is better than getting capped. We got another tape. The last one Blatstein made before he disappeared. It's our best shot at Nicky."

"Who's on it?"

"Eamon McMeekin."

Lamps' Bar, a north side dive at the heart of AC's no man's land on Tennessee Avenue, was named for its owner. Archie "Lamps" Washington's sobriquet derived from the condition of his eyes, which bulged from their sockets. Archie has explained on occasion to the curious that it has something to do with his thyroid. As long as his customers were buying drinks, eating pickled pigs' feet plucked from the floating gallon jars lining the bar, and playing the policy game he ran out of the backroom, Archie cheerfully obliged their good-natured jibes about his prominent orbs.

Lamps' Bar was Jake's and Alfie's location of choice for hammering out issues between them that they both knew could become animated. Jake, from their usual table in the back corner facing the bar's only entrance, motioned Lamps to send over two bottles of Schmidts when his partner walked through the entrance.

"I'm listening," Alfie said, pulling up a chair.

"How much do you want to know?"

"Meaning…?"

"Do you want deniability?"

"What I want is to know what my partner is doing freelancing and risking both our shields."

"Perry confirmed Nicky had Blatstein hit. Perry and his team have been trying to leverage someone close to Nicky and Blatstein got elected. The feds had him in the middle of a cigarette-smuggling ring and used that to put him in front of the grand jury. They kept him before the grand jury all day to create the impression he was cooperating. The son of a bitch got to the point where he answered "Five" to every question because he was tired of repeating the full Fifth Amendment mantra his lawyer had written out for him.

"Perry wished him a 'nice day' when he was leaving the courthouse at 6 p.m. Blatstein must have figured it was fifty-fifty whether he'd live out the week. That night, he called the number Perry slipped him on his way out the door."

"Bottom line, Jake, Blatstein is not our case. Eddie was a federal witness. His murder is a federal matter. Let Perry handle it."

"McTierny is likely in a footrace to arrest those two bozos from Bayonne before the feds can turn them against the higher up that ordered the hit. My guess is once McTierny has them, they'll both run into some terminal bad luck. Case closed."

"Jake, you know I'm all in with you when it comes to making our case. But what you're asking here is for me to go way outside the lines. Based on what we know as of now, we have no justification to disobey a direct order from McMeekin, his status as a corrupt shit bag notwithstanding."

"You're right, Alfie."

"About what?"

"Our captain's a shit bag."

"He's the feds' problem, not ours. Leave it alone."

"Yeah."

Outside Lamps', Jake watched his partner pull away from the curb and drive south on Tennessee. He had made his decision. He would provide Alfie cover, deniability. He'd work the Tunnel Queens case with his partner and keep his interactions with Bill Perry to himself. He was convinced that the feds' investigation of mob infiltration of the gaming industry and his murder case were not coincidental, that they shared more than the tunnel as a crypt for murder victims killed seventeen years apart.

His meeting with Michelle intruded on his thoughts. Her heart had scarred over. She seemed distant. What had he expected, that showing up after nearly two decades of absence from her life, confessing his regret for deserting her when she needed him most would erase the hurt, that they would fall into each other's arms and live happily ever after?

He turned the key in the ignition. For Michelle, he would risk his shield, and Alfie's.

* * *

Special Agent Bill Perry and Detective Jake Harris stared through a fifth-story window across Atlantic Avenue from the building where Arthur Gomberg's offices occupied the top floor. The room was empty of furniture except for a card table and two metal chairs. Each wore an earpiece that would enable him to listen in on conversations occurring in Gomberg's office, thanks to the bugs installed in ceiling light fixtures and the baseboard behind Gomberg's desk.

It was a warrantless bureau black bag job reserved for organized crime investigations. Perry wanted leads; admissibility in court was not his objective. Both men knew the tapes would prove an effective persuader when played during a sweat session to flip any participants, particularly the public officials who visited Gomberg to kiss his ring.

An hour earlier, Jake had gotten the call from Perry inviting him to sit in on the surveillance. The FBI bug had picked up Gomberg's call to Vincent Nicastro. It was urgent, Gomberg demanded.

A tape recorder was on a table between the two men. Perry was fiddling with it when Nicastro walked around the corner at South Carolina and turned right on Atlantic to the front of Gomberg's building. Jake tapped Perry's forearm to alert him and then focused high-powered binoculars on Vinny. Nicastro paused before entering the building. He felt the knot of his tie and ran a palm over his hair. Jake knew these last-minute groomings were not out of any respect for the man who had summoned him. Vinny simply liked to look good.

Nicastro's face glistened fresh from his daily facial. His fingernails, perfectly manicured as usual, shone with lacquer. The trouser cuffs of his navy-blue suit broke over black banker-cap shoes polished to a high shine. The dimpled knot of his Italian silk tie centered the collar of his white monogrammed dress shirt.

Minutes after Nicastro disappeared into the building, the voice-activated tape recorder crackled alive.

"What the fuck is going on, Vinny?"

"Take it easy, Fish. Sorry, I got to do this."

Both men listening knew Nicastro was running his hands in the creases of Gomberg's groin, around his back, checking for a wire.

"What the fuck is that noise?" Perry asked.

Jake laughed. "That's Gomberg trying to breathe. Adnoids. It happens when he gets excited." Jake pictured Fish gulping oxygen, jaw protruding, opening and closing, forcing air over his lower lip, out his nose, eyes bulging.

"Don't tell me to take it easy. Why was Blatstein hit?"

"The judge got himself into the middle of a ring of yahoos smuggling untaxed cigarettes up from North Carolina. He had the feds tailing him for months and never knew it. He was high risk. If he gets indicted and flips, it gets sticky. Plans get jeopardized."

"Okay. Eddie had to go. I get that. But who's the Einstein that dumped him in my construction site?"

"Yeah, well, that's a problem. Coupla cowboys. Good guys, but not the brightest lights. They grabbed the judge outside his girlfriend's place, and he got nuts on them in the car. They tried to calm him down, but they had to whack him in the back seat. They needed a temporary spot till they could get him up to the Meadowlands for a proper burial."

"That's crazy. You hit a judge, you don't get a coupla goombas to do it! I got the Casino Control Commission up my ass with a proctoscope and a drill. Our friend in Trenton is spooked. Since Eddie turned up dead, the senator don't wanna know me. I made that scumbag. He was walking around, looking at tall buildings, when I got the county committee to run him. I financed his campaign. Now the fuck is ducking my calls."

Nicastro stood, signaling the end of the discussion. He was a half foot taller than Gomberg, who stood from behind his desk and stared up at his visitor. "You tell our friend to get his nephew under control. That crazy guinea bastard is gonna bring us all down."

Vinny turned his head slightly to the left then to the right to crack the stiffness from his neck and smiled. "Our friend will take care of his end. You worry about yours."

"Vincent, remember who you are. I made you. I took you out of the pool hall where you'd be just another small time union fixer. Things go south for me, they go south for you."

Nicastro's smile broadened. "Arthur, you'd do well to remember your part—you know, upstanding citizen, public benefactor. Leave the Blatstein problem to others to manage. You don't want the Little Guy to worry that you can't take the weight, that you might crack and cause problems. People that cause problems become replaceable."

"Just do what I pay you to do."

Nicastro shot his cuffs, touched the knot of his tie, turned, and left Arthur Gomberg to gaze at the awards and photographs on the wall behind his desk for whatever comfort they would afford.

Jake had become an expert on Arthur Gomberg. As teenagers, Jake had been drawn to Fish—like a visitor to a circus sideshow who can't look away from a sad, freak of nature—trying to imagine what was going on in his mind, trying to imagine what it was like being Fish.

Arthur "Fish" Gomberg had always been a collector. He sorted and inventoried his possessions like a merchant fussing over a display window or arranging his shelves of goods. It started with baseball cards, then cars, then people. Vinny Two-Tone, Joey, Toad, even Sammy Dorfman. Each object, each person had a place, a function. His was a perfectly ordered world, and as his collection of things and people grew, so did Fish.

What Jake didn't know of Fish from their summers on the boards, he got from newspaper and magazine articles as Fish gained prominence. When he became Mr. Gomberg and his money demanded respectability, Fish turned his interest to collecting *honor*. After all, Fish figured, honor could be acquired like anything else. Fish had learned that at the auction gallery. The men that made a living using shills and fast talk to separate yokels from their money filled their grimy little offices with awards from the synagogue, the mayor, and the Policemen's Benevolent Association.

Fish purchased respectability with his millions. It was a kind of money laundering except Fish didn't turn dirty money into clean. He used his money to cleanse himself.

The Press ran a feature on Fish when he was named the Greater Atlantic County Federation of Jewish Charities Man of the Year, another when he became president of *B'nai Brith*, yet another when he was elected president of *Avoda*, the most prestigious of Jewish men's organizations. His prodigious giving to Israel Bonds and the Atlantic City

Medical Center landed him the chairmanships of their boards. He was on the board of Beth Judah Synagogue, and a past president of the board of the Down Beach Jewish Community Center. He even had an honorary degree from Temple University and served on its board too.

Fish's favorite backdrop for press photos was his office. It was like a man looking in a mirror, looking in a mirror. Each new press photo would capture the framed pictures of Gomberg with mayors and governors, senators and congressmen, Israeli generals and ministers—photographic echoes, redundant preservation of Gomberg's validation. The walls and tables held dozens of framed certificates with calligraphic script and gold seals, plaques and gavels inscribed in his honor. To authenticate them all, to make his honor irrefutable, unassailable, there was the centerpiece of it all, a gold-framed photograph of Gomberg at Gandolfo Palace in an awkward half bow before the Pope, complete with rosary beads blessed by the Holy Father himself.

When he died, his obituary would take up the entire page of *The Press* above the fold. This thought, above all others, pleased him.

Round and shiny, hair and skin and nails glistening with oils and treatments, he kept everything new, showcased, on display: his clothes, his cars, impeccable, in perfect order.

Jake knew it hadn't always been so. Often, a feature story on Gomberg would include details of his humble beginnings.

Fish's dad started out curing kosher pickles in wooden barrels and supplying the local delis and supermarkets.

AC

He'd drive vats of his pickles to his customers in the back of a beat-up Ford station wagon. Fish's dad and the wagon smelled of garlic and pickle brine. His customers liked his prices and asked what else he had. So he expanded into meats and cheeses, kosher and nonkosher, condiments in bulk, blintzes, knishes, and other specialty pastries. He was a middleman and made a few pennies over the suppliers.

His father's money had gotten the Gomberg family to Margate, the toniest of the three downbeach towns south of Atlantic City. The Gombergs had been fortunate. They were able to flee the inlet section of AC where lower-class Jews and Irish had to live side by side with Puerto Ricans and Negroes. They joined the Linwood Country Club, the wealthy Jews' answer to Seaview, the exclusive *goy* club that wouldn't have them.

Fish never felt comfortable around the country club set. There was something unrefined about the Gombergs. They lacked grace, especially father and son. Having met Fish's mom once, Jake assumed she was uncomfortable at the club with the wives of the other members. Fish referred to his mom as the *Minimum* because his father insisted she have lunch at the club at least two Saturdays a month so he could meet the monthly food minimum. When Fish's mom resisted, his father would grumble at her that if she didn't eat at the club, he'd have to pay regardless.

Jake recalled the one time Fish got the crew laughing so hard they had tears in their eyes. Fish's dad forced him to play golf every Saturday morning during the summer. One Saturday night, Fish arrived at the Texas Avenue boards more agitated and flustered than usual. He no sooner reached the others hanging on the rail than he launched into an animated account of that morning's round of golf.

A golf club in Fish's hands might as well have been a sledgehammer. The game mocked him. He dreaded the first tee, surrounded by foursomes watching, waiting. He silently implored God to allow him to strike the ball down the fairway. He didn't care about distance. Just get the ball into the air and down the middle.

A successful golf swing was a series of fluid, connected movements, programmed through disciplined repetition into muscle memory. Each golfer had a personal, preset ritual of visuals, paces, and waggles as precisely timed as the ignition sequence of a rocket launch, culminating in a mental mantra, a *swing thought*, essential to lock in the hardwired sequence of movements. At this point in his narrative, Fish demonstrated his setup routine. Toad almost fell over the rail he was laughing so hard. Fish managed to make contact, but the ball rarely got airborne and squirted into the rough, a snake killer.

Fish just wanted to pick up his ball and run to the next tee to put some respectable distance between the foursome behind them, but his father insisted on playing every shot, which included interminable ball hunts in the deep rough. "Fuck 'em. They can wait. I pay my dues. Artie, don't pick up that ball. We got as much right to be here as those cocksuckers." As his father openly defied course etiquette, Fish looked back at the trailing foursome. One of them, apparently tired of waiting, hit his tee shot well beyond Fish and his father. Fish's dad ran out into the fairway, hollering and shaking his fist, yelling "Cocksuckers!" at the top of his lungs.

By now, Vinny and Joey were rocking with laughter too. Fish wore a tentative grin. For once, Fish seemed to escape his usual role of the sad clown. This time, he was the funny guy, the others waiting for him to continue. Then the unexpected happened. Fish joined the others and began laughing. He motioned with his hands for them to quiet down and pay attention. He was setting up his big finish. But first he had to stop his own laughing and catch his breath, which was not easy for Fish, given his adenoids. He took the five iron he'd been using to part the weeds, looking for his ball, walked out into the fairway where his father was still hollering and heaved the club with all his strength at the foursome behind them. Then he turned, dropped trow, mooning everyone with his big white pimply ass. By now all five boys were holding their sides, trying to talk but unable. Fish delivered the last line of his story with the timing and tone of a comedic genius: "I think that's the last round of golf I'll be playing this summer."

Poor Fish. Jake wondered how bad it must have been with a man like Hyman Gomberg for a dad.

Men like Fish's dad gave everybody around them the jumps. Men like him lived forever, while all around them others succumbed to heart disease and aggravation. But middlemen eventually get squeezed, and Fish's dad was no exception. The wholesale food business slid into the crapper along with AC's economy. Fish's dad was tapped out at his banks.

In the end, unable to run his business or pay his club dues, he blew his brains out with the forty-five he kept in his car. According to the story in *The Press*, he stuck the barrel in his mouth and squeezed the trigger. He'd bought the gun as protection for his weekly collections, mostly cash. He visited each customer personally. He trusted no one when it came to money. If his mattress paid interest, he would have avoided banks.

As Fish told it, he heard the pop of the handgun and followed it to the garage. His father was slumped behind the wheel of his Cadillac Deville. His mother stood at the driver's side window, staring at the jagged opening in the back of her husband's skull. She was in her nightgown. A streetlight shining through the garage door windows shadowed her sagging breasts. Fish said she wasn't crying, not even a whimper. Her face was blank. Neither acknowledged the presence of the other. Neither made a move to console the other.

After the death of his father, Fish took to the boards. Jake caught glimpses of him at his new vocation: boardwalk pitchman. He was a quick learner, and he had *seykhl*. He watched the *goyim* from Indiana, Ohio, Kansas—to Fish they might as well have been from Mars—parade up and down the boardwalk, falling for every come-on. They stood with wide eyes and mouths open in thrall to pitchmen hawking cheap blenders and food processors and magic knives that would never need sharpening. With rapid-fire spiels, peppered with Yiddish insults, the pitchmen promised convenience, health, and vigor with each purchase.

But fleecing *goyishe kups* at twenty-five dollars a pop for a blender or a set of miracle knives was small-time. The boardwalk auctions promised bigger scores and required finesse, talent. The auctions appealed to Fish on several levels. He liked to get the better of people, to take advantage of them with his cleverness without their ever realizing what he was doing. Fish liked to cheat people, probably because he had been cheated. Life wasn't fair, wasn't meant to be.

Fish got himself hired as a floor boy in one of the "joints," as they were called by the auctioneers. One summer night, Jake wandered into the gallery where Fish worked. Fish was in his element, Jake noticed immediately. On a break between lots, Fish pulled Jake aside and, with no small amount of pride, explained the business to him. Shills, phony grandmother and grandfather types, were salted in the audience to drive up the bidding. Fish's job was to walk up and down the aisles showing the marks the item on the block, as the bidding was about to begin. The shills would *ooh* and *aah* and open the bidding at the ask.

Fish studied faces in the crowd. He saw them flush with excitement at the chance to acquire an estate object at a price "so low it was like stealing." "Estate Sale Tonight," read the permanent sign in the window. They'd tag some Mayflower-old-money sounding name to it for effect: Farthingham Estate sale or Carrington Estate auction. In truth, there was no estate. All the goods were cheap and mass-produced. *Chotchkes.* The joint had a few semi-valuable items—silver table settings, crystal, some jewelry—but overpriced, another element of the scam. Those pieces were fobbed to the *whales* in the back by the closer.

Fish explained to Jake the hierarchy in the auction business. The *hook* stood out front of the joint and pulled the marks inside with promises of *unbelievable deals*. The *opener* sold lower-priced items to get the marks interested and keep them around for the bigger pieces. The *lead* handled the big-ticket items after the metal folding chairs were occupied by an acceptable number of marks. And there was the *closer*. He was the most important player in the auction flimflam. The closer worked in the back. Once the bidding ended on a higher-price item, the lucky winner was escorted to the back to sit down with the closer to finalize the paperwork on the sale. Small-time bidders were never taken back to the closer. To meet the closer, you had to have some money worth stealing.

Fish was the escort. Jake watched him walk the mark to the back of the joint, like leading a lamb to slaughter. Once alone with the whale, the closer would work him.

"Arthur, would you please get Mr. and Mrs. Wilson some coffee?"

"Yes, Mr. Stephens."

Fish explained that everyone who worked in the joint had a phony name. At that time, Fish hadn't earned a new name. Floor boys didn't need one. Usually, auctioneers took their first names and made them their last. They figured the tourists from the Midwest wouldn't trust anyone named Grunberg or Gurwicz or Plotsky. So Stephen Grunberg became Mr. Stephens, Robert Gurwicz became Mr. Roberts, Michael Plotsky became Mr. Michaels.

Fish would never be a stand-up auctioneer. A front man needed to talk fast and project his voice in a rhythmic cadence that soothed and mesmerized. The nasal twang Fish's adenoids produced grated on the ears. The way Fish explained, he preferred the back room anyway. Closing was a higher art form. In time, Fish mastered the close and became Mr. Arthur.

Mr. Arthur had a special talent for his trade and made serious money for his employer, enough for Fish to negotiate a piece of the business. He dropped out of Temple University and worked auction full-time. When the joints in AC closed for the winter, he worked an auction gallery in Lauderdale. Mr. Arthur visited whales in their homes on the Gold Coast of Florida and on the Upper Eastside of Manhattan. He brought along his case of estate pieces for their consideration. "Long-term investments," he'd say like a wealth management professional to a silk-stocking client. He knew how to make them feel special, flatter them, pander to their need to be treated as old money even though they were only a generation removed from the *shtetl*.

The money Fish made working auctions gave him the stake he needed to get into real estate. Casino gambling was inevitable, Fish—and everyone else with a brain— knew. AC was on the economic ropes, and gambling was the easy fix. Fish was a bottom feeder. He made his first move with three "spoiler" lots in the Inlet, narrow wedges and alleys not good for anything except blocking someone else's development plans. Then he picked up the tax liens on five properties in the Italian Riviera: Ducktown South, the beach blocks of Texas, California, Georgia, Florida, and Mississippi Avenues. The old hotels along the boards were obvious. Big outside money, mainly Las Vegas and New York, took them off the table early. Steve Wynne, Del Webb, Bob Guccione, Hugh Hefner, Merv Griffith, Donald Trump: not one had sand in his shoes.

Their casinos were planned for entire blocks from Pacific Avenue to the boardwalk. The decrepit walk-ups and trattorias that shared the beach blocks with the old hotels were leveled. They were reminders of family, hard work, the grind, responsibility—and they had to go. The neighborhoods across Pacific north to Atlantic Avenue would be turned into parking garages.

The only locals who would get a real taste were those who had hung on to the old hotels. For their pieces of the beach block, they were given points in the casinos that would rise in place of the Shelburne, Traymore, Blenheim, and the other *Grand Dames.* And it didn't take much of a piece to be set for life.

Fish leveraged his deeds, with their metes and bounds that cut across five planned casino projects, into the purchase of the *La Concha,* a beachfront motel faded and cracked with neglect. It was four blocks down beach from the epicenter of casino development but close enough to the action that he figured second-wave money would want it. He was right. He flipped the agreement of sale before he went to settlement and bought two more and did the same then did it again. He optioned property up and down the boards, pieces the big money overlooked. Before his fortieth birthday, Fish was worth several million dollars on the books and a few more off.

He kept one spoiler. It ran behind the Blenheim and along one side with an easement for access. He needed to negotiate a piece of the Blenheim with the family that had built it and owned it from the day it opened in 1906. For these negotiations, he enlisted the aide of his friend, Vincent Nicastro, who went to his friends in the back room of Victory Billiards.

Nobody had bothered to think about what would be lost. Everyone bought into Trenton's promise that casinos would bring jobs to AC—without asking what kind of jobs. No one was concerned about what would happen to the bits and pieces of AC that were good and healthy—the restaurants that had been owned by the same families for generations, the pizzerias, Jewish delis, and corner candy stores in the old neighborhoods.

Instead everyone would work for the gambling industry—the company store—as valet car parkers, kitchen workers, busboys, cocktail waitresses, maids, and bellmen. The dream jobs were on the casino floor: dealers, croupiers, pit bosses. But most of these would go to carpetbaggers.

By 1979, the boardwalk had become one huge construction site with no place for the Dorfmans or other locals who had hustled a living from the beach and boardwalk each summer for more than a century. Ducktown was the first of the neighborhoods to go. The Atlantic City Expressway originally connecting Philadelphia to Pleasantville was extended to run through Atlantic City's heart, no less a presage than the first wagon train through the Dakota prairie. Bernie Dorfman lost his sports book, Tessie lost her luncheonette, and Sammy lost his paper stands and numbers game. The insiders got fat on real estate and graft. The politicians got pieces of deals for voting the right way, the mob ran the unions, and everybody went along.

* * *

Jake got into the cruiser and handed Alfie a cup of coffee.

"How's your mom doing, Jake?"

"She can't remember her own name. She's gaining weight and coming on to Mr. Feinstein in the room down the hall. The nurses have to keep an eye on her, or she'll hop in the sack with him. But I guess it's better than remembering everything you lost."

"Maybe," Alfie said.

"I found Bernie Dorfman," Jake said.

Jake couldn't say exactly why he needed to see Bernie. He just did. And Alfie didn't interfere by asking.

The Hebrew Old Age Home took up the entire beach block between Brighton and Chelsea Avenues. It was where old Jews with no family, or whose children couldn't or wouldn't pay for a private nursing home, went to die. Jewish charities paid the bills, and though its Board of Trustees had good intentions, the place was a warehouse. Its residents ran the spectrum from physical illnesses to mental—organic brain syndrome, senility, loss of cognitive ability. Mother boards erased.

"Bernie Dorfman," Jake said.

He and Brathwaite did not take out their credentials.

The receptionist, intent on placing checkmarks on the jackets of manila files piled on her desk, did not look up or otherwise acknowledge the two men. After a minute watching her flip through files, Alfie placed both hands on the gray metal desk and leaned in close to the receptionist's face.

"Ber-nie-dorf-man."

She looked past Alfie at Jake. "You family?"

"Friend."

"Ain't seen you here before. What about him?" She nodded toward Alfie.

"He's family."

The woman smirked.

"Only his brother and sister are on his list, and they don't come anymore. I need some ID."

The men complied. She scanned the shields. "This should be something to see. Wait over there."

She pointed to a rattan love seat with floral-patterned cushions and a matching chair in the dayroom just beyond her desk, picked up the phone, and punched an intercom button.

Sunlight, which by now had burned through the morning clouds, flooded the room. Except for the smell and the look of the occupants, it could have been the lobby of one of the remaining cheap motels that lined Pacific Avenue, faux tropical motif, lacquered bamboo furniture, faded floral fabric.

Waiting for Bernie, he understood why he had come. The old man was a portal to a time before strangers took over his hometown. With Bernie sitting beside him, he'd click his heels three times and be hanging on the rails again, feeling the sea air on his skin before heading to see Michelle.

Is this how it ended, crossing the barrier from youth to the rest of your life; a desperate longing to go back, to be anywhere but where you were? Long after the arrogance and resilience of the young had been squeezed from them, old men walked the streets wondering at the joke that had been played on them. They railed at ghosts, profane solil-oquies, outbursts of grief for lives unrealized. Street mum-blers. Few among them had the means to do little more than eat enough to keep from starving, sleep in a bed most nights, live another angry day. Yet they keened at the sky for a second chance, certain they could make it all come out right.

Bernie Dorfman shuffled into view behind one of the attendants, a large black woman who looked like she was leading a farm animal into a stall. Thorazine had taken from him whatever senility had not.

"What's on his shirt?" Jake asked.

"Huh?"

"What's on the front of his shirt?"

Jake looked hard at the woman who'd brought him.

"Looks like pea soup to me. Yeah, pea soup. That's what they was fed today."

Bernie wore white orthopedic socks and paper slippers. His shirt, buttoned unevenly, was stuffed carelessly into his trousers. A corner poked through the fly, which had been zipped about a third closed.

"You want to clean him up, go ahead clean him up. He just gonna spill his dinner all over hisself anyway." The escort looked at the receptionist. "Miss Lupe, call me when these gentlemens is done."

Jake took Bernie's hand and sat him down on the couch. Bernie was smiling at whatever was in his head, but it was not the smile Jake remembered.

Jake sat, holding the old man's hand, and neither spoke a word.

Live Nude Girls, Private Viewing Booths, the neon in the front window promised. Each time Jake passed that sign, he thought, *What else? Dead nude girls?* The building on Atlantic Avenue midblock between Pennsylvania and Virginia had once been the home of Homberger's Department Store, an upscale ladies' apparel shop.

Sammy Dorfman, unchanged by time, sat just inside the entrance behind a glass case filled with adult novelties. When the two detectives entered, he did not look up from the tout sheet he was studying.

"No jerkin' off in the booths," he said flatly around the soggy brown-black stub in the corner of his mouth, cognizant of the futility of his admonition.

"I went to see Bernie," Jake said.

Sammy looked up. "I know you. You worked the beach, didn't you?"

"And sold papers for you," Jake added.

"Yeah. I recognize you. They were good days. We all made a living. Right, kid?"

"Yeah, Sammy, we did."

"This fuckin' town. Ain't like it used to be. I don't know nobody no more. Everybody's a stranger now."

147

"Let's talk about Arthur Gomberg."

Sammy eyed the butts of the service pieces holstered under their shoulders, peaking around the lapels of their jackets. "You a cop now, eh kid?"

"Yeah."

"Gomberg, eh? Mr. Big Shot? I taught that little bastard everything I knew. What do I got to show for it? I ask for a little something to get me through a slow period, and he puts me here. What kinda thing is that to do? I was like a father to the little prick. I says, Artie, let me work real estate for you, you know, sell condos. He don't say yes. He don't say no. Just says he's got somethin' else. I end up cleanin' jism off the walls of nudie booths. So who's the schmuck? Me!"

Sammy was still answering his own questions.

"What do you remember about Gomberg back then when he was running numbers for you?"

"You kiddin' me? I can't remember to take my putz out of my pants to piss. How am I supposed to remember some kid?"

"Anything," Jake pressed.

"You here about the bodies they found in my sister's tunnel? Is that what this is about?" He didn't wait for a response. "You know what I remember about Artie? When he wasn't workin', he was pullin' his pud. I don't mean sometimes. It was like a sickness. Every goddamn night, I'd find him in the tunnel with that punk he ran with. The kid that killed his uncle and chopped off his hands. Once I saw one of Tessie's boys with them. I go in the tunnel to lock down the gate, and these two would be in there, whackin' off."

"Joey Nardo," Jake said.

"I don't remember names. Scary-looking kid." Sammy reached down and picked a scab from his shin.

"Did you ever see them in the tunnel at night?"

"Not in the tunnel. Some nights after making my rounds at the paper stands dropping late editions, collecting the money—you remember, kid. Sorry. Officer. I'd circle back to make sure the tunnel was secure—you know, the pads locked down proper, Bernie's chair and table okay. Bernie liked me to do that. I'd sometimes see them sitting on the steps down to the tunnel."

"See anyone with them?"

"It was early, around ten, ten thirty usually, when I'd see them. I never saw anyone with them. The only reason I even looked for them is I spotted Arthur's car parked at the ramp."

"Ever say anything to them?"

"Yeah. Stay the fuck out of the tunnel—like it would do any good."

"Sammy, you just told me you saw one of Tessie's boys with them."

"Did I say that? Maybe I just got confused with what I read in the papers or somethin' maybe Tessie said. My memory's not so good. I think I got some of that *old-timer's* disease, the one where you have trouble remembering if you brushed your teeth or who you been married to for fifty years. Maybe that's not so bad. New piece of ass every night."

"How's Tessie?" Jake asked.

"She wants to move to Miami Beach. She says she can't take the winters here no more. You get old, the cold gets to you. I tell her she can't move to Miami. It's not real down there, something not right about the sand. And I hear they got pelicans. One of them takes a shit on your head, you'll know it."

"She ever say anything about her boys? The ones that disappeared?"

"Tessie has a big heart. Those boys of hers would come and go. She'd get upset if they didn't come back. She knew something bad had happened. Guess she was right."

With his tongue, he pushed the soggy stub of the cigar to the other corner of his mouth.

"My sister was mother to every queen in this town, at least the ones who spent time in her place. Back then, the boys would get beat on just for laughs. Cops didn't care. Cops would beat them up too. She would bring some of them home, fix them up, let them stay on the couch until they healed up, make them tea and toast. Heart of gold, Tessie.

"They'd cry to her about their boyfriends, this one and that one. They'd ask her advice, and she was always willing to give it. Their families—their own mothers and fathers—wanted nothing to do with them anymore. So they came to Tessie."

"You got a way to contact her?"

Sammy scrawled a number on a corner of his tout sheet, tore it off, and handed it to Jake.

"Listen, do me a favor. Don't tell Mr. Gomberg what I said. I'm gonna ask him for a job in his casino when the new one opens. You know, kind of a greeter, local color."

Jake pictured Sammy at the entrance to the casino floor in his soiled shorts, eczema, too-large newsboy's cap, big blocky Roy Orbison shades, chewing on a cigar stub.

"Don't you want to know how Bernie is?" Jake asked.

"I know how he is. He's like this town."

A few nights later, Jake was summoned back to the home. Mrs. McKenna told him it would probably be that night or early morning. She was an expert at this type of death, the nontraumatic kind that came in the quiet of night. Wide eyes glazed, increasingly fewer rasps of air passing through the lungs, the temperature of the skin, the expression fixed, mask-like. Mrs. McKenna detected these signs of a life nearing its end, always earlier than sons and daughters, husbands and wives.

"She's peaceful," said Mrs. McKenna. "She's not in any pain. You're a good son." Intended to comfort him, her words were instead a recrimination.

He was struck by the quiet of the place. There were no moans, no manic, angry diatribes directed at unseen family members, husbands who left, daughters who'd ruined their lives by marrying *that man,* sisters who'd stolen jewelry. In each room, he glimpsed a tiny figure under a top sheet, curled in the fetal position. The head angled up and back on its pillow, seemingly disconnected from its torso, a gaunt tortoise-like appendage unable to withdraw to the safety of its shell.

Jake had become good at the violent street death that was the regular fare of a homicide detective. He was at his best when it was too late. He took his mother's hand. It was dry and cold. He spoke of scenes from their life as a family and told her she would soon be with her Buddy. It didn't matter whether she could hear his words.

He wondered at her love for his father, what it must be like to want to stop living, to care nothing for any other person, to acknowledge she had no life without her one love. He wondered whether true love, if that was what it was, was worth the pain of losing it.

Her breathing slowed and the rale in her chest softened. She wasn't fighting or struggling; she took each breath dutifully. She had waited twelve years to die; a few more minutes wouldn't matter. He began to mark the seconds between her breaths. He would remember the long delay before her final one, thinking she had died when she hadn't. When her last breath came, it startled him. After it, he waited and waited some more. He looked at his watch: 1:06, to the minute the exact time his father had died.

On the drive from the nursing home to the Venice Apartments, his mind drifted. Alfie had gotten the lab results on the Louisville Slugger. *Jesus.* His mother had just died, and he was already thinking about Joey's Louisville Slugger.

* * *

Alfie pushed the cup of black coffee poured moments before by Hairnet Mary across the table as his partner walked toward the booth.

"You look like shit."

"I hear that a lot lately. I don't spend a whole lot of time looking in the mirror."

"Good thing. How's your mom doing?"

"She died last night."

"Sorry, Jake. You okay?"

"Yeah. I was with her. My father's death—he suffered until his last breath. It was a struggle. I guess that's the way with cancer. Mom just went to sleep. No gasping for life. That's all she wanted since my father died."

"You want to knock off, I got you covered. Anything you need, I'm here."

"Thanks. I need a couple hours to see my brother. He's got some papers I need to sign. You bring the labs?"

Alfie handed Jake the manila envelope. The report said there were hair fibers embedded in the barrel. These had been removed at the lab and sealed in evidence envelopes to prevent further contamination. The handle, black with pine resin Joey had rubbed in to give him a better grip, yielded mint condition prints. Joey's had been identified. But a second set of latents didn't have a match in the data bank. The Kastle-Meyer color test of the stains on the barrel revealed human blood in the wood fibers. Preliminary typing tests showed the blood came from at least three different human sources.

"What about running the hair fibers from the bat against the strands from the skulls? Did any of those geniuses think to do that?"

"Guess not," Alfie responded.

"Those lab guys won't wipe their own asses unless you tell them."

"McMeekin's sitting on Dougherty, Jake. Kind of chills his enthusiasm."

"Alfie, we need Bill Perry to get these analyzed by the FBI."

"You got a death wish, partner?"

"I'm not asking your permission. You can run to McMeekin, or you can stay out of my way. I'll swear we never had this conversation if it all goes south."

"I'm your partner, Jake. What you do, I do."

"Looks like my dumb is contagious."

Ben lived with Linda, his second wife, their two sons, and three cats in Linwood, an upscale community across the bay from Margate. Their home was a five-bedroom center hall colonial complete with backyard pool and an unobstructed view across the marshes to the barrier island on the Atlantic Ocean.

Jake knocked then opened the front door without waiting for a response. He never waited for his brother to let him in.

Ben leaned across the couch and poked his head around the corner of the den to see into the foyer.

"Oh, Jake."

Ben never greeted him with "hello," "hey," or "yo." It was just "Oh, Jake"—as if Ben had just woken up to find his brother standing by his bed in the very spot he had been the night before. They always seemed to be in the middle of the same conversation.

He noticed lately an edge to his brother on those occasions when they interacted, which were becoming rarer. They didn't socialize. Ben's wife, Linda, was aloof, even cold, not just to Jake but to everyone. He chalked it up to her Protestant gene. Ginny from outward appearances got along with Linda, but neither got very close to the other. Ben was intelligent, witty, loquacious, and to Jake anyway, unhappy. Ben was a self-taught musician, on guitar and piano. He was also a cynic and an atheist. Jake, only of late, gave any thought to his brother's amalgam of traits and how that stew might explain his behavior.

When he looked for reasons, Jake realized how little he really knew about his brother. His understanding was dependent on stitching together snapshots of Ben's life. When Jake had gone off to college, Ben was left behind to cope with their demented grandmother. But what it always came back to, in moments of brutal honesty, was that Jake knew he had not been much of an older brother. Maybe that explained Ben's occasional flashes of resentment.

They sat on the L-shaped sofa in the family room. The Sixers game was on the tube. Ben pushed the power-of-attorney forms across the coffee table. Jake spied the photograph of Ben's two boys with Charles Barkley. His brother was a big fan of professional basketball. Jake had no interest in a sport he associated with prima donnas, whiners, and instant gratification.

On his eighth birthday, Buddy had taken Jake to a minor league hockey game at convention hall. He hadn't understood all the rules, especially the zone violation penalties but the players charging hard, up and down the ice, digging for more speed made him think of his father racing toward him on the street ice, the orange ball on the horizon framing Buddy's entire body as if the sun had spewed him onto the earth.

To Jake, hockey players were true warriors, grace and stamina, selfless courage, and brutality, faces notched by high sticks and elbows, smiling through a puck-size gap where their front teeth should be. Their blood turned the ice red. Gashes stitched, they returned barely missing a shift. They didn't whine and pout about bad calls, missed ones, or cheap shots. Stone-faced stoics, they dropped their gloves and settled things with their fists. The primal code of hockey enacted and enforced on the ice enthralled the eight-year-old, and he resolved to grow into that kind of man.

Jake signed the power of attorney without reading the document. "Where were you last night?"

"Here."

"Mrs. McKenna told me she couldn't reach you."

"Tell me, Jake. How'd you feel alone with Mom in the dark holding her hand while she died?"

It was a question he should have been able to answer. His mother had died in his presence. How did he feel? He was able to recall perfectly his life with Buddy, an eight-millimeter home movie production—skating on street ice and learning to hit a baseball, field a ground ball, and make the pivot throw at second base to complete a double play. Buddy was tireless. He'd hold four scruffy hardballs in his glove—seams torn, cowhide beginning to peel—and pitch to his son. Then there was infield practice. Buddy hit hot grounders, one after another. As soon as Jake fielded one and threw it to Ben at first base, another was screaming his way.

"Head down! Look it into your glove. Take the bad hops in the chest or your face, but keep your head down!"

The realization that he would never again do anything with his father crushed him. His father was still young when he died. He was strong and handsome until the moment the cancer took over his body then his mind. He and Buddy were cheated of being men together.

But his mom?

"She got her wish."

"I asked you what you felt."

"I felt relieved that she didn't have to lie in that bed by herself any longer."

"You felt relief for yourself. You wouldn't have to imagine Mom in that bed, and you're not feeling much of anything."

Jake was about to say he loved her and missed her but he stopped himself. "She was our mother. You should have been there."

"And spoil your performance? I'll tell you what you really felt last night, Jake. You felt virtuous."

Ben was right. He'd nailed it.

"She deserved to have you there. She should have had more than just me."

"Bullshit."

"It was the right thing to do, for both her sons to be with her."

"The right thing? You sound like Dad. Is that what you're after? To say and do what you think our father would? Support your family and be there for birthdays and Little League, come home for dinner, not get drunk, and not smack your wife around? Isn't that what husbands and fathers are supposed to do?"

"Is that all he was to you?"

"Everything else he did—the money he gave to his sister and her kids, the daily visits to his mother, the drop-everything-for-the-aunts-and-uncles and run their errands—all that he did for himself, to feel good. He had this image of himself as the good son, husband, and father."

"And?"

"Fight, fuck, and die, Jake. That's all we're required to do."

"So our father's life was bullshit?"

"Not to him. And that's all that really mattered. He was sincere. He wasn't looking for praise."

"He lived for others."

"That's what it looked like. But that wasn't true. He'd knock himself out for everyone else, so he didn't have to think about what else he could have done with his life."

"He didn't hate his life, Ben. He was content."

"His whole life was a placebo."

"When did you get so smart?"

"Four years at home after you went away to school, Dad was cleaning up Nana's shit and tracking her down on Ventnor Avenue. She would walk down the white stripe in her nightgown and bare feet. When he wasn't looking after Nana, he was sitting with his mother in the old-age home, listening to her rant about his failures as a son, the worst being marrying *that woman*. He could never do enough. She died, and he spent his mornings and evenings saying *kaddish* at the synagogue—every goddamned day."

Ben picked up the powers of attorney and tapped them on the table to straighten their edges before replacing them in the file folder.

"You know why Mom didn't want to go into the home, Jake?"

"She didn't want to end up like Nana."

"Do you know *how* Nana died?"

"Hardening of the arteries in her brain."

"That was her medical condition. She was in the state hospital at Ancora. A real medieval snake pit. I'm not sure why she ended up in that place. Probably because facilities like the one mom was in couldn't handle her. I heard Mom crying one night late soon after Nana died. Dad was trying to assure her it wasn't her fault and there was nothing she could do about it. They couldn't prove it, but they were sure Nana had been beaten by one of the attendants. That's how our grandmother died, Jake, from a beating by a ward attendant at a state mental institution. That's why Mom didn't want to go into a home."

Two lanes of cracked, potholed blacktop traversed the short span of wetlands from the mainland to the Margate Bridge. The stretch of road leading to the bridge afforded an unobstructed view of the entire island. Jake drove that route home from Ben's house, even though there was a half-buck toll and Absecon Boulevard at the uptown end was free.

The demolition of the beachfront hotels was nearly complete. He scanned the horizon across the marshes from the Brigantine Inlet to lower Chelsea. The city grinned back with the gap-toothed grimace of a hockey player at the end of a long shift.

* * *

Tessie Dorfman lived on the top floor of a six-story apartment building on Chelsea Avenue surrounded by lots strewn with the rubble of demolished boarding houses. The orange brick structure midway between Atlantic and Pacific was destined to become a parking garage. It had an elevator, but Jake took the stairs. At her door, before lifting the brass combination bell and knocker, he cleared his throat, stood erect, shoulders back, and ran a palm over his hair in a vain attempt to smooth unruly curls.

"Come. Sit."

He entered a time warp, back to 1962. Tessie had scavenged the counter and stools, even the soda spouts, which she had arranged and mounted as they had been in the old luncheonette. The Coca-Cola and Nathan's famous signs now hung on the wall above the spouts and stools. The long rectangular mirror etched in one corner with the image of Rosie the Riveter flexing her bicep muscle and swigging a bottle of Coca-Cola hung over the living room sofa.

"Do they work?" Jake asked, gesturing toward the soda spouts.

"No. The plumbing was too expensive, and my kitchen isn't big enough."

"Looks just like it did," he said.

He walked to the old lunch counter and ran fingertips along its worn surface. He recalled the aroma of lotion, the press of bodies. He'd stood at this counter and met his uncle and his lover. He remembered the squeeze of Jamie Wescott's strong handshake.

"I saved what I could. They thought I was crazy when I had them bring it here. The super tried to stop me, so I had it all brought up in the middle of the night. It comforts an old lady. Nobody else cares much."

"I like it," he said. "It's nice to have something to remember by."

She motioned him to the sofa where she pushed aside piles of black-and-white photographs, postcards, and what appeared to be handwritten letters whose pages were worn to near transparency.

"Sit, sit," she said, patting the bare space next her. The gold lamé muumuu she wore rode up and pulled tight against drumstick thighs. "Not much left of the old queen is there?"

"Not too much, no."

"I wouldn't give you spit for the whole town. Sammy called. Told me to expect you—and what you wanted to talk about. Not sure I have much to offer. Tell me, Jake. How's Sandy?"

"He's in New York. He's very sick."

"I'm sorry. I know how close you were to him. They were all good boys, but Sandy was special. He was handsome, beautiful really. But more than that, he had taste and style. I guess it came from living in New York. Nothing flamboyant, if you know what I mean. Not a swish. Oh, I shouldn't use that word. I loved all my boys, even the swishy ones."

"He considered this town his home. If you're born here, you never get the sand out of your shoes."

"So they say. I'll never forget the first summer you started working for Bernie. You were his favorite, you know. He always said, 'That Jake will be somebody.'"

"And the day you discovered Sandy in the luncheonette. *Oy*! You came in with an order. Sandy spotted you and panicked. 'Tessie! Hide me! That's my nephew!' He was certain you'd hate him if you found out he was a fairy. Oh, I shouldn't use that word either. Back then nobody was as sensitive as they are today. Still. He ran behind the counter and ducked down until you were gone."

"I could never hate Sandy."

"His brother Harry made his life miserable."

"Now Harry I learned to despise."

She laughed. "You had on these tight lifeguard trunks, hung down around your *pipick*. And no shirt. You turned everybody's head, and the queens wondered who that beautiful boy was. I could see Sandy since I was behind the counter. He was turning red. He was so angry. When you left, he made it clear that anyone who went near you would answer to him. And Sandy could handle himself with his fists. He was in very good shape.

"After that close call, we set up a warning system. The boys near the entrance would sound the alarm, and Sandy would duck behind the counter. Everyone enjoyed the sport of it—except Sandy. I know it made him sad."

"None of that was necessary."

"The day you finally saw him the place was so crowded, and there were new boys who didn't know the routine."

"I'm glad."

"So was Sandy."

"Do you remember Jamie Wescott?"

"Of course. He was Sandy's boyfriend. The wild one. He had a dark side that attracted Sandy. Moth to a flame. Opposites, you know what they say."

"Jamie was one of the bodies found in the tunnel."

"I read about it in *The Press*. Aren't you supposed to be taking notes? What? You think you could fool Tessie why you came? To see me for old times?" She smiled. "It's okay. You have a job to do."

He felt the skin of his face warm. He had come for information, but among the ruins of the luncheonette, that objective had somehow faded.

"In what way was Jamie wild?"

"Before he met your uncle, he cruised the leather bars and went to the baths. That wasn't so unusual, I guess, back then. Sandy did none of that. Your uncle had one boyfriend at a time. Sandy was refined and appreciated the arts. He was well-read. He exposed Jamie to classical music, theater, fine arts. Jamie was Sandy's Pygmalion."

Her literary reference surprised him.

She noticed his reaction. "I read, young man. You don't need a college education to enjoy literature. Sandy was an older man, but he'd aged well, movie-star handsome with a lean body. And Jamie fell hard, but he never entirely lost his taste for his wild ways. When they fought, Jamie would taunt him about how he would go to the baths and find a younger man. I don't know whether Jamie carried through with his threat, but that was his way to get at Sandy.

"It was a dangerous world for my boys. They were street prey. Queer baiting was just another weekend activity, like drinking beer. Gangs would beat my boys and not take a thing from them. I nursed more than a few. Nobody wanted them, least of all their families."

"What about the cops?"

She smirked. "The cops were as bad as the juvenile delinquents. They turned a blind-eye to get them off the streets. Some of the cops did their own share."

Jake thought of the summer nights he'd cruised the streets in Fish's Bonnie seated next to Joey, the Louisville Slugger at his feet. He was ashamed at the memory even though he'd managed to escape to Michelle before the nights had had a chance to turn violent.

"Do you remember a kid named Joey Nardo?"

"He came in the luncheonette once. Started trouble and I had some of my tougher boys escort him out. Then I read about how he killed his uncle. He was evil. You could see it in his eyes. They were the scariest thing about him. Yellow slits, like snakes. Not human. I never saw him again, but from the description I got from some of my boys who'd been beaten, I knew he was responsible."

"What about Artie Gomberg?"

"The great Mr. Gomberg? A runner for Sammy. My brother once told me Artie played with himself a dozen times a day. Sammy used to catch him behind the pads. Who'd a thought he'd turn out to be a big shot?"

"Yeah. Who'd a thought?" Jake started to get up from the sofa.

"Had enough of an old lady, Detective?"

"Those were good days, Tessie."

"Yes, they were. And this was a good town. Took care of its own. Now? I don't recognize it. When you get old, the people you know disappear. That's expected. But your home isn't supposed to vanish. You should be able to walk the streets through the old neighborhoods and remember. You're entitled to that when you grow old. What will I have? Look outside. Hiroshima. I got no place to go when the owner gets his price. It's so sad."

"You'll be okay, Tessie. You're a tough lady."

"Oh, I'll be fine. But this town, it's sad what they did to it."

* * *

She stood at her rear window, surveying the small backyard. She had begun to lay in a flagstone patio, big enough to accommodate a chaise lounge, padded deck chair, and a small round glass table. Summer nights she kicked back on her chaise and read. When the sun was low over the bay and the natural light faded, she would close her book and watch the red ball disappear into the marshes.

Her bedroom was at the rear of the bungalow. She slept with the window open unless it was raining or snowing, and then she'd close it only if the direction of the wind blew the precipitation into her room. She fell asleep listening to the sounds of the bay and would awake to gulls squawking at first light.

It was three thirty in the morning when Jake jolted upright on his couch, staring at a television ad for the Popeil Pocket Fisherman.

Buddy had been a walker. He walked everywhere, chewing up city blocks with long rapid strides. As a boy, Jake would run beside his father just to keep up. Buddy wasn't in a hurry to get some place. That's not why he raced around on foot like he did. Now Jake understood why his father walked; he could see more of the town on foot—the smell of it, the mix of ocean and bay, and the wetlands baking in the summer sun.

On bad nights Jake would walk to Sovereign Avenue where she lived. Her white-clapboard bungalow on the bay sat on a tree-lined street of cookie-cutter houses with postage stamp yards of crab grass flanking short concrete walkways.

The bay separated the island from West Atlantic City on the mainland. Rickety piers and runabouts bobbing with the tide lined the lagoon behind her bungalow.

Since his split from Ginny, he would watch Michelle, unseen as cops were trained to do. He was a stalker but one without an endgame, one who meant no harm, unable to approach. Years ago, when he read in *The Press* of her marriage to Jimmy Walcott, he'd smirked at his adolescent delusion. After that, he turned off his emotional switch. But then Jimmy disappeared, and Jake's own marriage crumbled.

A light glowed through the shear window drapes of the bayside bungalow. Jake stood outside, imagining her curled up on the couch with her books. A museum poster of Monet's *Jardin á Giverny* had hung on her bedroom wall in the old Texas Avenue walk-up. The hundreds of tiny brushstrokes created the illusion of a garden lane with no beginning and no end. When he saw it that first night they were alone in her room, the painting drew him in. He felt the garden's warmth, the safety and sweet aroma of the flora. He pictured them together, in her room, feeling his discovery of her as if it were the first time.

A white-marble moon threw his shadow across her front yard. The ebbing tide exposed the marshes, and he could smell the bay as it washed against the bulkhead. Finally, he turned away and started back to The Venice.

I need to see you. Those were the words he choked back. "Do you have time to meet?"

"What about?" Her tone had not softened from their last meeting.

He felt a rush at the sound of her voice over the phone. "Joey."

"All right."

They arranged to meet at Tony's Baltimore Bar and Grill, a family-owned restaurant—one of the last—on the corner of Iowa and Atlantic. Its location off the beach block and away from the strip of old hotels had saved it from the wrecking ball. He sat at a table tucked in a corner to the right of the entrance. She walked in and waited just inside the entry. He watched her, intent on the slow turning of her head, her gaze moving about the room, searching for him.

He stood as she approached and pulled the chair away from the table for her to sit.

"I visited my brother yesterday. He told me you'd been to see him."

Jake nodded. "I sat across from Joey for an hour. He never looked up. Stared at his hands the whole time."

"He understood everything you said to him. He talks to me, just like when we were kids. He decided a long time ago there was not much point to his trying to communicate with anyone else. I'm sure his file at Farview is filled with psycho-gibberish explaining why."

"I got up to leave. My back was to your brother. I signaled the guard at the door that we were finished. Then I heard it. Like we were kids again and he was telling me to get in the Bonnie. *Beach Boy.*"

"Back when we were kids, Joey would tuck me into bed at night. He always made certain I had brushed my teeth and washed my face. He said he didn't want my teeth to turn black like his. I would climb into bed—the *real* bed with a box spring and mattress. Before Joey moved out of my room, he'd slept on an old cot my aunt bought at the Army-Navy. Joey pulled the sheet and covers up under my chin, made sure they were even and smooth, then folded them back to just below my neck. Every night—no matter what had happened to him at school, with the priests, the nuns—he made me feel safe, like no one could hurt me."

The waitress hovered with the stub of a pencil poised to write on her order pad. "You need more time, hon?"

Jake looked at Michelle. "Hungry?"

"Not really. But if you are, feel free."

"Anything to drink?"

Jake looked at Michelle, and she nodded.

"Two Schmidts," he said.

"Do you still go to art galleries?"

She hesitated. "Mostly local ones at convention hall when a collection is on tour. Sometimes I take the Greyhound to Philadelphia and spend the day at the Art Museum and the Rodin."

"You ever go with anyone?"

"Look, Jake, I'm not here for small talk."

The sting he felt at the sharpness of her tone quickly yielded to the realization that it was well deserved. "Tell me about your brother, what I don't know, something that might help me help him."

"The Joey you knew when he was running with Toad and Vinny—he was the same boy who tucked me in at night. I know what he did, running the streets. It was wrong, and I'm not excusing him. He talked tough and acted worse. But he lived every day of his life afraid. There were nights when the only way he could get to sleep was to lay his head on my lap, curled up like a little boy. It was hard for me to put the two Joeys together in my mind. Toad, Vinny, and the other guys from the neighborhood— they laughed at Joey's craziness. But Joey would never back down, not from anyone."

"Vinny was different," Jake said. "He was a planner, even back then. Joey was entertainment. Vinny always kept a distance, never got too close. Vinny was always looking for his escape route if things went bad. With Fish, it was different. Vinny used Fish for his car. But he thought Fish might be good to know someday. Vinny had this thing about Jews being smarter than everyone else. And he was right about Fish being useful. But Vinny was looking out for Vinny, always. Joey protected Fish. He always jumped in on Fish's side when the punks got carried away busting on him. I never understood it."

"I didn't understand at the time either. Now I do. Neither of them fit. Both were outside looking in. Somehow, despite how different they were otherwise, they saw that in each other. Fish and Joey were sad kids, Jake, who found each other."

"What are you trying to tell me?"

"Fish scared me. Not at first. But the more I saw them together, I realized Fish controlled Joey. When I asked Joey about Fish, what they did when they went out, he just said, 'Fish's my friend.' I was concerned for my brother. He was on juvenile probation. I didn't want him to be sent away for something Fish got him into."

The waitress arrived with their beers.

"You haven't had a cigarette," he said.

"I quit. This time for good."

Michelle took a sip of beer. "One night, late, I heard Joey come in, heard him moaning. It was almost dawn. He was on the couch, his arms tight around him, rocking back and forth. I put him in my bed, his head in my lap so I could rub his temples. That's what I did on nights when he couldn't fall asleep. His T-shirt was drenched with perspiration and dirt. At first, I didn't notice the blood stains."

"What about the bat? Did he have it with him that night?" He knew he sounded like a cop. But he also knew she agreed to meet because he was a cop who might be able to help her brother.

"The night Joey killed Mario, the cops searched the apartment. They didn't find the bat because it wasn't in the apartment. Vinny had it. A year after Joey got sent to Farview, Vinny came by with the bat. He thought I would want it. Not sure what he was thinking. Helluva keepsake."

"I never thought of Vinny as sentimental," he said.

* * *

Bill Perry and Jake Harris slouched in a beat-up yellow-and-white Ford LTD on Arctic Avenue around the corner from Victory Billiards, out of sight of the black Town Car that slowed to a stop in front of the pool hall to discharge its passenger. The nights spent sitting up on Victory appeared about to pay off. Vinny Nicastro trudged up the flight of stairs to Victory's second floor.

The two men in the Ford listened to the crooning of Vic Damone emanating from the jukebox in the crime boss's backroom headquarters thanks to Boom-Boom, the dull-looking gofer who waited on Nicky and his lieutenants. When he wasn't serving espressos and cleaning tables for Nicky, Boom-Boom was muscle for Nicky's loan shark operation. One of Nicky's customers behind on the vig died after a beating administered by Boom-Boom and company. Perry was able to persuade Boom-Boom that giving the bureau's black-ops access to Victory's backroom was better than being charged with murder in aid of racketeering.

Jake imagined the scene as Vinny entered the room. Zitto would be seated at his table in the corner farthest from the door. In Nicky's line of sight, Toad would give Vincent the wiseguy embrace, a pat down for wires and weapons. Vincent would not be offended. He knew it wasn't personal. Not knowing how much damage Eddie Blatstein had done before he was whacked had Nicky on edge. He suspected anyone could be wearing and when Nicky got nervous things got bad all around. Audible footfalls signaled that Vincent was clean and sent on his way to Nicky's table.

The volume of the jukebox was turned up, but the FBI bug picked up the voices. Later, the FBI sound lab would be able to filter the background noise and enhance the conversation.

"Talk to me, Vincent."

"Gomberg's getting nervous."

"Tell me somethin' I don't know."

"He'll do what I tell him."

"Good. The Jew senator from up north says the tapes that rat-fuck judge made have everybody in Trenton divin' for cover. Nobody's takin' calls no more."

A wet sucking sound accompanied Nicky's slow sip of espresso.

"We got another situation. The cop came to see Toad a while ago—had a moolie with him—you know him?"

"Yeah. We ran a li'l bit when we were kids."

"Toad says he was in here asking about Gomberg. What's his deal?"

"Like I said, we used to hang out. Joey Nardo, me, Toad, and this kid Jake. He was seeing Joey's kid sister."

"You telling me the cop's got a hard-on for Nardo's sister, and he's gonna save her fucked-up brother?"

"Maybe that's it."

"I don't want any more heat on Gomberg. What's the cop's price?"

"No price. He came by the office himself to serve the restraining order to stop construction. He seems to be taking this case personal."

"McMeekin fucked up on that one. Timing is everything, Vincent." Nicky paused to drain the demitasse of liqueur-laced coffee. "You and Toad talk with your cop friend. Maybe you can persuade him to do the right thing here for everybody concerned, including the sister."

"Yeah. We'll do that."

"You and Toad are gonna have a drink with Dick Tracy. Keep your mouth shut. Let Toad do the talking. *Capiche*?"

"Okay, Nicky."

* * *

Rocky G's Bar and Lounge was a demilitarized zone on the corner of Atlantic and Mississippi favored by wiseguys, pols, and cops needing a safe place to meet. Rocky Giardello, an ex-middleweight, opened the place with his last purse. He was his own greeter. Tourists liked to come into the place to rub elbows with Rocky and Benny Leonard, a Jewish boxer who once fought for the middleweight championship. Benny's nose looked like the ridge line of the Grand Tetons. Rocky and Benny entertained the customers with tales of their glory days. The wiseguys knew they were okay in Rocky's place.

Toad and Vinny sat at a table in the back corner reserved for meetings like the one they were about to have. The view from the table to the bar's only entrance was unobstructed. Vinny gestured toward the open door with a hand barely raised above his shoulder. When the new arrival was seated, the barmaid came over to take their order.

"Espresso and black sambuca," Toad said. He looked at Vinny and Jake. "Three."

"How you doon, kid? Everything good?"

Toad would go through the ritual demonstration of friendship, no matter what the purpose of the meeting.

"I'm okay, Toad."

"Jake, no hard feelings. You wearing?"

The waitress delivered the espressos and sambucas.

He started to stand and lift his arms.

"Sit down, kid. Maybe I'm sentimental. Your word's good. Right, Vinny?"

Vinny nodded.

"We got a problem we thought we could discuss with you."

"I'm listening."

"That murder case of yours, the three bodies, how's it going?"

"Still some leads to chase down. Why? What does Nicky care about some dead queens?"

"Who said anything about Nicky?"

"So who cares then?"

"The case is embarrassing Arthur."

Arthur. Somehow the name did not quite fit.

"Fags turning up dead in his hole, and then Blatstein upped the ante. He don't need that with the upcoming licensing hearings, background checks."

"I didn't put the bodies in Fish's hole."

Toad shrugged. "True, very true. But many people have an interest in Arthur getting his license. They just want to be sure you understand."

Toad leaned forward, touched Jake's arm. "Jake, Nicky's upset. Word is, Eddie Blatstein was wearing for six months before he got capped. This has some public servants in Trenton concerned. Right, Vinny?"

Vinny nodded.

"Those guys in Trenton got no *cajones.* They'll be climbing over each other to cut deals with the feds. We don't want Fish to have any more weight on him. That's why we think you oughta wrap up the case."

"Joey Nardo?"

"Makes sense, don't it? His bat. He's never getting outta where he's at anyway. Crazy fuck chopped his uncle's hands off with a meat cleaver, didn't he?"

"And the Blatstein hit?"

"What's that got to do with the queers?"

"Same hole—Gomberg's. The case has some new moving parts that interest me."

"I thought the feds were working Blatstein?"

"They are. We keep in touch."

Toad shook his head. "Smarter not to get involved in that one."

"The labs could make things complicated."

"Don't worry about the labs. We'll have one of our lawyers represent Nardo. McMeekin will get him a deal that won't add any time. You get your stats—and keep your shield. Everybody's happy. Right hand to God, Jake."

Jake pushed his espresso cup to the middle of the table.

"Whatsa matter, Jake? You gotta problem with that?"

It was Jake's turn to shrug.

"Joey's sister is still in town, ain't she? Michelle, right? Teaches at the high school. Has a nice little place on the bay at Sovereign Avenue. You used to like her when we wuz kids. You started seeing her again, am I right?"

Jake cleared his throat, but he had nothing to say. The gloves had come off, and he wasn't going to react one way or the other. Let them think the message had its intended effect.

"I like you, Jake. Always did. You stayed outta trouble. Made somethin' of yourself. Now do what's right here, for everybody concerned. Know what I mean?"

The sound of Michelle's name coming from Toad's mouth thudded into his gut like a Ray Robinson upper cut to the ribs. On the street outside Rocky G's, Jake broke into a full run toward Sovereign Avenue and the bay.

The house was dark. He knocked and then again, harder. He went around back, hopped the fence, and gave the kitchen window several loud taps with his knuckles. It was a school night. She rarely went out on the weekends but never when she had school the next day. His adrenaline took over. Nothing was visible through the windows. He heard no sounds. With his elbow, he broke a windowpane, freed the lock, and climbed through into the kitchen. A sliver of light was visible on the hallway floor.

He followed the light. Michelle appeared in the hallway, coming from the bathroom. She didn't see him. Her robe, loosely tied, came to midthigh. She dried her hair with a bath towel as she walked toward her bedroom. Her skin glistened with beads of moisture in the backlight.

"Michelle, it's me, Jake."

"Jesus, Jake! You scared me! What happened?"

"When you didn't answer the door, I got worried and—"

"And you broke in? I'm a big girl, Jake. You can't just—" The initial jolt of surprise faded, and her voice softened. "You know I should call the cops. Oh—that's right, you are a cop."

"I broke your kitchen window."

"So you'll fix it."

"Okay."

She walked toward him, stopped a foot from him, and let her robe fall to the floor. "Are you here to protect me or fuck me?" Her damp hair trailed down the sides of her face to the tops of her breasts.

He reached a hand to her shoulder and gently traced a line to her neck with the tips of his fingers. Her skin was warm. He looked at her body un-self-consciously. Her nipples hardened in response. The air smelled of her, a piquant odor that overwhelmed the freshness of the shower she had stepped from moments before. She moved closer, parted her legs. He placed the tips of his fingers there. She was slick with heat.

She fumbled with his belt and zipper and then the buttons of his shirt. Their legs and arms contorting in

Houdini-like movements, they managed to shed him of his clothes. He reached under her bottom and lifted her. She braced her leg against his thigh, reached down, and guided him inside. She pulled him down to the bath towel spread on the floor and rolled on top, straddling him. When they had finished, they were folded into each other's arms, legs entwined.

"The night you and I walked on the beach to Lucy, the night Joey killed Mario—I keep playing it over in my mind."

"I knew I wouldn't see you again. Mario's murder was a convenient reason for you to stay away. That night on the beach when we walked to Lucy and we did it for the first time, you were such a gentleman. I didn't want to lose you when you left for college. I was so afraid I'd never see you again." She shrugged. "In the back of my mind, I must have thought that if we went all the way, you'd come back. How dumb was I?"

"You weren't dumb."

"Gallant of you to say. We were kids. And then things happened out of our control. I wanted to at least have that night. That was the most beautiful night of my life, Jake, and the saddest. Still is on both counts. Why didn't you try to see me?"

"It was easier to turn everything off."

"So we both sat alone in our special places in the past."

"I suppose."

"I came to the synagogue for your dad's funeral. I stayed in the back where I could get away without your seeing me. You were married. I didn't have it in me to pretend to be an old friend. I heard the eulogy you gave."

"I loved him. I knew what mattered—his flying, the Navy days, skating on the street after a freeze. This is what I wanted people to know about him."

"I cried. I don't have any pictures of my mom or dad."

"Pictures I got. Plenty. My favorite is one of my father in high school. He's slouched against a Packard sedan, looking like James Dean before there was a James Dean. My dad was dark, and Dean was light. And my dad's hair had tight waves, not like Dean's at all. But Buddy and Dean had that same look: edgy and cool. It was in their eyes and the curl of their lips. Like James Dean, I think my dad knew he was handsome and a little dangerous. I liked the look and what it promised about his life.

"When I knew he was dying, I leafed through *The Herald*, looking for each of his pictures—you know, the candid shots they take for the yearbook. Under his official senior photo, it said, 'Future Ambition: To be Ann Sheridan's bodyguard.' I asked my mother who Ann Sheridan was. She just shook her head and rolled her eyes.

"Turns out Ann Sheridan was a sexy blonde movie star. No sentimental crap for my father. I looked at that picture and wondered what happened to that part of him."

"Life happened."

"I remember being angry at my mother and the bridge game for mucking up my dad's lungs with their cigarette smoke. I was even pissed off at Max."

"Max? The old man with the numbers?"

"Yeah. When I was just a kid, my dad drove trucks for Max, delivering coal to the old man's buildings. Mountains of coal-filled open bins formed the perimeter of his coal yard. The windows in the shack that served as an office were covered with a gummy yellow-black layer of tar. Every gust filled the air with black soot. He took me with him a couple of times. My mom almost killed him when she found out. I came home after one delivery covered in black dust.

"Sometimes I went with my dad to Max's apartment buildings. Buddy could fix anything, including the boilers in Max's buildings. Flakes of asbestos insulation spilled from gashes and rips.

"The night your brother, Vinny, Toad, and I watched the parade in one of the rolling chairs my dad arranged for us, I went to the barn at Texas and the boardwalk where Max stored the chairs. Buddy was repairing motors and brakes on Max's fleet. I looked down at him sitting cross-legged in a pile of motor and brake parts. His face was streaked with grease and sweat. I watched him work for a few minutes, told him thanks, that the guys had a great time. He looked up, smiled, and said, 'I'm glad, Jake.' That was it. He looked back down at the parts spread on the floor in front of him."

"Joey told me about that night, watching the parade with you. He liked you, Jake. I think because you made him feel like he was normal. Everyone was either afraid of him or thought he was crazy or both. He knew that. But not you."

Jake smiled. "It was you. I was willing to risk everything to see you."

"Except angering your mother." She paused. "Sorry, Jake. That wasn't fair."

"Yes, it was."

She fixed his eyes with hers. "Tell me about Ginny."

"We've been divorced a year. But I see her almost every day because of Danny."

"That's not what I need to know. Do you love her?"

"We went through a lot together. I wasn't much of a husband—or a father. I'm not sure how Ginny really feels. She's not great when it comes to showing her emotions."

"And now? How do you feel now?

"Sad."

"Your marriage announcement in *The Press* took my breath away. I felt like a fool."

"Michelle, I love you. I've never stopped."

"But you married her."

He had no response, at least one that would answer how he could marry another woman. "Sometimes I think I married Ginny to spite my mother."

"Did you ever think that she married you for the same reason with her family?"

"Maybe."

Michelle was waiting outside her bungalow Saturday morning at the appointed time. "Where to, Detective? You've been very secretive about our date this morning."

"I need you to be with me. I want to find my grandfather's grave."

The top hinge of the iron gate to the Jewish cemetery outside Vineland, caked with rust, had pulled loose from the column of crumbling bricks. Jews were not supposed to visit cemeteries on the Sabbath, but Saturday was Jake's day off, and he wasn't visiting a grave; he was searching for one. His Aunt Debbie could remember only that her father, Isaac, had been buried in a Jewish cemetery near Vineland, New Jersey—*Rosen something.*

The woman at the historical society told him there were three Jewish cemeteries near Vineland where most of the agricultural colonists were buried. One of those was in Rosenhayn. *Agricultural colonists.* The notion that he was descended from farmers appealed to him. He took out the sepia photograph his aunt had given him and showed it to Michelle.

"Handsome couple. I can see where you get your looks, Jake. They look Italian."

His grandmother Belle, barely out of her teens, stood behind Isaac and to his side. Belle looked like a flapper, bobbed hair, pearls to her belly, and a foxtail stole. Isaac, dressed in his doughboy uniform, sat perfectly erect. His left hand, placed formally on his thigh, clutched a pair of leather gloves. He wore a Smokey Bear-style campaign hat complete with decorative cord. Buddy never wore hats, but there was no mistaking that the soldier in the photo was his grandfather.

"The night my father died, I was with him. I was desperate to learn about his father, the grandfather I never knew and no one seemed to remember—not even his daughter, my Aunt Deb. I needed my father to be lucid if only long enough to tell me something about Isaac. He wasn't. After my father died I found my grandfather's tallit and tefillin. The prayer shawl was faded, and the tefillin's leather straps and boxes were badly cracked from dry rot. A faded piece of cloth, a dry rotted tangle of leather, and the one photo were all that was left of him. It was as if he never existed. I've spoken with my aunt, but she's unable—or unwilling—to recall anything about her father. My mother had always told me Isaac was a dear and kind man. How can a daughter not know where her father is buried?"

"Oh, Jake."

She squeezed his hand, and they walked through the gate.

The cemetery was overgrown with weeds, its headstones angled and worn. Many had Hebrew inscriptions; some were in English. Few had pebbles on them, a sign that the grave had been visited and the deceased was loved, respected, missed.

They continued up and down each row, some twice, reading the inscriptions.

None was his grandfather's.

* * *

Jake sat down across from Alfie. "Nicky Zitto sent his messenger boys Carbone and Nicastro to deliver an ultimatum. Indict Joey Nardo for the murders. Case closed. Nicky will cover his legal fees and grease the judge so Joey doesn't take too hard a hit."

"You went without me. I told you before to cut the Lone Ranger routine."

"You weren't invited. No way the meet happens with you along."

Alfie sighed. "And if we don't tag Joey?"

"They mentioned Michelle."

"That's reckless, even for Zitto."

"The heats on. Blatstein turning up dead in the Blenheim construction hole is a big problem. Zitto's worried about New York thinking he can't control his own neighborhood. The commission might deny Gomberg his license. Nicky has too much invested in Gomberg to allow our investigation to go beyond Joey Nardo."

Alfie shrugged. "All we got is Joey Nardo. Nicky needs Gomberg clean so Gomberg can front a casino license for him. He's not going away easy. The man had a judge hit."

"A corrupt judge but still a major strategic fuckup, but Nicky had no choice. Blatstein was gonna bring it down on all of them—Nicky, Gomberg, their pals in Trenton, and their guy on the Casino Control Commission."

"Greed, Jake. It's a beautiful thing. Job security. You'd think these guys would've learned a lesson years ago when the feds took out half the pols in North Jersey."

"If Nicky had the stones to reach out to me, he must be all over McMeekin to get Joey indicted and pled out."

"First things first. What are you going to do about Michelle?"

"I'll sleep in her front yard, if it comes to that. You meet with Bobbins yet?"

"His secretary called to set up a prep session for the grand jury. They tossed him the Blatstein hit. He's the designated liaison with the feds, the official FBI jock sniffer. Bobbins begged for the case. He's betting this is his ticket to a judgeship."

"Joel Bobbins has been an assistant county prosecutor for ten years, and he still can't find his zipper in the courthouse men's room. He'll make a fine judge."

"Jake, they don't need you or me to get the grand jury to return a true bill against Nardo. We just make it nice and official. Bobbins can summarize the case, leave out any forensic evidence that raises questions, and the grand jury would indict Captain Kangaroo if Bobbins asked them to."

"Granted. They don't need us to get a true bill. But we can sure fuck things up on the road to justice. McMeekin knows that. It just might buy us some time."

Alfie looked down for a long while then back up at Jake.

"Remember when we were kids and I took you to the Coliseum to see Ray Charles? You were the only white boy in the place. I had your back, and you were cool because you were my white boy."

"Yeah. I remember."

"This isn't a Ray Charles concert, and McMeekin isn't some Northside brother that'll let you slide."

"Alfie, I keep telling you, you don't have to do this with me."

"I know. But you're still my white boy. McMeekin has been taking with both hands—from Little Nicky and Trenton. You and I did our jobs, kept our heads down. We didn't care what McMeekin was doing with Nicky and the senator. It didn't involve us. Now it does. Now he's messing with our case."

"Once we start, there's no turning back. It gets awful cold in the winter walking a beat. And that's the best we can hope for if all we do is piss off Zitto and McMeekin."

"We've already done that, partner."

The ring woke him. The digital clock by his bed glared 2:00 a.m. "Jake, I need to see you. Now, please." Her words carried a quiet urgency, resignation, and resolve.

He arrived at her door twenty minutes later. She looked as if sleep had been scarce for more than a few nights. They walked arm in arm, in silence, to the sofa in her living room. He waited for her to speak.

She paused and seemed to be deciding how to begin. She stared into his eyes. "Jake, I need to tell you why Joey killed Mario. Maybe it will help you better understand him—and me."

"Michelle, you don't have to. What happened is long past."

"I need to tell you, Jake. From the time our parents left us with Theresa, Mario tormented Joey. Every day Mario would do something to make Joey cry. He'd beat him for no reason, break his toys, lock him out of the apartment for hours at a time. Can you imagine what that did to a little boy? Mario stopped the abuse only when Joey got big enough to defend himself. But in spite of all he had suffered at Mario's hands, Joey never lifted a finger against him.

"Mario hit my aunt. But as far as Joey was concerned, that was between Mario and Theresa. She'd always take him back.

"The night Joey killed Mario—after you left me at the door—I saw Mario passed out drunk on the floor. At least, I thought he was passed out. Joey hadn't gotten in yet. I went to my room, shut the door, and took off my clothes. Before I was able to get into bed, Mario was behind me. He threw me down on my back and straddled my head. He was naked from the waist down. He used his knees to pin my shoulders. He tried to force himself into my mouth. Joey must have gotten home just as he heard me struggling. My brother broke my bedroom door off the hinges. Then he killed him."

"The night Joey killed Mario—after you left me at the door—I saw Mario passed out drunk on the floor. At least, I thought he was passed out. Joey hadn't gotten in yet. I went to my room, shut the door, and took off my clothes. Before I was able to get into bed, Mario was behind me. He threw me down on my back and straddled my head. He was naked from the waist down. He used his knees to pin my shoulders. He tried to force himself into my mouth. Joey must have gotten home just as he heard me struggling. My brother broke my bedroom door off the hinges. Then he killed him."

"Why didn't you tell me then?" His tone sounded as if the attack had just happened.

"I was so ashamed. I was afraid of what you'd think of me."

"I loved you."

"There's more, Jake. I need to get it all out. I was nine the first time Mario molested me. Just with his fingers. Later he began rubbing himself on me, forcing me to touch him, coming on me."

She knew his questions without his asking. "Even if I had wanted to talk with someone—anyone—who would understand? Who *could* understand? Even I blamed me for what he did. I was certain it was my fault.

"When I got my first period, I was no longer the little girl. I know it must seem silly to you, but I felt like a woman. I resolved he would never touch me again. I threatened to tell someone at school, a counselor. I had no intention of telling anyone, but of course, he didn't know that. I managed to scare him off, until the night Joey caught him."

Jake pulled her close and gently kissed the top of her head. She fell asleep in his arms. He carried her into her bedroom and tucked her under the covers. He needed to clear his mind of every thought except Michelle and what she had related about Mario. He left her asleep and carefully locked her front door behind him with the spare key she had given him. Pacific Avenue was deserted. Graffiti-sprayed plywood covered shattered windows of abandoned restaurants, theaters, jewelry stores, and haberdasheries. Torn plastic sheeting nailed to windows and storm doors of rooming houses flapped and banged in cold gusts off the Atlantic. Newspapers, food wrappings, paper napkins stained with mustard, crumpled cigarette packs swirled along the asphalt and concrete, urban tumbleweeds.

The boardwalk was empty of people. Soon there would be palisades of reflective glass and steel rimming canyons of abandoned streets. There would be no neighborhoods, no places where people lived, no families with roots, no history. The ocean sounded different to him. Several casinos had opened. The whirr of gaming wheels, the clink and clatter of coins and chips, and the sharp riffle of a stiff new shoe of playing cards muffled the gentle break of the night waves against the shore. Smoke billowed from the revolving doors that fronted on the boards. The smell of the sea, too, had changed. Cooking grease from food courts belched from rooftop exhaust fans overpowering the familiar nostalgic aroma of roasted peanuts, grilled pork roll, and hotdogs.

He walked down the ramp to the street. Drifts of sand blown by winds off the ocean that had forever coated the asphalt just off the boardwalk were gone, blocked by the new construction. At the corner of Pacific and Ohio, he paused at Bally's Park Place Casino. The casino's lights illuminated the vacant lots and abandoned structures soon to be turned into parking garages. He stared at the elaborate mosaic decorating the street level walls. It was a scene of old Atlantic City, turn-of-the-century Victorian. Genteel couples and families strolled the boards, women in dresses, the men in high-collared shirts, bowties, and straw boaters. A thousand years from now, he thought, archeologists in deep-sea diving gear would uncover this wall and write learned texts on the civilization that created it.

He walked to Jackson Avenue, the border between Atlantic City and Ventnor. His Uncle Harry's house on Baton Rouge two blocks into Ventnor looked the same as it had thirty years ago. The awnings over its large front porch had been taken down for the winter, its windows dark, lifeless. He headed north on Ventnor Avenue and at the familiar street sign turned toward the bay. In the middle of the block, he stopped and stared across Aberdeen Place at his boyhood home. Inside, shadows passed in front of lighted windows. He imagined parents on their way to tend to a stirring child or to get a late-night snack from the kitchen. The trees were barren. A steady wind blew off the ocean to the bay.

Winter would come early. He could feel it. The narrow streets of Chelsea's bayside neighborhoods would soon be covered with hard milky sheets that would remain until April. They would buckle and crack with the thaw, and the receding ice would leave behind axel-busting potholes. But first, winter's new snow would lay down sheets of ice that in his memory were glistening surfaces as perfect as a hockey rink smoothed by a Zamboni.

His father had loved to skate on the frozen street outside their home. When a solid sheet had formed, his father would call to him from the utility room where he had gone to get his skates: "Jake, lace 'em up. There's good ice on the street." He would grab his black-and-tan hockey skates, miniatures of his father's, from the hook in the heater room where they hung by their laces. His father skated in a slow, deliberate glide to the end of the block getting the feel of the ice, checking for bare spots and potholes. Then, he would explode from a dead stop to full speed in three strides. He'd barrel down the street pumping, digging for more speed, straight at his boy. Jake was able to see his father's breath, staccato puffs of white, a human engine under full steam.

That was something, watching his dad skate, arms swinging in parallel, grace and power. He'd come out of the sun. Thirty feet, twenty, ten. *Whoosh.* An on-the-dime perfect hockey stop, spraying his son with shaved ice. "Okay, Jake. Your turn. Make it burn. Mind the glare and watch for the bare patches." The young boy did his best to match the powerful smooth glide of his father, but mostly he skated on the insides of his ankles. Buddy smiled at him. He liked that about skating with his father, too, seeing him smile.

* * *

In a windowless room in the FBI Philadelphia Field Office, Jake leaned toward the tape recorder in the center of the conference table. The FBI sound lab had improved the audibility of the Blatstein tapes by filtering out background noise and enhancing the voices. Still, portions crackled with static.

"Our friend from Bergen County says he needs fifty."

"That's Blatstein," said Bill Perry.

Jake nodded; he knew the judge's voice.

"What's that sound?" Jake asked.

"They're in a diner. McMeekin is slurping soup. Navy bean, if I remember correctly."

"Fifty? The Little Guy isn't going to like that the shake doubled."

"You think Nicky knows they call him the Little Guy?" Perry asked.

"Trenton is one large tight sphincter. The joint task force has everybody looking over their shoulders, wondering who's wearing. Jimmy Baugh too."

"Who the fuck is Jimmy Baugh?"

Perry smiled, pressed the rewind button, then play.

"I had to listen a half dozen times before I got it," Perry said. "City hall."

"Judge, our friend on the commission needs to get his colleagues to back off Gomberg's association with Nicastro."

"Can I get yiz anything else, gentlemen?"

"Not for me, hon. Judge, you want something? Slice a pie maybe?"

"No, thanks. I'm not feeling too good."

"Yeah, the wire Eddie's wearing must be wrapped around his nuts," Perry cracked.

Only the clinking of silverware, slurping, and a belch were audible for the next half minute.

"I got more news for the Little Guy. The fifty's just for our guy on the commission. The senator will need another hundred for his trouble."

"He likes round numbers, our friend the senator. I'll get back to you."

"You do that, Captain."

Bill Perry hit the stop button.

"We got seven meets on tape before Eddie got whacked, three with the senator, two with McMeekin and two with a commissioner. The senator is hanging tough, for now anyway. The commissioner is already looking to deal. The second McMeekin tape has your captain delivering Nicky's hundred-fifty K to Blatstein. With Blatstein ten toes up, McMeekin is the only one that can make Nicky for us."

"When do you sweat him?" Jake asked.

"Soon. We've got a few pieces to put in place first."

"Anything we can do at our end?"

"Keep your head down."

* * *

Jake's Aunt Anne warned him when he called. "Sandy is so weak, his mind goes in and out. But he would love to see his favorite nephew." Her voice over the phone transported him back to family gatherings: breaking the fast, clouds of smoke, the drone of ordinary conversation, cackling laughter and clinking ice in tumblers of scotch, trays of smoked fish, cream cheese and bagels, dishes of warm noodle kugel, and urns of freshly brewed coffee. Her meticulous enunciation, vaguely British, lent elegance to her two-pack-a-day throatiness.

His aunt had been the only member of the Gordon clan other than Sandy who embraced Sally Harris. It made sense: the spinster (lesbian?), the queer, and the unworthy woman who took Buddy away. "She had been such a vibrant woman," Anne said. "And you must tell me all about Ben. He never calls. How are those boys of his? I am so sorry to hear about you and Ginny." Her interest seemed genuine, not small talk to fill uncomfortable silence or segue to a hurried good-bye. That was what set her apart from the others and had endeared her so to him. She cared.

Jake arrived at West End Avenue, a wide canyon of mid-rise prewar apartment buildings in New York City's upper Westside. He checked the address and climbed the three steps leading to the iron-gated entry. He pushed the intercom and spoke his name, which Anne Gordon had left at the desk. He pushed open the door to the lobby at the sound of the buzzer, nodded to the doorman, and headed to the elevator.

Her sun-weathered face had a few more lines, but she had stayed trim, and her posture was erect. She wore a cream silk blouse and pleated black trousers. Her steel-gray hair, still styled in the *Jean d'Arc* he'd remembered from childhood, retained a healthy sheen; so, too, had her eyes and smile remained undimmed. She greeted him at the door to the apartment with a glass of scotch in one hand and a cigarette in the other. She was backlit by two large windows at the end of the entry foyer. The apartment overlooked Roosevelt Park and had a view of the river.

"Jake. Oh, it *is* good to see you!"

She closed her forearms around his shoulders with her wrists bent back, careful to avoid spilling her drink or nicking him with her cigarette. After a gentle squeeze, she pushed back from him.

"My god, Jake, you *are* Buddy." There was marvel in her voice. "Sandy needs a few minutes. Roy is with him. Hasn't left his side. You remember Roy. He was Sandy's guest for *Yom Kippur* at your parents's. Let's sit in the kitchen, and I can finish my cigarette. I can't smoke around your uncle."

Jake had always been aware that Sandy had another life in New York that no one else in the family acknowledged, except Jake's mother. She adored Sandy, the black sheep of the Gordon clan. Harry, the eldest of the Gordon siblings, always appeared on edge in his younger brother's presence, ready to erupt.

"Tea, coffee, Jake? Or something stronger?"

He looked at the counter to see a pot brewing.

"Coffee, thanks, Aunt Anne."

"This is not an easy time for you, Jake."

He liked that about her. Straight talk with grace. "No, it's not." He looked into the cup of black liquid. She was brave enough not to offer platitudes, so he felt he owed her something honest in return. "You wake up one morning to a different life. It's not a bad dream. It is your life, and you will live it every day from then on, and it will never go back to the way it was."

She reached for his hand and gave it a gentle squeeze.

Jake wondered if, from the start, he and Ginny were wrong for each other. The first thing he bought after their wedding was a Harley. He long ago admitted to himself why he bought the motorcycle. He needed it to keep from slipping into the ordinary, or what he believed was ordinary. New husbands starting a family didn't ride motorcycles. They bought station wagons and life insurance. Ginny should have known something was wrong with him when he went from college graduation to the Police Academy. She claimed that was part of his appeal, being *a half bubble off*, as she put it. Now, all these years later, she'd corrected their mistake, and he was alone in his shabby apartment. He visited his son every day if even for only a few minutes in the morning, but the child was becoming a stranger to him.

"Sandy should be ready," she said, motioning her nephew to follow her down the hall.

The air in Sandy's bedroom was heavy with a sweet odor vaguely like burnt almonds spiked with disinfectant. Roy sat in a chair by Sandy's bed, which could be cranked up and down at the head and foot. Tubing ran from his uncle's nostrils to an oxygen tank; an IV line dripped a clear liquid into a vein. Anne had described the purple and pink blotches—she called it Kaposi's sarcoma—and the weight loss, but Jake was still shocked by the sight of his uncle. His immune system had been compromised, the doctors said. He had contracted pneumonia, and sepsis had set in, which they had only recently been able to get under control.

Anne and Roy had been taking care of Sandy night and day, trying to keep him comfortable and his mind occupied. Roy had a brave face on, but the strain Sandy's condition had taken on his partner showed in the clench of his jaw and the slump of his shoulders.

His uncle's skin, translucent, appeared brittle, rice paper thin, as if it would crack at the touch, the ashy patina of the gravely ill. Purplish maculae covered Sandy's arms and face. He was shaven, but it was not the clean shave of a healthy man. It was the uneven work of a caregiver, with patches of stubble in the difficult areas of the face under the nose, lower lip, and just below the chin line.

Although Anne had described Sandy's appearance, Jake was not prepared for his uncle's eyes. They had let go of fear and anger and betrayal—the emotions of the living. His were the eyes of a man who knew he would soon be dead and had gone about the business of dying, occupying that space in time between resignation and nothingness.

Looking down at his uncle, Jake regretted the reason he had made the trip to New York or at least not telling Anne the truth about it.

"Roy dear, let's give Jake and Sandy some time alone, shall we? I'll put up some tea."

As Roy passed, he stopped and looked at Jake with kind eyes then patted his arm.

Jake sat in the bedside chair vacated by Roy. Sandy's breathing sounded like air being sucked through a water pipe. Raised nodules were visible on his face, arms, and hands. Sandy smiled weakly and lifted his hand an inch or so in greeting. Jake put his hand under Sandy's, feeling the slight pressure of it closing on top of his. His uncle's palm was not clammy as he had expected, but cool, dry, and soft. He attributed that to the bottle of lotion and container of baby powder on the night table.

"Sandy, I'm sorry I haven't come before now."

"No one from the family has, Jake. Fanny hasn't come in nearly a year. Don't be hard on yourself. You didn't know I was sick."

"You weren't at Buddy's funeral. Anne didn't say anything."

"Your father was a beautiful man. I miss him." He turned his head toward the window and raised his chin to its light. "The sun feels good. I've lost my tan. I must look dreadful."

Sandy turned back and managed another smile. "Jake, your father was not only the handsomest man I ever knew. He was the most decent."

Jake nodded. "I miss him every day."

"I was the family's not-so-well-kept secret. As long as I went along with the farce, I was welcome. Oh, it drove Harry mad to know his little brother was queer, but so long as I didn't bring it into his home, he tolerated me."

Sandy shifted under the sheet and lifted his head an inch or so off the pillow before letting it fall back. The small movements seemed to exhaust him. Dry, cottony filaments formed delicate hinges at the corners of his mouth.

Jake reached under his uncle's head, lifted it gently, and rearranged the pillows that had bunched to one side. He helped Sandy sip from the glass of water Anne had left on the night table.

"You're a sweet boy, Jake. Like Buddy."

"I appreciate you saying that, Sandy."

"Do you know what your grandmother Belle would tell people about her baby brother?" He managed a smile.

"What's that?"

"She said I was *different* because when I was a very little boy, I was bitten on the hand by a neighbor's dog. I had been. But that had nothing to do with my liking boys, of course. But she actually believed it. Anyway, I decided I'd had enough of the charade. I was a forty-five-year-old man. I brought Roy to the *bris* of Harry's first grandson. Your father and mother were there, along with all the aunts and the in-laws. Harry took one look at Roy and punched me in the nose. It being summer, I had on a beautiful pair of white linen trousers. The punch knocked me down. Blood all over me, my beautiful white shirt, the carpet. What a mess. You know, Jake, you really do see stars."

His lips formed a sad smile.

"Your father picked me up and used his clean white handkerchief to stop my nosebleed. When he was sure I could walk, he escorted Roy and me to his car. Your mother and Buddy drove us to Roy's apartment in Chelsea. Your mother put up a pot of coffee. Your father went across the street to Ginsberg's Bakery for pastries. Buddy could see that Roy was upset. He took it upon himself to make amends for Harry's behavior. That was your father's way. That's when we began breaking the *Yom Kippur* fast at your house. Roy was always welcome. Buddy made him feel like part of the family. That was Buddy's gift."

Jake could see the shift in his uncle's mind.

"Well, Jake, should we get to the business at hand? We *do* get *The Press* here. Have to keep up on the hometown news."

"I'm sorry, Sandy," he said.

"Don't be. I'm glad it's you, someone who will care and understand. Where do you want to start?"

"It's your story."

"Is it? It's been our secret. Hasn't it been, Jake?"

Our secret. He hadn't thought of it that way. Back then, he had been the only one who knew how Sandy spent his summer days and nights. The others in the family had suspected, of course. He recalled things said in whispers or code and things unsaid. But Jake knew.

"In sixty-two, September, just after Labor Day, you filed a report with the police, a missing person's report. Jamie Wescott. We found his remains under the Blenheim. We've identified him from dental records."

"I knew you'd call. As soon as I read the accounts in *The Press*, I knew you'd found Jamie. So, Detective Harris, what would you like to ask me?"

"Let's start with some background. When did you first meet Jamie Wescott?"

Sandy looked up at his nephew. "Jake, I appreciate your sensitivity to my circumstances. But I think it is important that you record what I have to tell you."

"Sandy, next time." Ten years had passed since he had last seen Sandy. His uncle was dying. Jake had no stomach to be a police detective at this moment.

"Jake, please, for me—for Jamie and those other poor boys. Take down what I say."

Jake felt the weight of the microcassette recorder in the side pocket of his sport coat. On the drive to New York, he had struggled over whether to ask his uncle to record their conversation. But Sandy was right. He took the cassette recorder from his coat pocket, and switched it on.

It was midnight when Jake got back to the Venice Apartments. A note from Ginny taped to his door reminded him he had missed his visit with Danny.

She launched a preemptive strike to avoid a scene inside the house and stopped him at the front door. "Before you hear it elsewhere, I'm seeing Norman Laskey."

"Rabbit, Ginny? Really?"

"Norman," she corrected. "And lower your voice. Danny will hear you."

She and Jake had been officially divorced for a year. How had Rabbit won over Ginny—the tall, blond *shiksa* doctor whose ancestors fought in the American Revolution? Jake's first thought was of Rabbit's two front teeth. *Oh, Norman, do that thing you do with your teeth. Please, Norman, please.*

Ginny explained they'd met at the medical center's annual holiday black tie dinner. Rabbit had been retained by the medical center's board to handle negotiations with the unions (his experience prosecuting and then defending wise-guys proved useful in labor disputes), and he soon was called in on all of the medical center's important litigation matters.

"What about Danny?"

"Meaning?"

"C'mon, Ginny. Do you want our son growing up around Rabbit as a role model?"

"I didn't say I was marrying him."

Rabbit was an unapologetic, in-your-face, street-smart kid from the Inlet. There was no nuance to him; there were

no halfways; there were no maybes. If he was your friend—
and Jake was—then you'd know he'd be there for you. He
had a long memory and a primal sense of justice. Ask Gail
Liebgott's father. These were qualities that Jake admired.

Jake didn't see Rabbit being with Ginny as a betrayal
of their friendship. But Ginny, a preppie debutante from
Sparta, whose family wintered in Aiken, South Carolina,
and summered in Bar Harbor? What could she see in him?
Then it hit him. Rabbit and he weren't that different.

"Does he stay over? Our bedroom is next to Danny's."

It's not our bedroom anymore. She didn't need to tell
him. "You're Danny's father. Nothing can change that."

Nothing can change that. It came out sounding more
like a wish than a fact.

* * *

Rodef Sholem was an old-style orthodox synagogue
with the *bimah* in the center bordered by pews on three
sides. The women sat in a balcony ringing the main sanctuary. He was twelve when last there. He, his brother, and
his parents had come as guests of the Gordon clan for High
Holiday services. He'd asked another boy why the women
sat upstairs.

"They're unclean, or they may be, you know, having
their periods. Don't you know anything?"

Now Jake sat in a back pew to avoid Harry and the
other Gordons. As the service was ending, he waited for
Anne and Roy to pass through the vestibule on their way
to one of the limousines parked at the curb.

Anne's eyes struck that balance between grief and love, the province of the honest mourner. She was relieved that his suffering had ended and was free now to remember her little brother the way he had been before his illness. She gave her grandnephew a gentle hug. Roy, clinging to Anne's arm and sobbing, reached out a hand and squeezed Jake's forearm.

"Thank you for being here. Sandy would be so happy you came," she said.

Only platitudes came to mind, so he said nothing.

"Sandy asked me to give this to you," said Anne.

Back in his apartment, he placed the box Anne had given him on the kitchen table. It was not much larger than a shoebox. He ran his fingers softly over the surface of alternating light and dark hardwoods finished to a high gloss. A pearl inlay bordered its hinged lid. He nudged the clasp with a fingertip and raised the lid.

Hairnet Mary was pouring her final hour of burnt coffee for AC's *café societé*—rootless stubble-faced men, cigarettes smoldering between yellow-stained fingers. Jake slid into the booth across from his partner.

"Bacon looks a little greasy."

"Yeah, but it's good."

"I read somewhere bacon fat and eggs are bad for your heart."

"Can't be bad, Jake. Good protein."

Jake nudged Sandy's box across the table.

Alfie turned the box, so he was able to read the notation on the evidence tape sealing the lid: "Received from

Anne Gordon, February 25, 1980. D/Sgt. J. Harris, badge number 225."

"The D-ring is pretty much all rust, and the shirt looks like somebody used it to wipe the floor after a bar fight. The trunks and T-shirt are what my ex-wife's family would call second-class relics. Any fluids are first class—the whole body and blood thing. I called Bill Perry. He'll run these through the lab at Quantico. Under the radar. The bureau's got so many black box ops going one more won't matter."

Alfie wrote the date and time and signed his name and badge number under Jake's entries to preserve the chain of custody. He put the box in the satchel on the seat next to him.

"What'd you do that for?"

Alfie smiled. "I'm not about to let you claim you made this case all by yourself. Besides, we're partners. Remember?"

"And all this time I've known you, you had me fooled. I thought you were a smart guy."

"Jake, there's no guarantee this won't get back to McMeekin. He will be one pissed-off captain."

"We crossed that bridge when we paid Vinny a visit."

"This is different, Jake. We're taking evidence in an ACPD case to the bureau without passing go. We haven't even logged these in at the hall. This blows up on us, we get put on admin, and your uncle's stuff becomes worthless in court because we broke procedures."

"We log this, and it has to go through Dougherty. That means McMeekin knows about it lickity. Doc's a good man, but he's got his kids, a wife, and a girlfriend to think about. My uncle's stuff could all of a sudden become accidentally lost or contaminated. At least with Perry, we got a chance for another move before we have to go to war with McMeekin."

"I got a call from Bobbins about the presentment to the grand jury. McMeekin put a deadline on returning an indictment against Nardo."

An oily film had formed on the black liquid in the cup Hairnet Mary had plunked down in front him. Jake took a sip and winced. "Damn, that's awful. Alfie, I'll take the box to Philly."

"If you think you're gonna keep me out of this, forget it. Besides, I'm starting to enjoy getting under McMeekin's mick skin."

"Anything more from Dougherty?"

"Not much. A bat could have caused the skull fractures."

"They're really sticking their necks out on that one."

"They haven't been able to match blood from the bat to blood on the T-shirts and bathing trunks. Same for the hair samples from the vics with the hair recovered from under the splinters of the barrel."

"Either they can't, or they won't. All the more reason not to trust them with my uncle's stuff." Jake pushed the cup to the side and waved off Hairnet and her pot. "Bobbin's counting on this case never going to court. He just wants his ink when the indictment is returned. McMeekin will engineer a plea bargain, and Joey will never leave Farview. And nobody will give a healthy shit but us."

"Can't really blame Bobbins, Jake. The case is ancient history, and the victims are nobody's husband or father. Nardo was adjudged incompetent to stand trial for the murder of his Uncle Mario, and he's still downing Haldol like M & M's at a pot party. So why not take the headline and easy stat? I mean, how do we know he didn't do it? I want the truth too, Jake. But maybe we're looking for something that isn't there."

Jake felt a pang of guilt as he left Alfie. He had not brought his uncle's tape. His gut told him to keep it to himself a while longer.

The receptionist sat behind a wall of bulletproof glass. She motioned with her head and buzzed him through the security door.

"Have fun, darlin'. And please try not to upset the man. He's been driving us all crazy with this damn case— and it's only Tuesday."

Jake had known lots of guys like Joel Bobbins. The prosecutor's office was full of grousers with nowhere else to go. The assistant prosecutor was a sulker who was certain everyone had conspired to deny him his proper due.

Bobbins, a graduate of Seton Hall Law School's night division, had all the insecurities that went with a night school law degree. He signed on as a contract lawyer with a mega-firm in New York and was buried alive in rooms full of documents in an antitrust case that had no beginning and no end—the Bataan Death March for new lawyers, robots expected to bill twelve hours a day, six days a week on "document review." Straight-lining, associates called it, for the uninterrupted line on the timesheet from 8 a.m. to 8 p.m. A Harvard snot two years ahead of him stuck out his hand to welcome him to the fold: "Congratulations. You just got a license to eat shit."

Two years at the New York firm gave Bobbins's résumé just enough shine to get him hired as an assistant prosecutor for Atlantic County. That and the fact that the Atlantic County Prosecutor, himself a Seton Hall grad, liked the idea that Bobbins had gone to the night school. He figured Bobbins would be hungry, feel the need to prove himself worthy every day, not like the Ivy Leaguers who wanted their asses kissed just for showing up.

Joel Bobbins never got the big cases in the office. He was the permanent second chair, passed over for chief of homicide and relegated to half-bundle, hand-to-hand drug buys. Bobbins told anyone who would listen how unfair it all was. After learning he wouldn't get the chief's position, he moped for a month and said he was going to quit, start his own firm, and make some real money. But he hadn't the confidence to go out on his own, and everyone knew it.

Bobbins's facial tics were legendary. They had set sequences and rhythms. He had learned to control them in court, but when Jake appeared in the doorway to his office, Bobbins's face started jumping.

"We're gonna streamline the Nardo presentment. Brathwaite got his shield before you, so he'll do the dog-and-pony for the grand jury. But you'll be up at the podium with us for the press conference."

"We're not ready to present to the grand jury."

Bobbins's tics were doing the Charleston. "No way, Detective."

"We don't have all the forensics back."

"Yes, we do. Here." Bobbins slid a thin folder across the desk.

"Like I said, Joel, we don't have all the forensics yet. We sent specimens to the FBI lab at Quantico."

"The feds have no jurisdiction. That shoulda been run by me."

"We don't have the capability to analyze the samples. The bureau has access to national databases. We were sending the bat anyway for the latents, so it made sense to get the stains and hair analyzed while we were at it."

"And Brathwaite agreed with you?"

Jake would've liked to give his partner some cover, but Alfie's name was on the paperwork. "It was my call."

"I thought Brathwaite had more brains than that."

"Nardo wasn't alone in the tunnel the night of the murders."

Bobbins's face jumped. "I'm waiting."

"It's just a theory, but I don't think Nardo could've killed three grown men by himself."

It was hard to tell from Bobbins's expression whether he was seeing bigger headlines and a judgeship or the premature end of his career. "You're dumber than I thought, Harris. I'm not interested in your theories. I'm only interested in what we can prove. And what we can prove now is that Nardo did the murders."

"From what I hear, Norman Lasky is going to take Nardo's case. Criminal Justice Act appointment." Jake tossed out Lasky's name just for effect. Rabbit had agreed to a meeting but no more than that for now.

"Lasky? For ninety bucks an hour?"

"Maybe he owes Judge Winkleman a favor."

Bobbins had been counting on steamrolling some over-worked, underfunded public defender into a quick guilty plea. Prosecutors relied on defense attorneys being bluff-ers who caved when it came time to pick the jury because the fees had dried up or they lacked the stomach for trial. Rabbit never bluffed. He was an adherent of the scorched-earth school. Opposing counsel knew if they didn't settle on Rabbit's terms, they'd bleed at trial. Rabbit considered it better to lose than blink.

Jake knew Bobbins's thought process. Negotiate a sweet deal for Nardo or face the possibility of a humiliating loss in the courtroom.

"If I find out you had anything to do with Lasky tak-ing Nardo's case, I'll have your shield, Detective."

A denial would confirm his involvement. Jake simply shrugged.

"Nardo's a violent psychopath. His bat is the murder weapon. Nobody cares about the victims, and nobody cares about Nardo. Keeping him locked up is a public service. Guys like you, Harris, always have to find a way to make things difficult."

"For whom?"

"You better find a way to unfuck this, Harris."

As soon as Jake got the call from Perry, he hustled to City Hall to find his partner.

"Saddle up, Alfie. Bill Perry just got the labs from Quantico on my uncle's stuff and the vics' evidence we asked him to compare. He'll meet us as soon as we can get to Philly."

Alfie grabbed the sport coat from the back of his desk chair.

"Any preview?"

"Just said to hustle."

Forty-five minutes out the Atlantic City Expressway, and they were crossing the Ben Franklin Bridge into Philadelphia. Perry picked a Dunkin' Donuts near the federal courthouse at Seventh and Market for the hand-off.

The FBI special agent was seated at a booth in the rear, nursing a cup of coffee. Perry was taciturn, a classic Westerner from a small town on the prairie. Although only thirty-nine years old, his hair was iron gray. His features could have been chiseled from the Black Hills of South Dakota, where Perry grew up. His pale-blue eyes were wolf-like, wary, and penetrating. Jake called him colonel because that was what he had been in the Air Force. He'd flown F-4s, spewing napalm over North Vietnam.

Jake and Alfie slid into the booth.

Perry smiled. "You two must be feeling the heat to close out your tunnel case. We're hearing Nicky is getting very impatient. Gomberg is Nicky's date to the dance. Gomberg gets no casino license. Nicky doesn't go to the ball. The tapes Blatstein made before he got capped could take Nicky down. We need a live witness to link Nicky to Blatstein. What about Nicastro or Carbone?"

"Known them since we were kids," said Jake. "They're not muscle. If Nicky's off the street, Vinny and Toad may come over. But I'm betting they'll never turn on Nicky while he's walking around above ground."

"We've been closing the net on your captain for months. McMeekin has been spreading wiseguy money in Trenton, at the control commission, and in the department."

"When will you sweat him with the tapes Blatstein made on him?"

"Soon, Jake. But both of you watch yourselves for now. Here ya go, pal," Perry said.

Jake took the manila envelope.

"Your uncle's clothes have traces of fluids, blood, maybe semen. Degraded. Not worth much."

"Any hits on the latents?"

"A set matches Gomberg's. The ones from his casino license application file. We got a positive on three other sets: Vinny Nicastro, Franco Carbone, and Joey Nardo's sister." Perry got up, signaling the end of the meeting. "Keep in touch, boys. And happy hunting."

In the cruiser, Jake unsealed the envelope and thumbed through the report, stopping at the results section.

"The hair and blood of victim 3 matched specimens recovered from the barrel of the bat," Jake said. "The stains on victim 3's clothing were too degraded. Results inconclusive. The same for the stains on my uncle's trunks and T-shirt."

"We got positive prints on Nicastro, Carbone, and Gomberg, Jake."

"All three have an answer for that. The bat was under the front seat of his car all summer, and their prints are on it because they handed it to Nardo many nights. There are plausible, innocent explanations for Nicastro, Toad, and Gomberg to have handled the bat that won't work for Joey."

"That's all we got, Jake. What else is there?"

"Joey Nardo can tell us what happened that night in the tunnel. I just need a way to reach him. Right now his brain is fried from electric shocks and the daily drug cocktail he gets at Farview."

"He'll make a helluva witness. Killed, then mutilated his aunt's boyfriend after beating him unconscious. And it's his bat." Alfie hesitated. "What about his sister?"

Jake hesitated. "Let's leave her out of this, Alfie."

"Jake, what the hell is that supposed to mean? We don't have the option to leave anyone out. We can't make a stupid mistake here. I don't see what you see, Jake—or what you want to see. We have no evidence that anyone other than Joey was in the vicinity of the tunnel the night the vics were killed. I got to be honest here. Your judgment is clouded by your relationship with Nardo's sister. That's dangerous—for both of us. Jake, we been together a long time. Why don't you tell me what you're not telling me?"

Jake looked at the lab report then back up at his partner.

"There's more. Victim number three. Jamie Wescott. He was my uncle's boyfriend. My uncle was the one who reported him missing seventeen years ago."

"Pretty thin—and that's being charitable. Your uncle's dead. Who else do we have other than Joey? Get real, Jake. Without solid, admissible evidence to prove Nardo did not act alone, Joey's going down."

He had his uncle's taped statement recounting the night Jamie Wescott went missing. There was Michelle's account of that night. And there was the glint of chrome under the streetlight at the boardwalk ramp. For now, he would keep these cards close to the vest until the feds' case came into better focus.

It had been forty-eight hours since Jake had heard the tape of his captain slurping navy bean soup and talking payoffs with the Honorable Blatstein. Detectives Harris and Brathwaite were at the end of their shifts and headed back to city hall when the radio squawked alive. Alfie hit the flashers and the siren at the same time he burned a one-eighty back down Atlantic to Missippi.

The bodies were stuffed in garbage bags dumped in the alley next to Victory Billiards, fresh kills, the blood still draining from their skulls. It was another ten minutes before forensics arrived. Soon the staccato click, pop, and flash of cameras wielded by Doc Dougherty's team peppered the carcasses in a strobe-like shower of light. Their hands were bound with duct tape behind their backs, wrists connected to ankles, forcing them into a kneeling position reminiscent of World War II photographs of Japanese executions of POWs. Each of the deceased had two .38 caliber bullet holes behind the ear.

Jake, responding to the tap on his shoulder, turned to face the silver-haired FBI Special Agent who moments earlier arrived unnoticed in the alley. "Just happen to be in the neighborhood, Bill?" Jake cracked.

Alfie nodded a greeting before turning away to join Dougherty, who was busy directing crime scene photographs and evidence retrieval. Jake made a mental note that Alfie had chosen deniability. Jake didn't blame him. He'd do the same if Alfie were out there chasing a personal demon.

Perry flashed a quick smile at Jake. "New York put the hit out on Nicky and Crazy Walter. Our CI told us New York was losing patience with the little guy. Nicky's mistakes and excesses were drawing unwanted attention to all family business and threatening the mob's stake in the casinos and unions. Blatstein was the last straw. The body showing up in the Blenheim site put Gomberg at risk. No Gomberg, no finger in the casino pie. Nicky had outlived his usefulness. He became a liability. The rest you know."

Jake pointed to the bodies of Nicky and his nephew. "What's this do to your investigation?"

"When Blatstein got capped, we lost our eyes and ears. With Blatstein and Nicky dead, McMeekin's a key guy for us. McMeekin will try to position himself as Gomberg's guardian angel. New York will eventually figure out they don't need him, but it will buy him some breathing room. When he starts feeling heat from New York, we'll pay him a visit. See if we can't bring him to Jesus." Perry paused and looked at Jake square on.

"I'd say you look like you lost your best friend, if you ever had one. Something happen I should know about, partner?"

"How long do you keep allowing McMeekin to believe he's still a real police captain?"

"A while longer. Be patient. And watch your back."

"I'm not worried about *my* back."

"I don't think you have to worry about New York getting to you through Michelle—at least for now. That was all Nicky. New York hit Nicky to restore some order and calm things down. Last thing they want to do is stir up a shit storm by going after you."

"How did you know about Michelle in all this?"

"C'mon, Jake. We got a small army of CIs on the inside, all of them wired up like a New York switchboard."

"So why do I have to hear about Nicky's threat to Michelle from Toad?"

"We had her back—and yours. Our boys would've stepped in if it came to that. Jake, you need to get small for now."

"Meaning?"

"You're making people nervous."

"Glad to hear it."

"Jake, we're nearly there in making a case against the mob for ITAR bribery of public officials, murder, and labor racketeering all tied up in a RICO indictment. But there's still a lot that can go wrong."

"So how's that different from every other mob case you've ever handled?"

"It wasn't, Jake, until you began rattling cages and made my job tougher."

"We're on the same side, I thought."

"Jake, I don't know why you're acting like a vigilante, and I don't want to know. I'm telling you to stand down before you step in a deep pile of shit."

"I don't deserve that from you, Bill."

"I don't care what you think you deserve or don't deserve. I've got my hands full just trying to manage the county prosecutor. At my request, the county has back-burnered its case on the Blatstein hit to avoid disrupting what the tristate federal task force has ongoing. You walking into Bobbins's office and kicking him in the balls didn't help that situation. That stunt you pulled a few weeks ago with your visit to the backroom at Victory followed by one to Nicastro's office shut down our access to the inner circle. Our guy—that's right, we have a CI close to the key players—had been providing critical intel on meeting locations that enabled us to set up surveillance—that is, until you spooked everyone from Nicky on down and things went dark."

"Bill, I—"

"I'm not finished. When you met with Bobbins, you nut-punched him with Lasky possibly representing Joey Nardo. I don't know what you're sharing with Lasky, but as far as I'm concerned, Lasky's a mob lawyer. Your partner, he's a smart man. He's working his case—your case—by the book. Take a lesson. You and I want the same thing. If you let us do our job, all the bad guys will go down hard."

Jake was far less certain than Bill Perry of the outcomes. But he held his tongue.

* * *

Joey Nardo sat in a metal chair, his ankles shackled to chains embedded in the cement floor, his wrists cuffed to a ring soldered to the tabletop. Expressionless, his eyes showed no recognition of the man sitting across from him. Despite the apparent futility of doing so, Jake pressed on. He knew instinctively that engaging in social convention with Joey would reduce whatever slim chance he had of a breakthrough. Better to go right at the reason for his being there: to convince Joey to be a cooperating witness to the tunnel murders.

"In two weeks, the county prosecutor is going to the grand jury for three true bills of murder one against you." He fixed an unblinking glare at Joey, who continued to stare past Jake. Jake resisted his urge to brace Joey with a forearm shiver to get his attention. "I want to shove this case up McMeekin's ass, but I need your help. You need to get your head straightened out, Joey."

Nardo's face remained blank. "Do you love Michelle? Do you want to see her dragged into court as a witness? Because that's exactly what is going to happen if you don't work with me."

Jake pushed his chair back from the table. He'd said what he'd come to say. He moved toward the door, but stopped midstride and turned back at the sound of the voice behind him.

"Keep my sister out of this." Nardo's eyes left little doubt what he would do to Detective Harris if only he could get free of his shackles.

Jake met Joey's glare with his own. "You're not giving me any choice."

Nardo shifted in his seat. His chains, pulled taut in anger at the mention of his sister's name, eased against the table. He looked at Jake, the rage in his eyes gone. "If I testify, then Michelle won't have to be a witness?"

Jake knew that withholding from the assistant county prosecutor Michelle's recollection of what her brother told her the night of the murders violated about half a dozen felony statutes, beginning with obstruction of justice. "I swear to you. If you cooperate and testify, Michelle will not have to."

"The night they took me away, you were at the bottom of the steps. I looked you in the eye and told you to take care of my sister. You deserted her. So why should I trust you now?"

"I can't give you a good reason."

"Right answer, Beach Boy."

He was Beach Boy again. Jake sat down and slid his chair back to the table.

"You were always the smartest of us. I knew that, even if the others didn't. You had lines you wouldn't cross."

"Maybe that's not always good. Being safe and being happy aren't the same."

"I liked you. I figured I didn't have to worry about Michelle with you around."

"I loved your sister."

He wanted to say *love*.

"You left her when she needed you."

Jake wanted to make excuses for himself, but he didn't. He was done making excuses. He was a kid back then, sure, but age didn't matter. Courage was an instinct; it was in you, in your gut, your body chemistry, or not. Jake could face down an armed dealer in a stash house on an under- cover buy gone bad. He'd done that more than once. But he had failed when it really counted. Michelle, Ginny, Danny—he had failed the real tests.

Jake said, "I was scared."

"So was I. So was Michelle. I never figured you for that. You had the stones to challenge me when we rode together. You had guts."

"You scared the crap out of me, Joey."

"The shrinks in here tell me I'm a sociopath. No feelings, no remorse. But most of what I remember about growing up is being afraid. I loved my sister. I hated the priests and the nuns at St. Mike's. I hated Mario. Those are feelings. And I felt things when I killed Mario. When I was beating him, I was thinking of those fucking priests. I chopped off his hands because of what those hands had done to my sister."

"Michelle never told me about Mario. I would've killed him myself."

"She couldn't. You were the best thing in her life. Why do you think I didn't kick your scrawny little ass?"

"Joey, what happened in the tunnel?"

"Why're you doing this, Beach Boy? Who're you trying to make things right with?"

"Does it matter?"

Joey took a deep breath. "Fish and me were in the tunnel with three faggots. Usual shit. Fish watching the action, the faggots doing what they do with each other. Like always, we planned to roll them for cash. That's all we ever did. Only this night, one of them started laughing at Fish. You know how Fish got when he was excited, gulping air, talkin' fast, sounding like his nose was filled with snot. This guy laughed at him, called him chubby, and mocked his voice. Fish went nuts. He grabbed the bat and swung at the guy. Caught him in the head. The guy went down. Didn't move. The other two had their pants around their ankles. Before they could move, Fish was on them with the bat. Two swings. They didn't move once they hit the ground.

I grabbed Fish and took the bat from him, but it was too late. He'd already bashed their skulls. We went to get Vinny and Toad. When we got back to the tunnel, blood was still coming out of their heads. The bodies hadn't moved. They helped us bury the bodies. Took all night."

Joey paused, looked down at his manacled hands.

"That it, Joey?"

"Before we went looking for Vinny and Toad, Fish made me promise not to tell them he did it. Everybody would think it was me anyway."

"You kept it secret?"

"For seventeen years. Until today."

"All this time and you told no one?"

"No one."

Except Michelle, Jake thought. To keep his promise, he would have to allow Joey to commit perjury about his sister's knowledge of that night. Adding one more felony to his lengthening list mattered little to him.

Jake caught a jitney uptown and walked the three blocks north on Tennessee Avenue to meet Alfie at Lamps' Bar. Alfie was at a table in the back, hunched over a beer, turning the bottle absentmindedly between his fingers.

"That looks like it's been sitting for a while. How about a fresh one? I'll buy."

Alfie looked up. "Yeah. I'll have another."

Jake signaled for two of the same, threw down a ten, and grabbed the two bottles of Schmidts that Lamps placed on the bar along with his change.

"This place takes me back to when we first joined the force, busting hopheads for nickel bags. We used to think a half bundle was the fucking French connection. One-stop shopping and we always made our quota."

Alfie forced a smile. "Simpler times, Jake. You could tell the good guys from the black hats." Brathwaite wiped beads of condensation from the bottle and took a long swig. "Jake, McMeekin pulled the plug. You're off the case."

"He thinks that's going to shut us down? Circle the wagons so the mob gets a seat at the table? He overplayed his hand, Alfie. We'll work it off the clock."

"You're not listening, Jake. *You're* out."

"What are you saying, Alfie?"

"You heard me."

"Fuck you, Alfie. It's my case."

"You're in the middle of a shit storm."

"You finished?"

"Just telling you what you already know."

"So he takes me off the case, and you go along. Joey gets to take the fall, Gomberg gets his casino license, and the New York mob skims the cream."

"Who said anything about me going along with McMeekin?"

"I didn't mean that, Alfie. Look. McMeekin's dead meat."

"It looks to me like McMeekin has been stepping in clover, what with Nicky and Blatstein gone."

"We just need to ride it out—together."

"You're still not listening, Jake." Alfie took another long swig, put the bottle down, and fixed Jake with his eyes. "You're a target."

"For what?

"For one thing, obstruction. Like you always said, Jake. Truth, like beauty, is in the eye of the beholder. Right now, McMeekin is the beholder."

"I never thought you'd be his messenger boy. What else did he want to tell me?"

"I'm not his fucking messenger. You know McMeekin would bust me in a minute if he thought he could beat the union. He put a tail on you weeks ago. He's got pictures of you and Michelle at Tony's Baltimore and you meeting with Carbone and Nicastro at Rocky's."

"I was working the case."

"That's not the way McMeekin spins it."

"How do you see it?"

"You know how I see it. Don't make this something between you and me. Nothing's changed. McMeekin plans on calling you in tomorrow to deliver the news."

"So I get sent to Siberia?"

"Working the night desk is the best you can hope for. He wants your shield."

Jake took the last swig of beer. "How about a lift home?"

Four stories below his apartment windows, Ventnor Avenue had begun to stir with traffic, mostly cops in squad cars ending their shifts and construction workers starting theirs. Jake had turned the TV off before midnight and climbed into a freshly made bed. Sleep came easily, an airy somnolence. He'd slept straight through to five and awoke feeling refreshed, not his usual exhaustion-induced stupor. He decided to walk the twenty blocks uptown for his appointment with Rabbit.

Norman F. Laskey's law office on the fifth floor of the Realty Trust Building looked across Atlantic Avenue directly at city hall. The office walls were bare except for two black-and-white photographs behind his desk. The first was an aerial shot of the Inlet taken in 1954, according to the date written beneath it, AC's centennial. The second was of the same section of the Inlet a quarter of a century later. In the more recent photo, two structures remained near the tip of the island where the ocean and bay converged—the old blue-and-white lighthouse, a quaint prop that hadn't operated in anyone's memory, and a grime-caked eight-story brick building, an anomaly, a mistake left standing after everything around it had been leveled. This had been Rabbit's home for the first eighteen years of his life.

Upon graduation from Harvard Law, Rabbit clerked for Judge Weinstein. When his year clerkship ended and on Judge Weinstein's advice, Rabbit joined the Atlantic County Prosecutor's office as an assistant, a brief rèsumè builder before seeking a highly prized appointment to the United States Attorney's office. Judge Weinstein had been the United States Attorney before being appointed to the bench. A clerkship with Judge Weinstein was a ticket to the federal prosecutor's office, Rabbit's penultimate step to establishing himself as the premier criminal defense lawyer in the state. Rabbit knew all this ahead of time. He'd planned his career moves. *The Press* ran a puff piece on Rabbit's appointment to the United States Attorney's Office in Newark. TOUGH COUNTY PROSECUTOR SIGNS ON WITH THE FEDS, the headline read.

Rabbit bought a home in the Parkway section of Margate, the wide avenue of large brick colonials and field-stone Tudors that ran parallel to the beach. He bought the home from the Liebgott family, who'd run into financial trouble. Rabbit's revenge, part two.

Mr. Liebgott had the contract to supply cars to the State of New Jersey. He made kickbacks to the state's contracting officer, who was also bagging for the state senator who controlled the deal. Mr. Liebgott recouped the money for the kickbacks with phony warranty claims to General Motors. One of Rabbit's federal prosecutor colleagues convened a grand jury. Mr. Liebgott, Penn grad, president of Avoda, B'nai Brith, and Linwood C. C. was indicted. He cut a deal and pleaded guilty. Rabbit attended the sentencing. Defense counsel presented letters of good character, and Liebgott begged for probation, expressing his remorse and asking the judge to consider how he and his family had been punished enough by their ordeal.

But Liebgott had drawn the meanest bull in the rodeo, a judge the prosecutors called "Toothbrush" because defendants had better have theirs ready. Liebgott got four years in the Federal Correctional Institution at Allenwood, the so-called country club for white-collar criminals.

He was allowed to remain free on bail to get his affairs in order before he had to report to the US Marshal's office in Camden. To cover his legal fees and the civil claims against him for fraud brought by General Motors he had to liquidate everything, including the center hall brick colonial on the Parkway in Margate. Rabbit didn't have the money, but he borrowed all he could from a bank for the down payment and went on the street for the rest. He got the house for half the asking price. Mr. Liebgott was out of time. Norman "Rabbit" Lasky sat across the settlement table from the soon-to-be incarcerated felon and smiled his gap-toothed smile.

Rabbit leveraged his headlines as a federal prosecutor into a lucrative private practice. That was what young prosecutors did like military fighter pilots who had left the service for six-figure salaries flying for the airlines. Rabbit worked alone, taking on big-fee organized-crime cases, the same thugs he used to prosecute. They were low-overhead, money-no-object clients. He drove a black Benz 450 SEL with "NFL" plates (his middle name was Fredrick), wore custom shirts and suits, and four-hundred-dollar shoes handmade in England (complete with steel shanks and McAfee heels).

And that was why Jake concluded that Norman Lasky—meter-juicing, pussy-eating Rabbit—was the only person he could trust to do what must be done: defend Joey Nardo.

Rabbit motioned toward two wing chairs and a coffee table.

"Let's sit over here, Jake. It's less formal that way, without the desk between us."

"I'm here for legal advice. This is a privileged conversation." Jake had uttered the formulaic words that bound Rabbit to secrecy.

"Agreed."

"I want you to represent Nardo. He was there in the tunnel that night, but he didn't swing the bat."

"Who did?"

"Gomberg."

Rabbit flashed a half smile. "Gomberg was always a strange kid. Never would've thought he had the chops to do something like that, though. Who's your source?"

"Joey."

"And you buy it?"

"Yeah. I buy it." Jake decided against telling Rabbit about Michelle. Letting Rabbit in on Michelle would mean Rabbit would have to choose between allowing Nardo to lie under oath to protect his sister or withdrawing from the case as Joey's lawyer.

"What are you after here, Jake?"

"Gomberg."

"The New York wiseguys are not gonna sit by and let you foul up their plans by taking out Gomberg."

"Bobbins could get a true bill from the grand jury against Joey for felony murder. All Bobbins needs to do is include a robbery charge. The grand jurors will buy that Joey and Gomberg lured the victims into the tunnel to rob them."

"Bobbins won't do that. He's got no case against Gomberg, at least not one he'd risk his career on. And there's McMeekin. He's got a heavy thumb on the scales of justice."

"McMeekin's gonna have other concerns he doesn't know about yet. My guess is Bobbins would blow you if you promised to cop Joey to one count of manslaughter and time served."

"Why you doing all this, Jake?"

"Just an honest cop doing the citizenry's business."

"In this case, doing the right thing comes with a lot of risk to your health. Gomberg's friends from New York won't go down without a fight."

Both men sat in silence, neither moving to get up and end the meeting.

"Alright, Jake. We'll do it your way. I'll set a meeting with Bobbins and see if he'll buy in. Be careful."

"I'm way past careful."

The call came out of the blue. Ninety minutes later, Jake arrived at the Ben Franklin Hotel, a block from the federal courthouse and the Philadelphia field office of the FBI.

"Hey, partner." Jake followed the familiar voice to see Bill Perry emerge from the bar off the lobby. "Glad you could join us."

"I needed a break from busting policy books and hookers. Besides, once McMeekin took me off the tunnel case, he lost interest in making my life miserable."

"The worm is about to turn." Perry walked to the elevator bank with Jake in tow.

The elevator doors opened on the tenth floor, and Jake followed his escort down the corridor to room 1035. Perry put the key in the lock to open the door. "How'd you like your old job back?"

Inside the room, a youngish, earnest-looking man in a white shirt, sleeves rolled to his elbows, and loosened tie stood over a figure seated against the far wall. "Jake, say hello to assistant US attorney Mike Pease."

Pease turned away from the figure in the chair and extended his hand. "Detective Harris, nice to finally meet you. Heard good things from Perry about you. Of course, you already know Captain McMeekin."

McMeekin looked up from his hands and stared at his detective sergeant. "What's he doing here?"

Mike Pease's expression was deadpan. "Who might that be, Captain? Nobody else is here but Special Agent Perry and me."

"I'm not saying anything with him here."

"Bill, I think we're ready now to play for Captain McMeekin the tape of his conversation with Judge Blatstein."

Perry pressed play on the machine sitting on the small table. At the first sound of his static-laced voice, Eamon McMeekin slumped in his chair. Perry stopped the tape after McMeekin had said enough to send him to jail for a decade.

"Blatstein's dead. That tape isn't admissible without him," McMeekin said, his defiance returning. "You got nothing. You're violating my rights."

Pease turned to Perry. "Bill, show the captain that piece of paper you have in your breast pocket. I'll save you the trouble of reading it, Captain McMeekin. It's a warrant for your arrest for extortion and bribery in violation of the Hobbs Act and Interstate Travel in Aid of Racketeering Act. Bill, cuff Captain McMeekin and take him across the street for processing. Oh, and let him call his lawyer."

Perry guided McMeekin toward the door using the cuffs, tightened just enough to cut into McMeekin's wrists, like a rudder on a boat. "You're fucked, Harris. Have you told your pal here, Special Agent Perry, about your girlfriend? Maybe he should know you've been playing him so you can be the hero and save her crazy brother. You thought she was letting you into her panties because she's in love? She's as fucked up as her brother."

Jake eyed his former captain impassively. "Bill, get this piece of garbage out of my sight."

Three days later, Rabbit called to say there had been movement from the prosecution to plea bargain with Joey Nardo. That was all he would say over the phone.

Jake arrived before Rabbit returned from court. His secretary escorted Jake into Rabbit's office, as she had been instructed to do. He waited for her to leave before walking behind Rabbit's desk. He stared at the two black-and-white photographs hanging side by side—Rabbit's old neighborhood in the Inlet section of the city, before and after. Tessie was right. Hiroshima by the Sea. He wondered whether AC would fare as well as Japan in its own aftermath of destruction.

"Bobbins wants to cut a deal."

Jake had not heard Rabbit enter. He felt awkward standing behind the desk.

"Sorry. Just looking at the photographs." Jake walked around the desk and sat at one end of the couch.

"I look at those pictures a lot, Jake. Was this town so far beyond redemption that it needed to be demolished? That's what's happened, you know. Atlantic City no longer exists. I don't know what this place is, but it's not AC. I know towns and cities change, but most don't lose their souls.

"New York will always be New York. And it's been that way from the beginning. Boston, Chicago, the same. Christ, even Philly. Can't get a decent cheesesteak in Little Italy, but it has the Italian Market, soft pretzels and the mummers. I don't know what we have anymore in this town—but it's not character. No turning back once you make a deal with the devil. We sold our collective soul to the casinos."

Jake had never heard Rabbit talk like this. He was the same Rabbit who'd ejaculated in Gail Liebgott's mouth and, before he even zipped his fly, told her he'd never see her again—just to get even with her father for slighting him. This was the same Rabbit who bought the Liebgott home at a bargain price when Mr. Liebgott was on his way to jail. Rabbit, the Attila the Hun of the trial bar, had sentiment.

"Casinos were the easy fix," Jake said.

"No guts, no vision," Rabbit agreed.

"The old hotels, they had style. Gone. Can never be replaced. Tearing down the Blenheim, Traymore, Dennis, Shelburne is like New York deciding to demolish the Empire State or Chrysler Building. The piers, Mr. Peanut, penny arcades—hell, we were the honky-tonk capital of America."

"At least that was something," Rabbit said.

Rabbit sat down at the other end of the couch. "Joey pleads to three counts of accessory to murder, agrees to cooperate, and gets time served," Rabbit said.

"Accessory to whom?"

"The usual: 'unnamed person or persons.' Bobbins gets some press, and Joey's plea won't foreclose charging others with the murders."

"What do you think?" Jake asked.

"Joey was in the tunnel. There is a factual basis for the plea."

"What about the plea colloquy? If Joey's present when the vics were killed and he didn't do it, he knows who did. The press is gonna want to know that small detail. How does a judge not insist that the killer be named by Joey?"

"We'll work that out with the judge in chambers. It's an ongoing investigation. The county prosecutor, the feds, and I will join in a motion to take the plea *in camera* and seal the record. The media will raise their usual freedom of the press fuss, but that story is forgotten before the newsprint is dry."

"What about the feds?"

"Bobbins's boss got a call from the United States Attorney in Newark. He agreed to stay the tunnel case until DOJ wraps up the grand jury. The way Bobbins had it figured, nailing Joey Nardo would up his standing with the feds. He would then be named to the joint task force investigating Eddie Blatstein's murder. You know Bobbins as well as I do. He figured he'd milk the Blatstein case to keep his name in the papers. Leak information to generate more ink. But his boss screwed him when he agreed to let the feds shut him down.

"Bobbins got on his knees and begged, and they threw him a bone. He could have his indictment against Nardo if he could get it pled out and avoid a trial. Bobbins gets his two-minute press conference and his name on the front page of *The Press*. Not what he envisioned, but it's not a total loss for him."

"Joey was found incompetent to stand trial for his uncle's murder," Jake said. "He's not going to make much of a witness against 'person or persons unknown.'"

"Standard cooperation requirement. Window dressing for the plea. Makes it look like the prosecutor is doing his job. Nobody's going to bring a murder indictment based on Joey's testimony."

"If Joey's competent to enter a plea, he's competent to stand trial for his uncle's murder."

"Yeah. That's a problem. I told Bobbins putting Joey on trial for the murder of Mario Cippolone is a deal breaker. But he's so hungry he'll find a way to get it done. Joey's served more than a decade and a half for a crime of passion he committed as a nineteen-year-old. Bobbins doesn't want him streeted, but that's what I got on the table: time served for voluntary manslaughter and reporting parole for life."

"You talk with Joey about this?"

"I want Bobbins on board, then I'll tell Joey."

The two men stood and walked to the door of Rabbit's office. Rabbit said, "My freshman year at F & M, whenever I told someone I was born and raised in this town, they'd get this stunned look. 'Nobody's *from* Atlantic City,' they'd say. Maybe they knew something about this place I didn't. I know what I know now. Whatever AC is, it's not mine. Ironic, Jake. I used to think we were the hustlers and the rest of the world the suckers. Now when I walk around town, finding myself looking for a building or a store from when we were kids, I wonder who the real suckers are."

On the sidewalk outside Rabbit's office, Jake thought of Michelle. He smiled in anticipation of her reaction when he told her the news that her brother would be released from custody. Finally, she would be able to care for him as he once had her.

Joey Nardo and the Tunnel Queens would become yesterday's news. Sandy's stained T-shirt and trunks would sit in the basement evidence room and, like the bones disgorged by the mud walls of Tessie Dorfman's tunnel in the ruins of the Marlborough Blenheim, wait to tell their story.

For the present, that left McMeekin, a corrupt cop owned by the mob. Bill Perry and his cohorts had closed the net on him. The feds would indict his captain. The tapes of his conversations with the late judge were powerful evidence of McMeekin's complicity in racketeering and bribery of public officials.

Jake had decided to walk from Rabbit's uptown office to Michelle's bungalow in lower Chelsea. As much as he wanted to savor the thought of what he had accomplished for Michelle and Joey, he could not let go of Gomberg. If the case ended with a corruption prosecution against McMeekin and a few state officials, Gomberg would skate.

The truth about the murders might never be told, and that sickened him.

He stood outside the bungalow. A full moon cast shadows across her small front yard. An ebbing tide exposed the marshes. He could smell the bay and hear it wash against the bulkhead.

Inside Michelle was waiting.

Her home was his refuge, a place of return. She greeted him in jeans and a plain white T-shirt. He wondered whether she'd remembered how he loved that look. They sat in the small nook in her kitchen by a window open to the backyard and sipped coffee.

"Your brother will be released in the next couple of weeks. Rabbit just needs to get the papers signed."

"Oh, Jake. How did you do it?"

"All I did was bring Rabbit in to represent Joey. Rabbit did the rest."

"I wanted him out of that place for so long, Jake. I want my brother back."

"He's coming back, Michelle."

"Where will they put him when he's released?"

"St. Nicholas of Tolentine—you know, the church on Pacific Avenue between Illinois and Indiana. A transition shelter for parolees."

"Joey won't go anywhere near a priest."

"I met with the head of the program. He's a good man, and the residents run the place. He went to see Joey. I think it will work out."

He had done it as much for himself as for Joey. A second chance for two old corner boys.

"I haven't felt this good in years, Michelle. That's worth a lot." He paused. "I don't want to lose you again."

"All that matters is we get things right this time."

"Is it too late?"

"We're here, aren't we? Who knows? Had we run off as kids, we might have ended up hating each other."

"I don't think so," Jake said. "The only person I've truly hated since leaving you has been me."

"What about now, Jake? Do you like who you are?"

"I'm getting there. When I couldn't sleep, which was most nights, I'd walk the streets. I'd stand across from your house and picture you inside, curled up with a book. Weird, huh?"

She smiled. "No. Well, maybe a little."

"Before heading back to my apartment, I'd always end up at the rail, looking out at the ocean. I love that smell and the sound of the waves at night. We let it disappear."

"People and places disappear. Happens everywhere."

He nodded but was not really sure she was right. "Every night I stood there at the rail, I thought of us back in high school. Did you ever? Think of us, I mean?"

"As bad as things were with Theresa and Mario and Joey, I'd put myself back there just to feel what I did those nights we were together."

"Do you still have the book?

She smiled.

The bedroom had different dimensions and finer appointments and furniture, but the warmth and feeling of safety were the same he had felt in the old apartment on Texas Avenue—her smell, too, a hint of baby powder. Michelle took down the familiar thin volume from the shelf. He lay next to her, his head on her pillow. On the wall at the foot of her bed was Monet's *Jardin á Giverny,* the same one from her old room on Texas Avenue. She opened to the first page and began reading.

He woke to the sound of gulls diving for their breakfast. Still asleep, she lay on her side, facing him. He studied the curves of her body moving with the slow steady rhythm of her breathing, her olive skin accented against the stark whiteness of the sheet draping her hip.

His thoughts turned, as they always did in the quiet of the early morning, to his son. As Danny matured, he became distant, and Jake's visits had dwindled. He had tried to see his son every day, even if only long enough to kiss him good morning or goodnight. Games and roughhousing and storytelling that had filled the early years following his split with Ginny had nothing to replace them. Jake had tried to be a father, but Danny wasn't buying. Ginny's move back to Sparta, New Jersey, did not help matters. Her father had gotten Danny admitted to Lawrenceville Prep, a feeder school for Princeton. Danny was becoming part of a world that was as removed from AC, Chelsea, and Ducktown as one could get. He'd have to fix that. He just didn't know how.

He threw on a pair of jeans and an old sweatshirt he had had forever. The streets were empty. Their Chelsea neighborhood had become a small island of life surrounded by corridors of plywood and chain-link security fencing separating the dispossessed from the abandoned. The story of his hometown was now told in spray-painted pictographs and neon. He understood, finally, why he continued to walk the streets in solitude. He was chasing a past that was threatened with oblivion. The ache in his gut as he walked alone was real, a lifeline to his past, palpable evidence of what had been. He welcomed the ache like a dying man might welcome a twinge of pain as a reminder that he was still alive and might stave off his end for one more moment. Some went peacefully; he could not.

It was not enough to conjure his own long-ago feel-ings as a young boy racing alongside his father, trying to keep up, as Buddy strode the sidewalks of his hometown. He needed to see AC through his father's eyes, understand what his father felt about this place where he was born, where he had lived his life. Despite the futility of it all, he continued, the ache of loss becoming proof of what was. He continued even after it had struck him on one recent late night walk that he hardly knew the man his father was.

Each solitary walk had ended the same: outside her bungalow on the bay. One day, he would relinquish his sadness to her, and when he did, the emptiness that plagued him would lift. They would talk of the past they shared, cherishing the good. The bad that they had endured would always be there, of course, but serving only to heighten the joy of their life together. He knew that day was coming nearer. He felt it. Back in front of her home, he smiled and walked toward the porch light Michelle had switched on for him.

Part Three

1994

Mayor Vincent Nicastro stood shoulder-to-shoulder with the president of the city council, a congressman, the governor, the chairman of the board of trustees of the Atlantic City Medical Center, and Arthur Gomberg. Each wore a shiny hard hat and wielded a never-before-used stainless steel spade poised to dig into the earth. The men smiled for the official photographer. They were gathered to commemorate the groundbreaking for the start of construction on the Arthur Gomberg Cancer Treatment and Research Center. Police Captain Brathwaite sat in the front row, watching.

With photographs taken, ribbon cut, and ceremonial spades of earth turned, the dignitaries dispersed. Alfie Brathwaite reached the mayor and Gomberg as they were about to enter the back seat of the waiting Town Car. Brathwaite removed a single piece of paper from his breast pocket, unfolded it, and handed it to Arthur Gomberg.

"You are hereby served and required to appear before the county grand jury to give evidence on the day and time specified." Alfie paused a beat before turning from the two stunned men.

Science had caught up with Arthur Gomberg. A breakthrough in forensic technology enabled analysis of degraded genetic material. Using mitochondrial DNA analysis, remains of crime victims that typically lacked nucleated cells could yield biological profiles. Crime labs now had a tool that had the potential to glean usable evidence from decades old shafts of hair, bodily fluid stains, and bones. The new science offered promise in the investigation of cases that had languished unsolved in archived police files for years, even decades.

The grand jury wanted DNA samples from Arthur Gomberg.

Clusters of ramshackle houses dotted the bayside in Chelsea and Venice Park, remnants of another time. They stood only because they held no present value to the developers, hoteliers, and casino operators. The candy stores, trattorias, dry cleaners, and corner barber shops that had made them neighborhoods were gone. The old high school, their high school—the white-brick castle on the circle at Albany Avenue—had been razed. The new one, an architectural approximation of a flock of Flying Nuns, was located offshore on Albany Avenue Boulevard in the no man's land between AC and Pleasantville.

The small pocket of neat, white bungalows along the bay on Sovereign Avenue in Chelsea, where Jake and Michelle Harris lived, remained untouched. Michelle and Jake had added a small bedroom and bath on to the side of the house for Joey. He stayed on his meds and was able to work during the week as a stock boy at the new Safeway Supermarket across the bridge in Venice Park. He was a hulking man, stolid but nonthreatening. He took meals with his sister and Jake. On weekends, Joey was a volunteer at St. Nicholas of Tolentine, helping to acclimate new residents transitioning from prison. On Sunday nights, he called "Bingo!" in the church annex. The anger was gone from him.

Jake entered the kitchen through the door that opened to the backyard. He wiped the potting soil from his hands and took the phone from Michelle. It was Rabbit.

"The presentment is set for next Monday," Rabbit reported. "Joey will be the only fact witness to testify before the grand jury. I'll prepare him over the weekend for what he'll face. Get him to my office on Saturday."

"I guess you're not going to want me to sit in when you prep him."

"You know the answer to that, Jake."

"Just making sure. I'll drop Joey at your office at ten Saturday morning."

Jake walked back outside to join his brother-in-law, who was on his knees, bent over a row of clay flowerpots in various stages of transplanting them to the small garden along the bulkhead.

"You ready to do some fishing, partner?" Jake asked.

Joey looked up at his brother-in law and nodded.

The county grand jury met twice a month in the basement of the courthouse located in Mays Landing, the county seat. The windowless room looked more like a junior college classroom than a courtroom. Bare cinder-block walls, painted government green, met a linoleum floor decorated with random black streaks. A clock of the kind found in every public school classroom in America was centered on the wall above a rectangular metal table at the front of the room. It was here that the prosecutor sat to examine witnesses situated in a chair at the end of the table next to an official court stenographer.

The jurors sat haphazardly facing the prosecutor and the witness in chairs with elongated hinged writing surfaces attached to the right armrests, giving the assemblage the look of middle-agers at a night school course for self-im-provement. In truth, there was nothing "grand" about the grand jury. It comprised twenty-five county residents selected at random, most of whom were retirees or unem-ployed. A quorum of thirteen was required to do business, and the vote of a simple majority of its total complement of twenty-five to return an indictment, which on those occasions when only a bare quorum was present, meant a unanimous vote in favor.

In practice, virtually all votes by the grand jury were unanimous and followed the recommendation of the pros-ecutor, which is not surprising since the prosecutor was the sole decider of what the grand jury saw and heard. After this one-sided presentation of evidence, the detec-tive assigned to the case would sum up the investigation followed by a closing statement by the prosecutor. In most cases, the grand jury never heard from the accused; and, defense counsel had no input to the grand jury. Originally conceived by the founding fathers to replace the King's Star Chamber, the institution of the grand jury quickly became a rubber stamp, known among the criminal defense bar as the "handmaiden of the prosecutor." The only jury that truly mattered was the petit jury—the jury of twelve peers that would decide guilt or innocence at trial.

When Jake arrived with Joey Nardo in tow, he saw Rabbit outside the grand jury room, talking with John Stein, the former United States Attorney for the District of New Jersey and now the newly appointed special prosecutor for the Gomberg investigation. Stein, a well-preserved fifty-year-old, had been the top federal prosecutor in New Jersey before leaving to join a prominent North Jersey law firm as a senior partner. In between, he did a stint as the number two man at the Department of Justice in Washington. Stein had the well-earned reputation of being a fearless and skilled crusader against the mob and corrupt public officials. As the top federal prosecutor, he personally tried the biggest and riskiest cases his office brought, which was unusual for the United States Attorney, usually thought to be a political appointee with little in the way of courtroom skills. Typically, the boss stood on the podium to announce the indictment to the media and grab the headlines with pithy sound bites about how *his* office has yet again sent the message that New Jersey would not tolerate (fill in the blank with whatever the defendants were accused of doing). But Stein was different. He was a true believer in public service and in locking up public officials who violated the people's trust. And he could try a case with the best of them.

When Jake first heard Stein had been appointed special prosecutor, he asked Rabbit why a lawyer of Stein's stature would take on the Gomberg case. Rabbit shot Jake one
of his worldly near-smiles and said, "To do justice." Rabbit
explained that when Stein was asked by the attorneys general of the United States and the State of New Jersey to
be the special prosecutor, he questioned the reason he
was needed for a decades-old murder case. Stein knew the
answer but wanted to hear it from the top: Gomberg was
the mob's front man in the gaming industry. The murder
charge, as weak as it was, represented the best chance to
eliminate Gomberg from the casinos and, with him, his
mob backers. Stein knew from his days at the Department
of Justice Gomberg's relationship with the mob. He listened
to the taped conversations Judge Blatstein made with state
legislators, a member of the casino control commission,
and Captain Eamon McMeekin. In the final analysis, Stein
had to first be convinced of Gomberg's guilt for the tunnel
murders. He was and he took a sabbatical from his lucrative
private practice to do what he saw to be his civic duty. The
statute of limitations had run on Gomberg's less salacious
criminal conduct, but there was no time limit on murder
charges. Kind of like convicting Al Capone of income tax
evasion, only in Gomberg's case the violent crime was the
road to justice, Rabbit explained.

Jake left Joey with Rabbit and walked over to the silver-haired figure standing alone against the wall opposite
from where Jake had entered. "Hello, Bill."

Special Agent Bill Perry's lips curved into the slight
smile of a man who has made peace with his lot. He had

come simply for the return of the indictment, hoping for some small sense of closure. He had no official role in the case against Gomberg. Perry's Tri-State Task Force investigation of organized crime's attempted infiltration of AC's gaming industry had been by all measures, except Perry's own, a success. The feds had obtained convictions of two state senators, a casino commissioner, three union stewards, four real estate developers, and Eamon McMeekin, former captain of the ACPD. All were incarcerated; none cooperated with the ongoing investigation, opting instead to trade a few extra years in prison for additional years of life after being paroled. Nicky Zitto's and his nephew's bodies turning up in an alley wrapped in trash bags had altered the calculus in favor of not testifying against more important targets up the food chain of the crime hierarchy. The murders of Nicky, his nephew, and Judge Blatstein went unsolved, but then again, they were scumbags; rough justice had been done.

Perry accepted Jake's extended hand and gave it a single firm squeeze. "Good to see ya, Jake."

"Same here, Bill. I heard you were hanging up the spikes."

"You heard right. I got my twenty in with the bureau, plus five flying jets for Uncle Sam. Can't beat the pension and the bennies. Same health care as the US Congress and the president."

"So when do you pull the trigger?"

"End of next month."

"Somehow, Bill, I can't picture you sipping piña coladas on a beach."

"I signed on with Del Webb as chief of security. So I'll be splitting my time between Vegas and AC." Perry nodded in Joey's direction. "How's he holding up?"

"He's fine. There's not much worse anyone can do to him that hasn't been done already."

Joey was to be the first witness of the morning session. A forensic geneticist waited in the corridor to provide the scientific evidence establishing that Gomberg's DNA was found on Sandy Gordon's beach trunks and T-shirt, which were worn the night of the murders. Alfie Brathwaite would be the cleanup witness to summarize the investigation he had conducted with Jake more than a decade and a half ago.

It was a razor-thin case but would be enough to get a true bill for three counts of felony murder against Gomberg. Proving the charges at trial beyond a reasonable doubt would take more—much more.

The final business of the day would be for the special prosecutor to ask the grand jury to return a true bill of indictment, which would then be presented to the presiding judge for signature. Copies of the indictment and a press release would be distributed to the media the moment the indictment was filed with the criminal docket clerk. The lurid headlines to follow would mark the beginning of the rest of Arthur Gomberg's life.

Rabbit took Joey aside to be certain his client was ready for what he would face in the grand jury room. As the grand jury foreman entered the anteroom and called Joey Nardo inside, Jake grabbed his brother-in-law's elbow.

"Just remember, he's still just Fish, Joey."

Both men smiled.

Gomberg had retained Gil Flowers, the former first assistant district attorney of Philadelphia, to defend him. Flowers had a well-deserved reputation for ruthlessness, a relentless adversary who used all means available to get his client off. He had honed his skills prosecuting high-profile murder cases. He knew the importance of the press and used it deftly in the DA's office. It was now his initial tactic as Arthur Gomberg's defense counsel.

Flowers had wisely decided against having his client waive his Fifth Amendment privilege and putting him before the grand jury in the hopes he could persuade the jurors that a man of his stature and good works could not possibly have committed the acts alleged by the prosecutor. How could any right thinking person take the word of a criminal psychopath over his? But there was the small matter of the DNA evidence, which would be presented to the grand jury without any judicial intervention. Flowers correctly concluded that the only way to deal with the DNA was to exclude it entirely, and that would have to await the pretrial hearing on a motion *in limine*.

The presiding judge scheduled the trial to begin Monday, September 12, which would allow approximately six months for discovery, motions, and trial preparation. After the spate of headlines announcing the indictment, there followed profile pieces on Arthur Gomberg, investigative reporting on connections between Gomberg and the mob, and rehashing of the criminal cases brought against public officials connected to Gomberg. Mayor Vincent

Nicastro was featured in one of articles even though he had never been charged in any of the casino-related corruption cases.

Then the case went dark, the media having for the moment sated the public's appetite for salacious stories. All that would change with the start of trial.

On the day the indictment was returned, Flowers began his media campaign to balance the negative press with his own narrative. "Arthur Gomberg is a man who has done so much for his city and its citizens. The charges are brought by an ambitious, self-aggrandizing prosecutor whose only concern is advancing his career even if it meant destroying the life of a decent man. Arthur Gomberg is innocent," went Flower's public mantra.

The Realty Trust Building was dark except for a single light at the corner of the top floor. Norman Lasky stared at the whisky coating the bottom of the snifter in his left hand and waited. "Hello, Jake."

Jake shook Rabbit's extended hand and then followed Rabbit into his office, where the two men sat on the lawyer's leather couch.

"Scotch?"

"No."

"Balvenie 21."

"It would be wasted on me. I used to drink Schlitz out of a quart bottle with Vinny, Toad, and Joey. Remember?"

"Yeah. I remember."

"Can Stein win a conviction?"

"The state's case is thin. Carbone and Nicastro are taking the fifth. Even if Stein immunized them, they'd prefer to go to jail for contempt over the alternative. Toad and Vinny are more afraid of the New York wiseguys than any special prosecutor."

Jake knew all this without hearing it from Rabbit.

"I need you to speak with Stein."

"I'm listening."

"The night of the murders Michelle asked me to find her brother. She was afraid for him, worried he'd get into serious trouble. He was on juvie probation. She never liked Gomberg and was sure Joey's hanging around with him would lead to big trouble for her brother. They weren't at Victory Billiards, so I walked to Indiana and the boards. I heard voices, loud, like an argument. I walked down to the tunnel's entrance. I heard moaning, grunts, hard to describe. Before I got too far in, I tripped on a board. Someone shouted 'Get him,' I think. I got scared, ran out of the tunnel and up the boardwalk stairs. At the top, I turned and saw someone run from the tunnel. At first, I didn't know whether someone was coming after me, but then the figure ran toward the water and turned down beach. I lost sight of whoever it was in the darkness.

"Then I saw Gomberg's Bonnie parked in the shadows at the foot of the ramp."

"How do you know what happened in the tunnel that night? You never saw anything. You heard voices, and you saw someone run from the tunnel. How do you know that was the night of the murders? You're speculating."

"The figure I saw running from the tunnel was my uncle. I didn't recognize him that night. I put that piece together much later when I went to visit him in New York and he told me what had happened to him the night he went searching for his partner. I never told Alfie Braithwaite. You are the first."

"What are you after, Jake? You want me to tell Stein that you, the detective assigned to the case, withheld material evidence? Do you *want* to go to jail?"

"There's more."

Lasky shifted uneasily from his end of the couch and reached for the tumbler of scotch on the end table. "Jake, I'm no choirboy, but you're putting me in a tough position. You're my friend, not my client. This conversation is not privileged. If what you're about to tell me conflicts with Joey's testimony given to the grand jury or at the trial, I've got an ethical duty to take some action. If I believe Joey has lied under oath, I'd have to persuade him to recant. If he won't, I'd have to resign as Joey's counsel, and that will be a red-flag alert to Stein and the court that Joey may have committed perjury. It will get awfully messy, Jake. You know that as well as I."

Rabbit's ethics might surprise some, but not Jake. "Joey has told the truth to every question he's been asked."

"I'm waiting."

"He has never been asked who else knew what happened in the tunnel that night. He will be asked that question by Gil Flowers at trial on cross-examination. Flowers will try to discredit Joey's testimony implicating Gomberg as a fabrication in exchange for his get-out-of-jail card. Flowers will hammer home to the jury that Joey's story that he kept secret all these years as a favor to his old pal is not worthy of belief."

"And how will Joey answer that question?"

"He will lie."

"To protect you?"

"No. To protect his sister. He doesn't want his sister on the stand. And I don't want that either. I promised Joey back when he was still incarcerated that if he cooperated, I'd protect Michelle. I failed at that once. I can't—I won't fail again."

"So you've known all along?"

Jake nodded. "Tell Stein I'll testify against Gomberg straight up. No immunity. No deal to keep my pension. But he can't call Michelle. If her name comes out on cross, it won't catch Stein by surprise, and you're covered too. Joey will tell the truth if he knows Stein won't call his sister. Flowers is a gambler, but even he would not risk putting the sister on the stand in his case. I'm asking you to get Stein to trade Michelle for me."

"Let's look at this from Stein's perspective. You're married to Joey Nardo's sister, which raises serious questions about your motivation to testify against Gomberg. And Joey has been living with you since his release, not an attractive package for Stein to buy into." Rabbit paused, swirled the snifter with a single slow turn of his wrist, and drained the last of the whisky.

Jake took a miniature tape player from his coat pocket and placed it on the coffee table in front of Rabbit. "I recorded my uncle's statement a month before he died." Jake reached over and pressed the play button.

"*This is ACPD Detective Sergeant Jake Harris, badge number 225. The date is January 24, 1980. My location is 810 West End Avenue, Apartment 507, New York, New York, the residence of Sandy Gordon. The time is 1:50 p.m. I am present with Mr. Gordon to interview him regarding the homicide of Jamie Wescott. Mr. Gordon, do you consent to this interview?"*

"I do."

"Mr. Gordon, do you consent to my recording of this interview?"

"I do."

"Mr. Gordon, what is your medical condition?"

"I am dying."

"Mr. Gordon, when did you first meet Jamie Wescott?"

"Spring sixty-one. We moved in together—this very apartment. We met at Lincoln Center. A film festival. We loved old movies, you know, from the glamour days of Hollywood. Big surprise—a queen who adored Garbo, Dietrich, and Monroe."

"Tell me about your relationship with Jamie Wescott."

"We had a few dates. Jamie was adventurous, fun. He lifted me out of myself. We became companions. Lovers. When I met Jamie, I was still under my brother's control. I was ashamed. Looking back, I came to realize I was ashamed— but not of being queer. I was ashamed of not being able to admit to my family who I was. I moved to New York, got a job in a salon, and rented this apartment. I was a living, breathing cliché."

"Did you know anything about Jamie's background?"

"Jamie had lived in the city for five years. He was a transplanted Iowa farm boy, one of a million self-invented souls. I could imagine the repression he endured. My own seemed trivial in comparison. He'd gone through it all before I met

him—the bathhouse orgies, the one-night stands, the police harassment and beatings. He was tired of the scene, and what I'd tasted of it had no appeal to me. I guess you could say he brought me out into the sunshine. He'd still liked to hit the edgier clubs, but he'd always take me with him. Is this difficult for you, Jake, to hear me talk like this?

"I've known since that summer I saw you in Tessie's. But I never really bother to think about the details. It's like knowing your parents have sex, but not wanting to know the specifics."

"Good. That's normal."

"Tell me about Jamie's disappearance."

"The last night I saw him, we quarreled, a silly argument over a boy he thought I was flirting with that afternoon in Tessie's. When Jamie stepped away to buy cigarettes, the boy came up to me. He was beautiful, cut, oiled. You know the type. Not very bright. Anyway, I wasn't interested, just amused. I never cheated on Jamie. That night, after a few drinks, Jamie brought up the boy, asked me how I'd like it if he played around. Then he stormed out.

"When he didn't return, I went looking for him. It was just after dark. I walked the half block to the boards, stood at the rail, and stared at the ocean. It was a new moon. The sky was black. The stars were brilliant. I always loved listening to the waves at night.

"A boy appeared below me on the sand at the entrance to Tessie's tunnel. He asked me if I wanted to come into the tunnel with him. I don't know what possessed me. I went down to the beach. At the entrance to the tunnel, I stopped. The boy came up to me. He was so close I could feel his breath. He smiled and gently took my hand.

"Deep in the tunnel, my vision had not fully adjusted to the darkness, but I knew we were near the gate to Tessie's. His grip became a vise. He pushed me to the ground, onto my knees. There was another boy with him, but he was in the shadows. All of us queers knew someone who had been lured by the promise of anonymous sex, only to be beaten and robbed. Looking back, I must have been so angry with Jamie and fearful for him that I was acting out. Stupid, really stupid."

"There was a second boy?"

"Yes. He came up behind me. I remember thinking that I was going to die in that tunnel. Did you ever think you were going to die, Jake? Really die? Everything around you moves in slow motion. There is a clarity of thought, your senses sharpen as if you have made peace with what is about to happen, and you savor your last moments. I think the boy behind me ejaculated. When I got home, I found what looked like semen on the back of my T shirt. I was so frightened I can't be sure.

"He and the other boy were distracted by a noise, and I got up and ran. I wanted to live and had a chance to get away, but my legs were heavy, sluggish in the dry sand. I looked back to see if they were following, and I tripped. I got a mouthful of sand."

"Was anyone else in the tunnel other than you and the two boys?"

'No."

"So Jamie was not in the tunnel?"

"He was not."

"Do you remember anything about the boys?"

"I can still see the face of the boy who escorted me into the tunnel. It was misshapen. The eyes—like he was in a trance.

One slightly lower than the other. He was tall and thin— gaunt, really. I should have known from his eyes to get away from him."

"Sandy, I want you to look carefully at these five photographs. Do you recognize the person who led you into the tunnel? Take your time."

"Yes, that's the boy that lured me into the tunnel."

"Turn the one you selected over and read the number I've written on the back."

"Three."

"Sandy, are you able to sign and date the back of the photo you selected?"

Jake reached into his breast pocket and placed the five photographs he had shown his uncle next to the tape player, numbers up. He turned the one marked "3" bearing Sandy's scrawl as if it were the winning hole card in a poker game. Like all mug shots, the subject appeared drugged. A greasy black forelock fell to just above his brow. Stark lighting accentuated the acne on his cheeks and chin. It was Joey the night of his arrest for killing his uncle.

"Do you remember anything about the other boy?"

"I never saw him. The second boy came up behind me after we were already inside, in the darkness."

"Anything, Sandy?"

Jake remembered back to that day in Sandy's apartment. The interview had exhausted his uncle. He was unable to keep his eyes from closing. Sandy had pointed at the large cup of ice water with the straw stuck in its lid. Jake held the cup while his uncle sipped water through the straw. Sandy's voice on the tape was weak, difficult to hear.

The two men leaned in close to the tape player's speaker.

"I do remember his voice. It was nasal, like his nose was clogged and he had to breathe through his mouth."

"After that night, did you ever see Jamie Wescott again?"

"No."

Rabbit looked up from the tape player and the photos arrayed on the coffee table. "You withheld evidence. You know the seriousness of what you did. You were the detective assigned to the case. Why didn't you turn over the tape as evidence?"

"McMeekin was Zitto's whore. He was railroading Joey to protect Gomberg. I couldn't risk the tape being destroyed. I thought I could make it come out right."

"Jake the question remains: what proof is there that your uncle's statement describing his encounter with Joey and Gomberg happened the same night Jamie Wescott and the other two victims were murdered?"

"You heard the tape. Sandy was in the tunnel just after dark. My uncle never saw Jamie again. The murders had to have happened later that night. My uncle's statement, Joey's eyewitness testimony, and my testimony put Gomberg in the tunnel the night of the murders."

"Your uncle's taped statement may not be admissible. It's hearsay and highly prejudicial to Gomberg. If I had to bet, the judge keeps it out. That leaves Joey and you. Stein may need Michelle for background to establish Joey's relationship with Gomberg."

"I want Stein to leave Michelle out of this. No interviews, no statements from her of any kind. I can testify about Gomberg and Joey as kids. I was there. I saw it every summer night. That's my deal. Non-negotiable. Leave Michelle alone, and Stein gets a cop witness willing to risk his reputation and pension."

"Maybe more than your pension or reputation, Jake." Rabbit hadn't asked the hard questions of his friend, challenging the gaps in his narrative, cross-examining him like he would a hostile witness, probing for the entire truth, digging for the reason Jake was willing to risk all for what was so little in return. "As far as Stein is aware, Michelle is a minor witness that he could do without. Trading her for you should be an easy deal to make."

Jake waited for Rabbit to ask him what Michelle knew about the night of the murders. The pause in their conversation was heavy with that and other unasked questions. Rabbit knew the questions. By not asking them, he signaled his acceptance of Jake's proposal. Rabbit knew he had enough to interest Stein.

"I'll talk with Stein in the morning, Jake."

He found Michelle curled up on the couch under her reading lamp with an open book tented across her chest. Her eyes were closed. He stood just inside the door, watching the small movements of her sleep, and marveled at his good fortune—yet undeserved in his mind. He imagined that the seemingly haphazard and unconnected events that marked the timeline of their lives were preordained from the moment he first saw her when he was a fifteen-year-old high school kid. The centrality of the brutal killings of three harmless human beings—at once the source of his guilt and his redemption—intruded. He knew he had much to do to purge the remnants of the shame he carried. He would not hurt Michelle again; he would not fail her. He covered her with the afghan draped over the sofa's back and switched off the reading lamp.

* * *

By the first day of summer, the media frenzy following the indictment and arrest of Arthur Gomberg had intensified. It seemed every day an article appeared, reporting on legal motions and many others speculating on who would be witnesses for the defense or prosecution. Gomberg had touched many lives for the good, and the salacious details of his alleged crimes sold newspapers. Jake and Michelle avoided all discussion of the case and seemed to will it from their thoughts. They would have this summer together and would not allow the upcoming trial to ruin it.

Jake knew Gomberg and his lawyers were hunkered down, preparing for trial. Important motions to suppress DNA evidence that could determine the verdict would need to be filed. Gomberg would have to be rehearsed for his role at the trial. He must be made to appear likeable, unthreatening, and beneficent. His clothing, facial expressions, his every movement in the courtroom would be scrutinized by the jurors searching for a sign of guilt or innocence. Gomberg would be torn down and remade by Gil Flowers, stripped of arrogance, anger, and any other personality tic that might influence the jury against him.

Jake knew all this. He had lived it as a homicide detective in his own cases. Despite his efforts to shut it out, the case intruded. He wondered at his life and Michelle's once trial began—and forever after.

He loved this time of year, the waning days of August. The southern New Jersey dirt farms produced ears of pearl-like strands of sweet white corn perfectly formed and savory beefsteak tomatoes that could be eaten like a ripened peach and were just as sweet. His mother had always said that it was the sandy soil and sea air that made the late summer harvest so unique. She was probably right about that, he thought. Soon, the humid heat of August would yield to an Indian summer that would hold the warm breezes and colors of the sky, water, and earth before fall's first frost.

Jake watched unnoticed from the kitchen doorway as Michelle stood over a cutting board piled with sliced Jersey beefsteaks, cucumbers, and bell peppers. Several shucked ears of Silver Queen corn sat to the side of the freshly cut vegetables. The sound of her knife against the wooden board accented the modulating buzz of cicadas and the wash of the incoming tide against the pilings off their backyard. He wanted to freeze time and live in that moment with her.

Sensing him, she turned. "How long were you standing there? You were so quiet. I guess I was daydreaming. Come here." She put her arms around his neck and kissed him softly. "It's beautiful, isn't it, this time of day?" They turned, he behind her, his arms around her shoulders. He pressed his face gently against her hair, and the two of them watched the last light of the day recede into the marshes.

He found a parking space near the corner on Atlantic Avenue and walked north on Mississippi toward the White House. The hunched heavyset figure exiting the sub shop was unmistakable. A half dozen submarine sandwiches wrapped in heavy white deli paper poked above the edge of an oil-soaked brown bag like so many warheads ready to launch. Jake decided not to avoid the encounter.

"Hey, Franco."

Franco "Toad" Carbone looked up into the face of his old corner boy. He smiled easily, not the wiseguy "fuck you" grin. "Yo, Jake. Been a while." There was no rancor or threat in his voice, no swagger. "You doon all right?"

"Yeah. I'm good. You?"

"Yeah, I'm good." There was an awkward pause before Franco brightened. "Nonno's almost a hundred."

Jake pictured the old man eating his fresh fruit, spitting the pips into the top of his fist, and tossing the peelings on the floor.

"The doc says he gotta watch his diet. Who's he trying to kid? 'Yo, Doc,' I said, 'he's been eating and drinking the same way his whole life.' I keep his glass filled with homemade jug wine and his plate with wedges of provolone and sweet peppers swimming in olive oil; and, fresh baked Italian bread to sop up the oil."

"That's the secret to his long life."

Toad laughed. "He still asks for you, Jake. 'Where's the *Morta Cristo* you used to run with?' I tell him you're a cop. He says, 'Yeah, I remember. He came to the pool hall that time with the moolie.' His mind's sharp as ever."

"It's good seeing you."

"Yeah. Toad looked down for a moment then back up at Jake. Same here. Nothing was ever personal, Jake. I'm kinda glad it came to this. Both of us are still walking around above ground."

Toad's refusal to testify was a badge of honor. He had been rewarded with a minor sinecure with one of the locals.

"I'll tell Vinny hello for you when I see him. He always liked you. He knew you were a smart kid. He'll be leaving town as soon as the *thing* is over. Vinny's planning to move down to Boca with his receptionist."

The thing. Their thing. The events that bound them forever had given way to the sheltering deceptions of time and selective memory.

Vinny had agreed not to stand for re-election on the condition that he would be permitted to finish his term and collect his pension.

Jake couldn't picture the old Vinny living out his days in Boca. Sammy Dorfman was right: there was something wrong with the beach sand in Florida—it was coarse and off-color—and then there was the pelican shit. And Boca had no White House subs on fresh baked Formica's Italian bread, guts out, dripping with olive oil and loaded with premium sandwich steak topped with melted provolone.

"Yeah. Give Vinny my best."

"Jake. I gotta get something off my chest."

"What's that?"

"It's about that night at Rocky's Bar. It was wrong to mention Joey's sister like we did, to bring her into our business."

"I knew it was Nicky, Toad. I wanted to rip his grease-ball head off his neck. You were messenger boys."

"We never would've hurt Michelle. Never. You gotta know that."

"I know that. Vinny and you were never muscle. It wasn't you I was worried about. When I left Rocky's, I ran to Michelle's house. We've been together ever since."

"Whadda ya know? At least something good come out of it."

"Would you have warned me if it came to that, if Michelle was in real danger?"

Toad looked down at his shoes.

"I think you would have, Toad. For old times."

"Thanks for sayin' that, Jake."

"See ya, Toad."

Jake was exhausted, but sleep would not come. He felt the emotions and physical reactions of a prize fighter alone in his dressing cubicle, waiting to enter an arena filled with bloodlust. As the trial date neared, his late-night walks took on an added urgency. It was as if he were racing some doomsday clock ticking down to when Atlantic City would be rendered unrecognizable, the first half of his life erased. He needed what was left of his hometown and his memories hardwired in his psyche. AC had once been a carnival of cultures and neighborhoods, each with some connection to the others, however tenuous. Italian trattorias, pizzerias, and bakeries fed the entire island. Jewish delis dotting the island from Margate to the Inlet supplied the island's residents their Sunday breakfast of bagels and lox and sandwiches of corned beef piled between two slices of freshly baked rye dripping with coleslaw and Russian dressing that defied even the largest of jaws to engulf them. And the White House. The Sacco family still made the best cheesesteaks in the entire world. The sub shop was an outpost under siege, surrounded by black-topped arterials, boarded-up storefronts, and abandoned walkups.

He found himself on Mississippi Avenue. At St Mike's, Spanish had replaced Italian as the *lingua franca* of the parish. Dante Hall had an imposing new entry that seemed to Jake less inviting than the worn wooden street level doors to the old bingo parlor and gym. Across the street, the front of the walkup that had housed Victory Billiards was boarded over; all outward traces of the pool hall and its denizens were gone.

He turned the corner at Sovereign and Atlantic just as dawn broke the horizon over the marshes.

* * *

The door behind the bench opened, and Judge Michael Winkleman entered.

The courtroom deputy rose. "All rise. *Oyex, Oyez.* All those having business before this honorable court, come forward, and they shall be heard. The Superior Court of New Jersey, County of Atlantic, is now in session. The Honorable Michael Winkleman presiding. Be seated."

The courtroom was closed to the public and the press. The jurors, selected over the course of the week, waited in a room adjacent to the courtroom. The judge arranged a sheaf of papers and several volumes of case books opened to pages tagged with yellow Post-its.

"The court has before it two motions *in limine.* I shall take up first the defendant's motion to preclude the state from introducing DNA evidence. Then I will address the state's motion to admit the recorded statement of Sanford Gordon. Am I correct, gentlemen, that these are the only remaining motions to be decided before I seat the jury?"

Both lawyers stood.

"Yes, Your Honor," Stein responded.

"That's correct, Your Honor," Flowers confirmed for the defense.

"Be seated, gentlemen. The court has heard three days of testimony from qualified forensic geneticists, two presented by the state and one by the defense. Counsel have stipulated to the qualifications of these experts, and there is no motion to exclude them based on training and qualifications. There is also agreement between counsel that the science itself is valid and the methodology meets the threshold of reliability required for admissibility. The court has received in evidence all the demonstrative exhibits prepared by the experts to illustrate the science of DNA imaging and identification, along with the written reports prepared by the experts.

"The court also heard testimony from law enforcement personnel presented by the state on the chain of custody and preservation of the articles of clothing, baseball bat, and remains of the victims. On this issue of the gathering, handling, and maintenance of the physical evidence, there is substantial disagreement. The experts have testified extensively on degradation and contamination of the physical evidence. The defense expert contends the state's handling of the remnants of clothing, in particular, has rendered the DNA analysis unreliable and inadmissible. The state's experts testified that analysis of mitochondrial DNA is not dependent on nucleated cells. They further testified that sufficient intact Y-STRs were recovered to enable reliable analysis of the cellular material.

"The decision of this court is to admit the expert testimony as it pertains to the baseball bat, the clothing of the three victims, and the remains of the three victims. The court finds merit in the defense's argument that the chain of custody and handling of Sanford Gordon's clothing renders unreliable any scientific analysis based on it. Both Mr. Gordon and his sister, Anne Gordon, essential links in the chain of custody, are deceased. Even if they were alive and able to testify, the court's substantial concerns about the reliability of these clothing remnants as the basis for DNA analysis because of the handling of this evidence outside normal law enforcement protocols for nearly two decades would remain. However, the court will reserve ruling on the admissibility of Sanford Gordon's clothing until the state wishes to proffer them to the jury. I instruct you, Mr. Stein, that you are to provide the court and Mr. Flowers with twenty-four-hour notice of your intended use of this evidence so that the court can hear any additional argument before ruling on the defense motion to exclude. I also instruct you that you are to refrain from making any reference to this evidence in your opening statement."

Stein stood. "Yes, your Honor."

"I will now turn to the state's motion for the admission of the tape recorded statement of Sanford Gordon.

"In January 1980, Detective Harris interviewed the deceased at his residence in Manhattan. Detective Harris recorded the interview with Mr. Gordon's permission. For purposes of this motion only, the court has admitted the transcript of that interview. In summary, Mr. Gordon recounted in a coherent and lucid manner the details of his encounter in the tunnel under the Marlborough Blenheim the night his companion Jamie Wescott went missing. There were two males in the tunnel with him. He identified Joseph Nardo from a photographic array shown him by Detective Harris as the male who lured him inside. Mr. Nardo has admitted he, in fact, was present in the tunnel. Mr. Gordon did not see the face of the second individual, who was standing behind him. He was only able to recall his voice, which he described as distinctive and having a heavy nasal quality that one associates with breathing through the mouth due to an obstruction of the nasal passages.

"Mr. Nardo testified that the defendant, Arthur Gomberg, was in the tunnel with him that night.

"The state offers the recorded statement under two exceptions to the hearsay rule—first, as the dying declaration of Sanford Gordon. In this regard, the medical records establish that Mr. Gordon was in the end stages of cancer and cardiopulmonary disease. Mr. Gordon stated on the tape that he knew he was dying. Within weeks after Detective Harris took his recorded statement, Sanford Gordon died.

"However, Mr. Gordon himself was not mortally wounded in that tunnel and gave his statement more than seventeen years after the event at issue. His death was from causes other than injuries he received in the tunnel that night. The textbook example of a dying declaration is a statement made at or near the time of the crime by a victim suffering from mortal wounds. The court is reluctant to extend this narrow exception beyond the carefully delineated boundaries of case precedent in this state.

"I will now address the second basis on which the state offers the recorded statement of Mr. Gordon: the residual exception to the hearsay rule. Within narrow confines, the residual exception will not exclude a hearsay statement even if the statement is not specifically covered by another defined exception. The requirements for admissibility under the residual rule are that the statement has equivalent circumstantial guarantees of trustworthiness. It is offered as evidence of a material fact. It is more probative on the point for which it is offered than any evidence reasonably available, and admitting it will serve the best interests of justice.

"The details and incidents disclosed on the tape were not such that one would want them revealed. The interview was difficult for both Detective Harris and Sanford Gordon, Detective Harris's great-uncle. There is credible evidence apart from the statement to support the conclusion that the defendant was in the tunnel with Mr. Nardo the night of the murders.

"The state offers the statement to establish that the defendant was in the tunnel the night of the murders and, in fact, was the second assailant standing behind Mr. Gordon during a sexual assault on him. The defense has argued that on this issue, the evidence is cumulative and non-essential.

"The court has determined that the wisest course is to take its ruling on the admissibility of the recorded statement under advisement. We will see how the evidence develops and take up the admissibility of this statement at an appropriate time during the presentation of the case to the jury. Mr. Stein, my admonition and instructions regarding the clothing apply to Sanford Gordon's statement."

Stein rose. "Understood, Your Honor."

"The court's memorandum opinion, findings, and conclusions will be filed today under seal with the prothonotary. If there is no other preliminary business, we are ready to bring in the jury."

Flowers rose slowly from his seat. "Your Honor, I have a motion before the jury is brought in."

"Yes, Mr. Flowers. Proceed."

"Your Honor, the defense withdraws its opposition to the admissibility of the DNA evidence obtained from Sanford Gordon's clothing. In light of the court's decision to admit the other DNA evidence, the defendant wants the jury to have all the available evidence, including the Gordon samples. We make this motion without prejudice to our position that none of the DNA evidence is admissible, and we preserve that issue for appeal."

"The court will take your motion under advisement. Regardless of your acquiescence to the admission of the Gordon evidence, the court still has an obligation as a gatekeeper to ensure that scientific evidence meets the minimum standard of reliability before allowing the jury to consider it. Bailiff, you may now seat the jury."

Norman Lasky and Jake met each evening after trial in Rabbit's office. Those meetings began with Rabbit's summary of the day's trial proceedings and ended with two old friends reminiscing over whisky and cigars. As the state's case wound to a conclusion, the evening sessions focused on what role Jake would have as a witness, if any.

"The DNA evidence establishing the presence of Gomberg's semen on your uncle's clothing is a thin reed without your uncle's statement. Unless Gomberg can be placed in the tunnel the night of the murders the DNA evidence is barely relevant and may be excluded by the judge depending on how the testimony develops. As it stands now, Stein will have to rely on Joey's testimony to place Gomberg in the tunnel the night of the murders."

"You believe Gomberg's going to walk, Rabbit?"

"A thin case is getting thinner. Flowers did an excellent cross-examination of the state's forensic expert. He kept it simple. Avoided the science. He focused on crime scene integrity, chain of custody, contamination, what should have been done, what was done, and what was done wrong during the gathering of the remnants tested. He kept it low key and then raised the suggestion that the mere fact that DNA was recovered from remnants of clothing didn't mean it was deposited during the commission of a murder.

"It was a textbook cross—tone and substance. And Flowers ended his cross with a masterful piece of misdirection. He used the state's expert to introduce into evidence that your uncle's DNA was identified on the remnants of Jamie Wescott's clothing placed into evidence by the state."

"That explains Flowers's motion to have my uncle's evidence admitted along with all the other DNA evidence."

"Jake, the state will rest tomorrow morning. Stein—and I agree—believes Flowers will keep the defense short—a parade of dignitaries attesting to Gomberg's charitable works and the many benefits he has bestowed on the city. Religious figures and heads of charities will testify to his good character. Then—because Flowers is no fool—he will call average folks, people just like the jurors.

"Flowers will end the defense by calling Gomberg to the stand. The direct examination will build quickly. Flowers will have Gomberg admit what he must—that as a teenager he ran with a group of toughs that, by the way, produced a mayor and an ACPD detective. He will freely admit he did some things back then that he regrets. But he is no murderer. Flowers will finish his direct examination by eliciting from his client what Flowers knows the jury must hear to acquit: Gomberg's categorical denial of the charges against him."

"What is Stein's prognosis?"

"If Gomberg survives cross without taking any hits below the waterline, Stein thinks the jury will acquit. He needs a killer cross-examination. He still believes it was the correct strategy not to call you as a witness in the state's case-in-chief. After tomorrow, he may have no choice but to put you on the stand as a rebuttal witness."

"What's his basis for calling me on rebuttal?"

"Stein is certain he will be able to force Gomberg on cross to deny being in the tunnel with Joey the night of the murders. That will open the door for your testimony about what you heard and saw that night. Gomberg's guilt or innocence will be in your hands."

The night air was freshening, and a breeze off the ocean carried the aroma of the sea. It was a new moon, and the stars formed a brilliant canopy. Instead of walking to his car, Jake turned the corner at South Carolina Avenue and headed toward the boardwalk. At the ramp, he was bathed in the headlights of the black Town Car that had been trailing with its lights off. The rear door opened, and the occupant of the back seat motioned Jake to join him in the limousine as he pressed a button on the armrest to raise tinted glass to close off the driver. "Franco told me he ran into you outside the White House."

Vincent Nicastro had lost his shine. His jawline sagged, and dark circles bagged beneath his eyes. Streaks of gray through his still-full head of hair lent an air of distinction that the oils, creams, and hand-tailored suits and shirts failed to supply. He was tieless in a white slightly rumpled shirt. Monogrammed cuffs peaked below the sleeves of his signature navy-blue chalk-striped suit jacket.

"Yeah. We caught up a bit. Nice to hear Nonno's going strong. I told him it's the olive oil, garlic, and the jug wine."

"True. We dagos had it right all along. They call it the Mediterranean diet. We didn't have a name for it."

"Franco said you were thinking of moving down to Boca. I told him I had my doubts. Too much culture shock."

"I need a change, Jake."

"Why didn't you get rid of the bat?"

"What?"

"Joey's bat. You had it the night it all happened. Michelle told me you brought it to her a year after Joey went away for killing his uncle. Why, Vinny?"

"I don't know why. It seemed like it was all Joey had. I was with him every night when we were kids. I never saw him use it to hurt anyone. I thought his sister should have it, decide what to do with it. I never expected what happened to happen. That we'd be here thirty years later and the bat..." Vinny's voice trailed off.

"Funny thing about Joey's bat, Vinny. We're all on it—you, me, Fish, Toad, Michelle. We all had our fingers around the grip, on the pine tar."

"The thing about Joey—I mean, when he went nuts on the fathers in the rectory, he had his reasons. He was just a kid. What was he—eleven? Twelve? Any of us might have done the same thing. Maybe not. I don't know. His uncle, as crazy as that was, it had a reason. It wasn't random. I knew he was not the violent head case he made others think he was. When I think back, I felt sorry for him. Maybe that's why I kept the bat and gave it to Michelle."

Vinny cracked a half smile and looked Jake in the eyes. "You wearin'?"

"No, Vinny."

"Fish was a strange kid, but I never figured him for this."

"When did you decide it was okay for Joey to take the weight for the tunnel murders?"

"I didn't. New York decided. Nicky decided. If it means anything, I felt bad about that. But Joey was inside, and he wasn't getting out. The tunnel murders weren't gonna make a difference in his life. It was an easy fix to a very big problem involving some very important people—and a whole lot of money. What about you, Jake? Why the big crusade against Fish?"

Jake paused. He realized Vinny had just asked him a question he had never asked himself. "It's not about Fish. I always felt a little sorry for him. I watched my hometown disappear and become a money machine for outsiders who cared only about squeezing every dime out of every square inch of sand they could get their hands on. The politicians in Trenton enabled this takeover by the mob and outside money. Look at Guccione's monstrosity. It's a rusting steel skeleton straddling a rickety frame walk-up that had been home to the same family for decades. The family refused to sell, so Guccione, with the blessing of the zoning commission, acquired the air rights. The family is still living there, and Guccione has walked away, leaving behind the mess he made of one family's life. I just got tired of them all getting away with it in the name of saving AC from financial ruin. Fish just got caught in the crossfire."

"And I thought it was all about Michelle."

Jake smiled. "You ever miss the old days, Vinny?"

"Maybe. But I look around and wonder what's left here. Nothing but strangers picking over the bones."

"Didn't have to be that way. We let it happen. Greed, corruption, carpetbaggers, and the mob doomed our town."

"And taking out Fish is gonna cure all that? C'mon, Jake. Corruption exists like the air exists. We all could've had a small taste. Now what've we got?"

Vinny paused. The rhythm of his breathing altered; his exhalation was audible, somewhere between resignation and a sigh.

"Are you gonna testify?"

"Vinny, don't go there."

"We have to go there, Jake. There's too much at stake for all of us. I'm here on my own. Hand to God. Nobody asked me to talk to you. I meet Fish at night after court. I'm all he's got left that is anything like a friend. Nothing much has changed since we were hanging on the rails. He's acting strange. Okay. He was always strange, but I mean different. He's in and out of reality. Like he flips back and forth between thirty years ago and his *situation*. Only I'm never sure he knows which is real.

"I don't go near the courthouse, of course. But Fish talks to me about the trial. His lawyer thinks the jury will hang, maybe even acquit. Keeping your uncle's statement out was a big win. Only one concern, Jake."

"Me."

"You."

"You know what this conversation becomes, Vinny, if it continues."

"That's up to you, Jake. I'm gonna say what I came to say, corner boy to corner boy."

"Okay, Vinny."

"Fish's image is all he has. The whiney kid that we ran with thirty years ago was dead and buried. Except now he's not.

"Franco and me are survivors. For us, it's not about what other people think, unless those other people are signing our paychecks. Fish? It's all about what other people think. Jake, if you testify, Franco and me become accessories, after the fact, to murder."

"It's not my call, Vinny."

"So I guess my movin' to Florida is gonna have to wait."

"Look at the bright side, Vinny. You can't get White House cheesesteaks in Boca."

"Yeah. True enough. Funny that the only thing left of our town worth having is a White House sub."

Jake Harris spent a long day waiting. Arthur Gomberg was the final witness in the defense case. Stein wanted Jake ready for rebuttal and squirreled him away in the witness room off the courtroom. Gomberg had done well on the stand in his own defense—perhaps too well. Flushed with confidence after parrying the prosecutor's toughest questions, Gomberg gave Stein what he needed to call a rebuttal witness. Stein had saved the setup questions for the end of his cross. In three crisp questions, he had Gomberg deny his presence in the tunnel at anytime the night of the murders. Flowers's careful finessing of that issue had been undone. Gomberg's lawyer kept his game face, but a careful observer would have noticed the slight slump of his shoulders at his client's mistake. He knew, as did Judge Winkleman, that the door for rebuttal testimony by Jake Harris and the admission into evidence of Sandy Gordon's taped statement had been thrown wide open.

At the knock on the door, Jake closed the six-month-old issues of *Time* and *Newsweek* he'd been thumbing absentmindedly waiting to be called to the stand. Stein's assistant escorted him from the sequestered witness room through the large double doors leading into the courtroom. John Stein stood at the podium and faced the jury.

"The State of New Jersey calls Jacob Harris."

Gomberg sat next to his lawyer at the defense table, his eyes straight ahead. Jake stood in the witness dock for the familiar litany with the bailiff. Gomberg continued to stare straight ahead, avoiding eye contact with his boyhood friend.

"State your full name for the record."

"Jacob Harris."

"Raise your right hand. Do you swear or affirm to tell the truth, the whole truth, and nothing but the truth?"

"I do."

"You may be seated."

Judge Winkelman turned to face the jurors. "Ladies and gentlemen, the state and defense have rested their cases-in-chief. The next evidence presented to you will be rebuttal testimony offered by the state. This is a natural breaking point even though it is a bit earlier than our usual stopping time. We're in recess and will resume promptly at 9:15 tomorrow with the testimony of Mr. Harris. I remind you of your oath not to discuss the case among yourselves or with any other person. Bailiff, please escort the jury from the courtroom."

The tide was out. He slowed to a stop on the dirt shoulder, rolled down his window, and inhaled the aroma of decaying crustaceans plugging the exposed bottom of the bay. The late September sun low in the sky painted strata of mare's tails in deep pinks and purples; the reflected light played through the swaying sedge. He imagined the long-ago scene, the marshes on the bayside emerging through a backlit blood-orange fog. Filaments burnished by the sun and salt air, presented a palette of washed tans, greens and reds. They glided in a twelve-foot sneak box, his father slowly pulling the oars across the rivulets of bay water that snaked through the grasses. His father and he made their trips across the bay to the marshes just before dawn or evenings as the sun dipped below the horizon, the best times to fish for flounder and black bass. The bay was eerily quiet, and the changing light enhanced the subtle hues of the grasses. Jake knew that when they had crossed the bay and reached the other side, what little conversation with his father would end until they were on their way back across. Until then, there would be only the whoosh of water and the brush of reeds against the hull.

He scanned the horizon, moving his eyes slowly south from the casinos to where Michelle waited in their bungalow. He loved his island, and he loved Michelle. He smiled, knowing he would soon be home. He closed his eyes, waiting for night to fall. He wanted to sit in the darkness under the stars, listening to the crickets and the night breeze. Michelle would understand.

It was after nine o'clock when he arrived at the house. Michelle would be inside, curled up on the couch, asleep with a book opened beside her. He wasn't sure whether Joey would be home. His brother-in-law had been spending a couple nights a week helping out at St. Nick's with new admissions to the halfway house.

The living room ceiling lights were off. The three-way bulb in the reading lamp by the couch was on low. He opened the door slowly so as not to startle her. She was sitting upright on the edge of the couch. In the shadows, he saw her glance up in his direction then back to the Queen Anne across from her just out of Jake's line of vision.

"Come in, Jake. You must be exhausted after today. I know I am."

From the doorway, Jake could not see the speaker, but the adenoidal wheeze was unmistakable.

Jake entered, glanced at the visitor, sat next to Michelle, and took her hand.

Arthur Gomberg was dressed in the suit he'd worn that day in court. He had not loosened his tie. A ring of grime edged the tightly buttoned collar of his monogrammed dress shirt, deposited by stress-induced perspiration. The front page of that morning's *Atlantic City Press* was on the coffee table between them. The headline above the fold seemed permanent since the beginning of the trial. It always began with his name, followed by a short phrase depending on the events in court. The morning headline spread across the coffee table read: Gomberg's Semen Found on Dead Man's Clothing.

The .45 resting on his lap in the casual grip of the fingers of his right hand vaguely pointed in the direction of the couch's occupants. He lifted the hand gun a few inches from his lap. "It was my father's, you know. Family heirloom of sorts."

Jake turned to Michelle. "Where's Joey?"

"Yes, where is my boyhood companion? He should be with us now, Jake. Don't you think? The three misfits together again."

"Why are you doing this, Fish?"

"Arthur," Fish corrected.

"Why, Arthur?"

"You remember the summers we ran together? I remember them. You and me—two Jewish boys—and the three wops from Ducktown. They were good days, weren't they, Jake? The boards, the clip joints, the streets—am I right? The *emmis*."

Jake nodded.

"We're a lot alike, Jake, you and me. Neither one of us belonged—not with our own and not with the others. Difference between us, Jake, is you didn't care. I was a fat kid with adenoids, but I had a muscle car. The Margate crowd saw me cruising Ventnor Avenue with the toughest guys from Ducktown, and they weren't laughing. They looked at me, and I was somebody. You ever been a fat clown, Jake? That's what they call a rhetorical question."

What could he say to Gomberg? *Arthur, don't make things worse? Killing us won't solve anything?* Just thinking the words was enough to know their absurdity. Jake knew that for Gomberg, there was no *worse;* for Arthur Gomberg, there could be no salvation. In Gomberg's world, people were cynics or suckers. He had been deconstructed, unmasked. All that remained was a sick, overweight, homely kid with adenoids.

"You know I had a private audience with the pope? I got the photo of me and His Holiness on the wall of my office. The rosary beads he blessed are set in the matte. And I have a photograph with Bill Clinton and one with Yitzhak Rabin. On my latest trip to Israel, we had lunch. That's right. I had lunch with the prime minister of Israel.

"That's all gone now, Jake. Cancer Center too. My name will come down. My name will be removed from all the buildings and scholarships I created with my money. Money got me all those honors. But at least I tried to use it for good. Now all the money in the world can't help me. My lawyer tells me even if I'm convicted, I won't go to jail because I was a kid when it happened and because of my life since then. "Of course, my casino license will be revoked. I guess that was the point of all of this. Am I right, old friend?

"You read the papers, don't you Jake?" He motioned the gun at the newspaper on the coffee table. "I have become a cliché, a series of adjectives. I'm Gomberg the fag, a sicko who clubbed three human beings to death to prove he wasn't one of them. You didn't have to do this to me, Jake. The past was buried, and nobody knew. It was always just us—Joey, Toad, Vinny, you."

He spoke their names in a prayer-like whisper, an incantation summoning the past to make the present disappear. It was like he willed himself to be someone else, anyone but who he was. Having left her off the list, he looked at Michelle then quickly away.

Looking at him, Jake imagined Fish was in a different place, a different time, cruising Ventnor Avenue in his Bonneville Coupe, its 389 V8 engine growling, Del Shannon riding shotgun. Fish's eyelids were half-mast, head tilting and rolling, grooving with Del. *I'm a walkin' in the rain, tears are fallin' and I feel a pain. Wishin' you were here by me, to end this misery.*

Jake inched his feet under the coffee table separating him from Gomberg. The arthritis in his knees had steadily worsened. Would he have the leg strength to propel the table with sufficient force then hurtle his own body at Fish? Jake's mental rehearsal of the sequence of movements required to disable Fish before he could get a round off, like the visualizations of a professional athlete at the end of his playing days, did not account for the ravages of time.

As if a switch had been thrown, Fish toggled back to the present and checked back into reality.

"In all the time we ran together, Joey never used that bat. He never hit anyone with it. I used to rag him when we were alone. 'Why you carry it? You never hit no one.' Joey just shrugged and said he carried it just in case. 'Just in case what?' I said. He said, 'You know, just in case I need it.' You got Joey a good lawyer, and he got Joey out for time served. End of story. Or shoulda been.

"I messed up bad on the stand today, Jake. My lawyer said I opened the door for you to testify against me. Tomorrow morning, Jake, you're gonna get on the stand and tell the jury that I was in the tunnel, like Joey said, that you saw my car parked at the ramp the night of murders. That makes me a liar. If I lied about being in the tunnel, then I also lied about who did the killing. False in one, false in all, my lawyer calls it. He thinks my fuckup on the stand could be enough to get your uncle's tape into evidence.

"What did I ever do to you, Jake? When McMeekin couldn't reel you in, Nicky wanted you hit. Toad and Vinny were summoned to a meeting with Zitto. Vinny came to my office right after. Crazy Walter was going to do it. Vinny just hung his head. Toad too. I said, 'No. Not Jake. I'll take care of it.' So I reached out to New York. Nicky and his nephew wind up in an alley, stuffed in garbage bags. I saved your life, Jake. Because I liked you. And here you and I sit."

Fish focused his eyes on the two figures on the couch across from him. Perspiration beaded on his brow and upper lip. He seemed to wilt in front of them. He gulped air like back in the day when Toad pretended he was going to drop cigarette ash on the Pontiac's upholstery.

Fish had always moved in slow motion, and the speed with which he lifted the gun from his lap and worked the carriage to chamber a round surprised Jake. Fish raised the gun. There wouldn't be time to reach Fish before he got off at least one shot.

Jake rose and moved to place his body between Fish and Michelle. "Fish, no! Not Michelle!"

Fish squinted, his expression quizzical. "Why would I want to hurt her?" Then he placed the barrel in his mouth and squeezed the trigger.

Epilogue

2015

Holy Spirit Cemetery was located west of Atlantic City, on the outskirts of Pleasantville. The two occupants of the black Ranger pickup drove in silence along Pleasantville's Main Street. The town across the bay from Atlantic City's casino district was deserted, a microcosm in faded black and white reminiscent of depression-era small-town America. Shadows cast by clouds whipped by gusts off the bay raced with time-elapsed swiftness along the corridor of plywood-and-steel curtains bookended by McDonald's and Dunkin' Donuts. Pleasantville remained what it had always been: a blue-collar town of failed businesses and near-full unemployment.

The Ranger pulled through the open gate and down the gravel lane toward a far corner of the cemetery that abutted the White Horse Pike. Passing marble markers adorned by cherubim and family mausoleums with filigreed wrought-iron fronts topped by Roman crosses, the Ranger rolled to a stop before a freshly dug grave and discharged its occupants.

It was April, but the air held the bite of winter, and Michelle Harris snuggled in close to her husband against the chill. The couple had brought no flowers. Instead they each found a stone and placed them on the simple granite marker. Jake Harris imagined, standing there, that Michelle thought of her older brother as the little boy with rotted teeth who made her brush hers every night before tucking her in bed and whispering to her of the beautiful little princess who brightened his world. Jake remembered the blood-spattered, handcuffed nineteen-year-old in the grip of two ACPD officers who told him to take care of his sister. Somehow, they had become a family.

The table tucked in a corner of the Down Beach Deli afforded privacy with a view of the Saturday morning bustle. It was *their* table, and the staff knew that between eight and ten every Saturday morning, no one was to be seated there but the three men who had just entered. The waitress had the usual fare ready as they walked through the door: a carafe of freshly made coffee and a plate piled with Danish and sticky buns warm from the oven.

Alfie Brathwaite spread the front page of *The Press* next to the plate of pastries. The headline above the fold read like an obituary: "Three Casinos Close Their Doors."

Rabbit Lasky reached for a sticky bun topped with walnuts and raisins. "You know when I knew the casinos were in deep shit? When I walked into Trump Plaza and saw empty five-dollar tables. The governor thought he was going to save the town by having the state take control of municipal services in the casino district. He forgot about the unions. The bosses reminded him."

Alfie snickered. "We don't need him coming in here, draining the last drop of life out of this old queen. Besides, he's got a better chance of becoming president than he has taking over Atlantic City."

Jake Harris smiled. "Right. We don't need his help to finish the job we started in '78."

"Seemed like a good idea at the time," said Rabbit.

"Bad planning."

Jake looked at his old partner. "What planning, Alfie? Turn over the city to speculators, bulldoze the neighborhoods, drive out the families and local businesses, add healthy quantities of cash for the pols, the unions, and the wiseguys, and presto change-o, Las Vegas by the sea. Except the ocean might as well not even be there. The gamblers check in, but they never leave the hotels until they're cleaned out."

"I think you got something there, Jake," Rabbit said. "That song. How's it go? You can check out, but you can never leave."

Jake Harris could not recall when he stopped taking his long, solitary walks through the streets of the old neighborhoods, but he knew why. At the corner of Atlantic and Mississippi, a Donald Duck look-alike adorned the sign over the entrance of the Duck Town Tavern. Back in the day, there had been no Duck Town Tavern. There had been only Ducktown, and it was gone.

On Mississippi Avenue between Atlantic and Arctic—the epicenter of his senses four decades ago—he could no longer remember. The smells and sounds and places were not even echoes. Formica's bakery was hanging on barely. Victory Billiards and the old neighborhood walkups had been bulldozed and buried deep beneath the foundation of Cabela's Bass Pro Shops. The facade of St. Mike's had been refurbished without any deference to the neighborhood church it had been. "Dante Hall" etched in the new stone lintel had no meaning to the current parishioners—newcomers part of the influx of migrants seeking employment in a gambling town. There was no purpose to walking the old streets. They mocked him.

The White House remained, bounded on one side by the twelve-lane terminus of the Atlantic City Expressway and on the other by decay. Inside, the Wall of Fame remained as it had been fifty years ago; the same photographs, faded by time, recalled the glory days of the Steel Pier, the Five Hundred Club, and the Club Harlem. The aroma of sizzling sandwich steaks, onions and peppers, olive oil and provolone; the bustle of the next generation of submeisters at the grill; the clipped jargon of customers ordering their favorites written on a green three-by-five grease-stained order pad by an inscrutable descendant of the efficient Maria of his youth abided still, frozen in time. The White House cheesesteak was still the best in the world.

Even the beach blocks of Margate and Longport were not spared. Many of the beachfront homes were bought as tear-downs and replaced with garish, outsized mansions squeezed onto postage stamp lots. Only Lucy had faired well. She was rescued from the wrecking ball by community activists, placed on the Historical Register, and renovated to her original splendor.

A new wave of real estate speculators would descend on the town to buy up failed casinos and the lots left vacant since 1978. What had been a seller's market when casino gambling was on the near horizon had become a trough for bottom feeders. Maybe this time they'd get it right.

Michelle met him at the door when he returned from his breakfast with Alfie and Rabbit. She was wearing her favorite pair of jeans and one of his old shirts frayed at the cuffs and collar. She smiled.

"It's a beautiful day. What do you say we take a walk on the boards?"

About the Author

Alan Lieberman, born and raised in Atlantic City, has "sand in his shoes." He is a trial lawyer specializing in white-collar defense. Earlier in his career, he served as a federal prosecutor and investigated major cases of public corruption and mob-related crimes. His first-hand experience in the FBI's fight against organized crime infuses *AC* with the authenticity only an insider can bring to this compelling story of greed, corruption, and murder on the eve of Atlantic City's casino era. He is an avid pilot and flies abused dogs rescued from quick kill facilities to loving homes up and down the I-95 corridor.

CPSIA information can be obtained
at www.ICGtesting.com
Printed in the USA
LVHW092305010620
657180LV00001B/240